MW00815127

CRIMINAL

Colors by Elizabeth Breitweise

IMAGE COMICS, INC.
Robert Kirkman - Chief Operating Officer
Erik Larsen - Chief Financial Officer
Todd McFarlane - President
Marc Silvestri - Chief Executive Officer
Jim Valentino - Vice-President
Eric Stephenson - Publisher
Corey Murphy - Director of Sales
Jeff Boison - Director of Publishing Planning & Book Trade Sales
Jeremy Sullivan - Director of Digital Sales
Kat Salazar - Director of PR & Marketing
Branwyn Bigglestone - Controller
Sarah Mello - Accounts Manager
Drew Gill - Art Director
Jonathan Chan - Production Manager
Meredith Wallace - Print Manager
Briah Skelly - Publicist
Sasha Head - Sales & Marketing Production Designer
Randy Okamura - Digital Production Designer
David Brothers - Branding Manager
Olivia Ngai - Content Manager
Addison Duke - Production Artist
Vincent Kukua - Production Artist
Tricia Ramos - Production Artist
Jeff Stang - Direct Market Sales Representative
Emilio Bautista - Digital Sales Associate
Leanna Caunter - Accounting Assistant
Chloe Ramos-Peterson - Library Market Sales Representative
IMAGECOMICS.COM

CRIMINAL, VOLUME SEVEN: WRONG TIME, WRONG PLACE. First printing. September 2016.
Contains material originally published in magazine form as CRIMINAL Special Edition, and CRIMINAL Tenth Anniversary Special Edition.

ISBN: 978-1-63215-877-2.

Published by Image Comics, Inc. Office of publication: 2001 Center Street, Sixth Floor, Berkeley, CA 94704. Copyright © 2016 Basement Gang, Inc..
All rights reserved. CRIMINAL™, its logos, and the likenesses of all characters herein are trademarks of Basement Gang, Inc., unless otherwise
noted. "Image" and the Image Comics logos are registered trademarks of Image Comics, Inc. No part of this publication may be reproduced or
transmitted, in any form or by any means (except for short excerpts for journalistic or review purposes), without the express written permission
of Basement Gang, Inc. or Image Comics, Inc. All names, characters, events, and locales in this publication are entirely fictional. Any resemblance
to actual persons (living or dead), events, or places, without satiric intent, is coincidental. Printed in the USA. For information regarding the CPSIA
on this printed material call: 203-595-3636 and provide reference #RICH–703266.

 Publication design by Sean Phillips

Ed Brubaker
Sean Phillips

CRIMINAL

Wrong Time, Wrong Place

Wrong Time

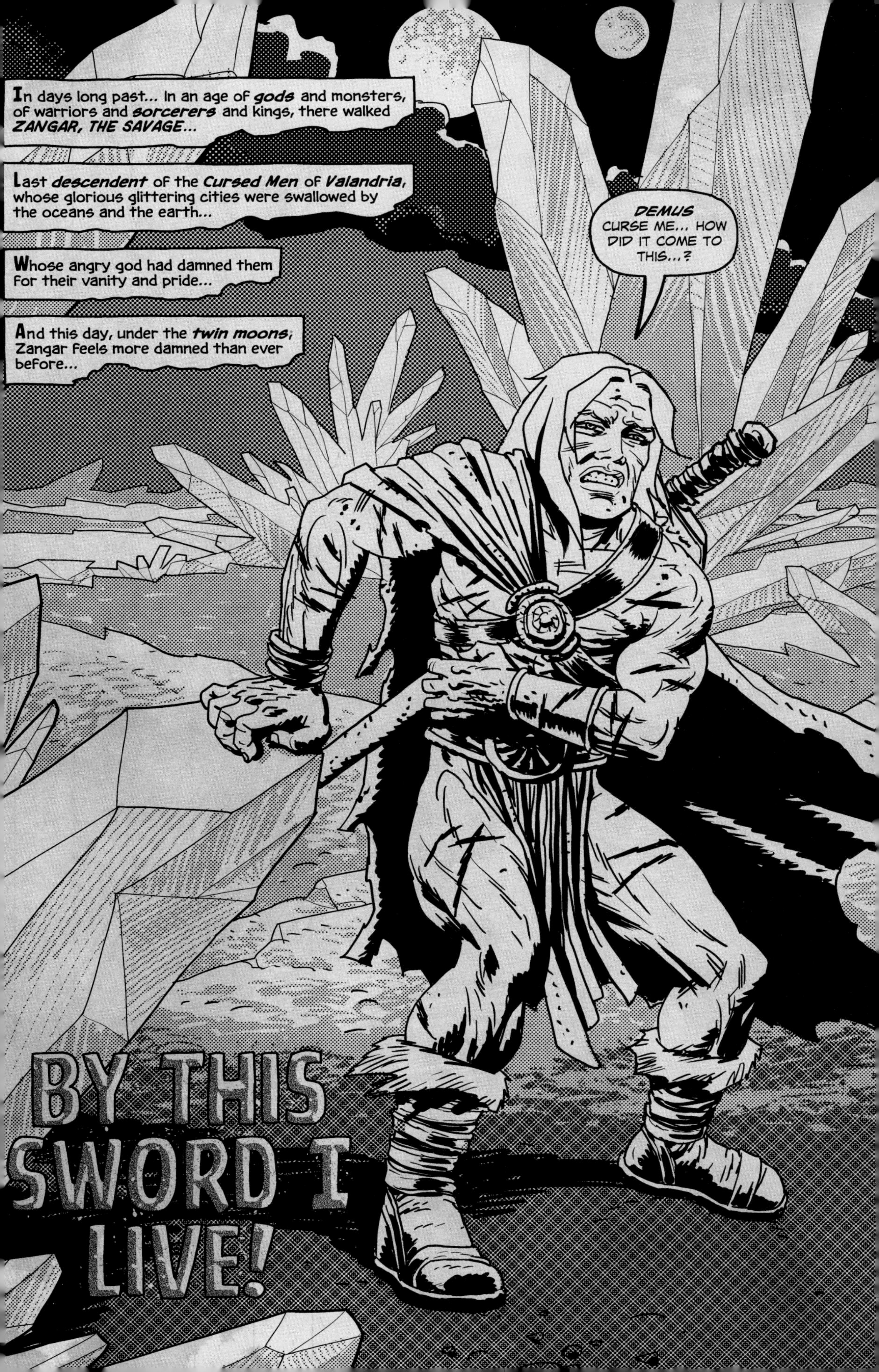

In days long past... In an age of gods and monsters, of warriors and sorcerers and kings, there walked ZANGAR, THE SAVAGE...
Last descendent of the Cursed Men of Valandria, whose glorious glittering cities were swallowed by the oceans and the earth...
Whose angry god had damned them for their vanity and pride...
And this day, under the twin moons, Zangar feels more damned than ever before...
DEMUS CURSE ME... HOW DID IT COME TO THIS...?
BY THIS SWORD I LIVE!

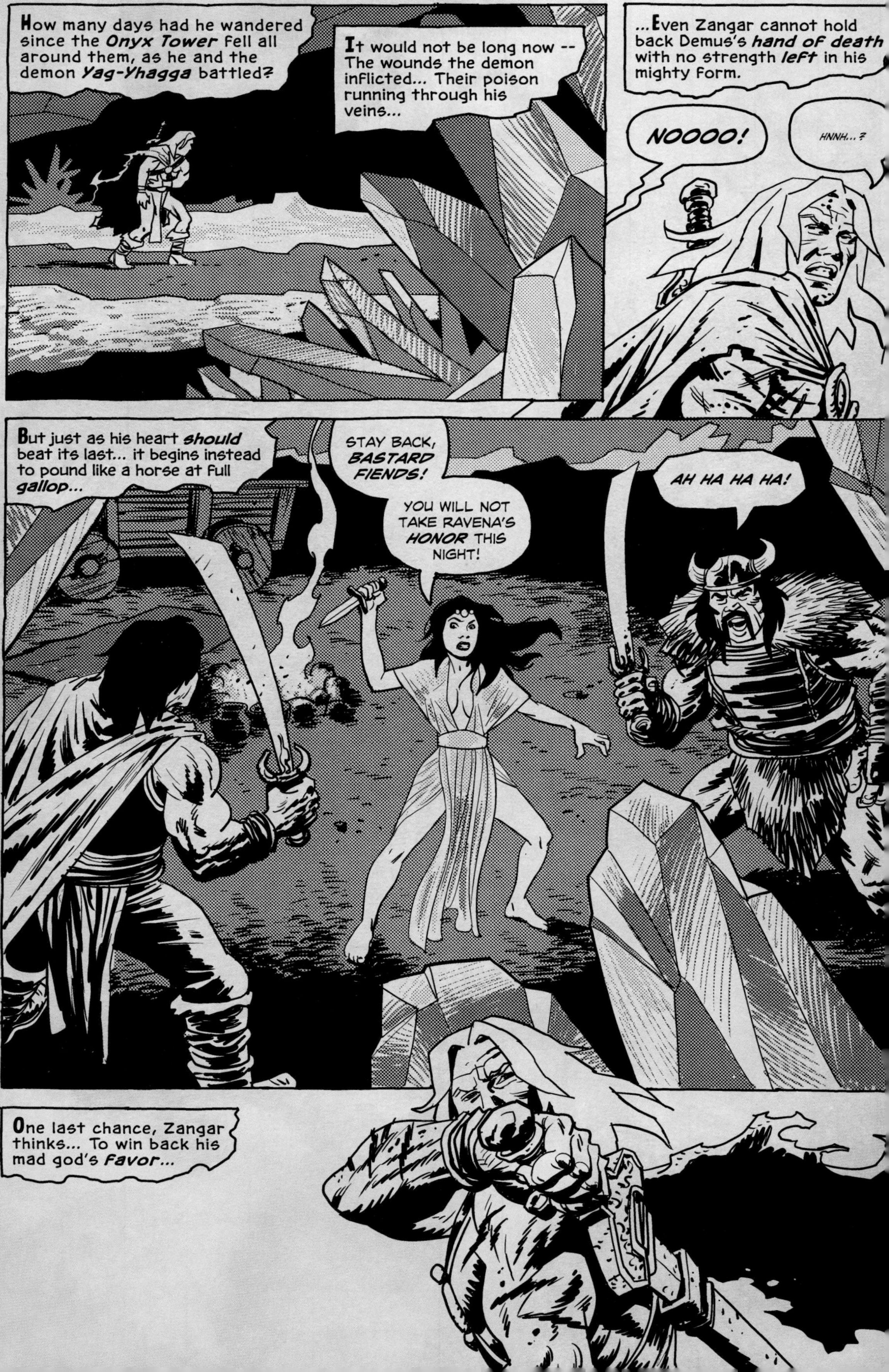
How many days had he wandered since the *Onyx Tower* fell all around them, as he and the demon *Yag-Yhagga* battled?
It would not be long now -- The wounds the demon inflicted... Their poison running through his veins...
...Even Zangar cannot hold back Demus's *hand of death* with no strength *left* in his mighty form.
NOOOO!
HNNH...?
But just as his heart *should* beat its last... it begins instead to pound like a horse at full *gallop*...
STAY BACK, *BASTARD FIENDS!*
YOU WILL NOT TAKE RAVENA'S *HONOR* THIS NIGHT!
AH HA HA HA!
One last chance, Zangar thinks... To win back his mad god's *favor*...

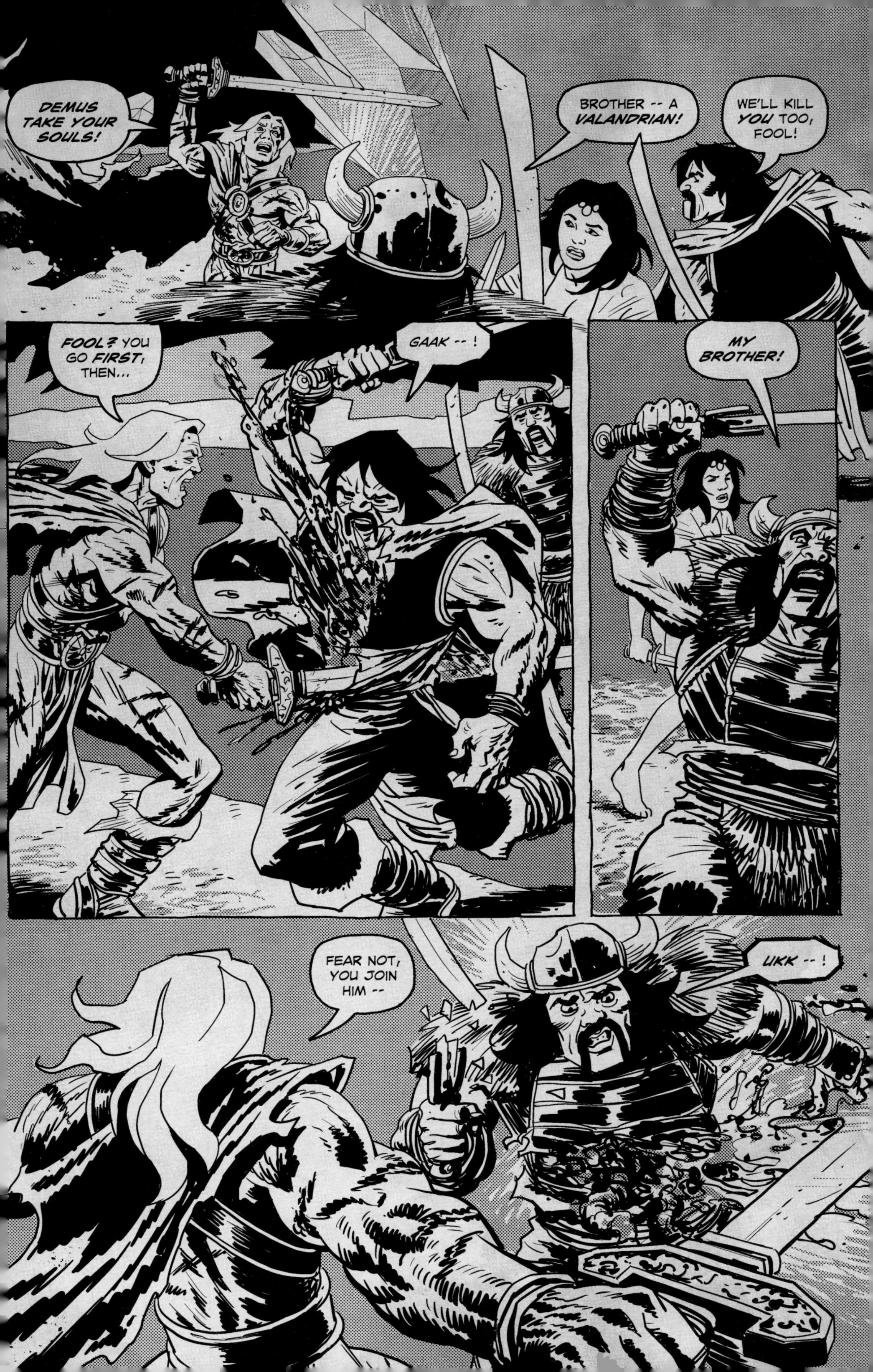
DEMUS TAKE YOUR SOULS!
BROTHER -- A VALANDRIAN!
WE'LL KILL YOU TOO, FOOL!
FOOL? YOU GO FIRST, THEN...
GAAK -- !
MY BROTHER!
FEAR NOT, YOU JOIN HIM --
UKK -- !

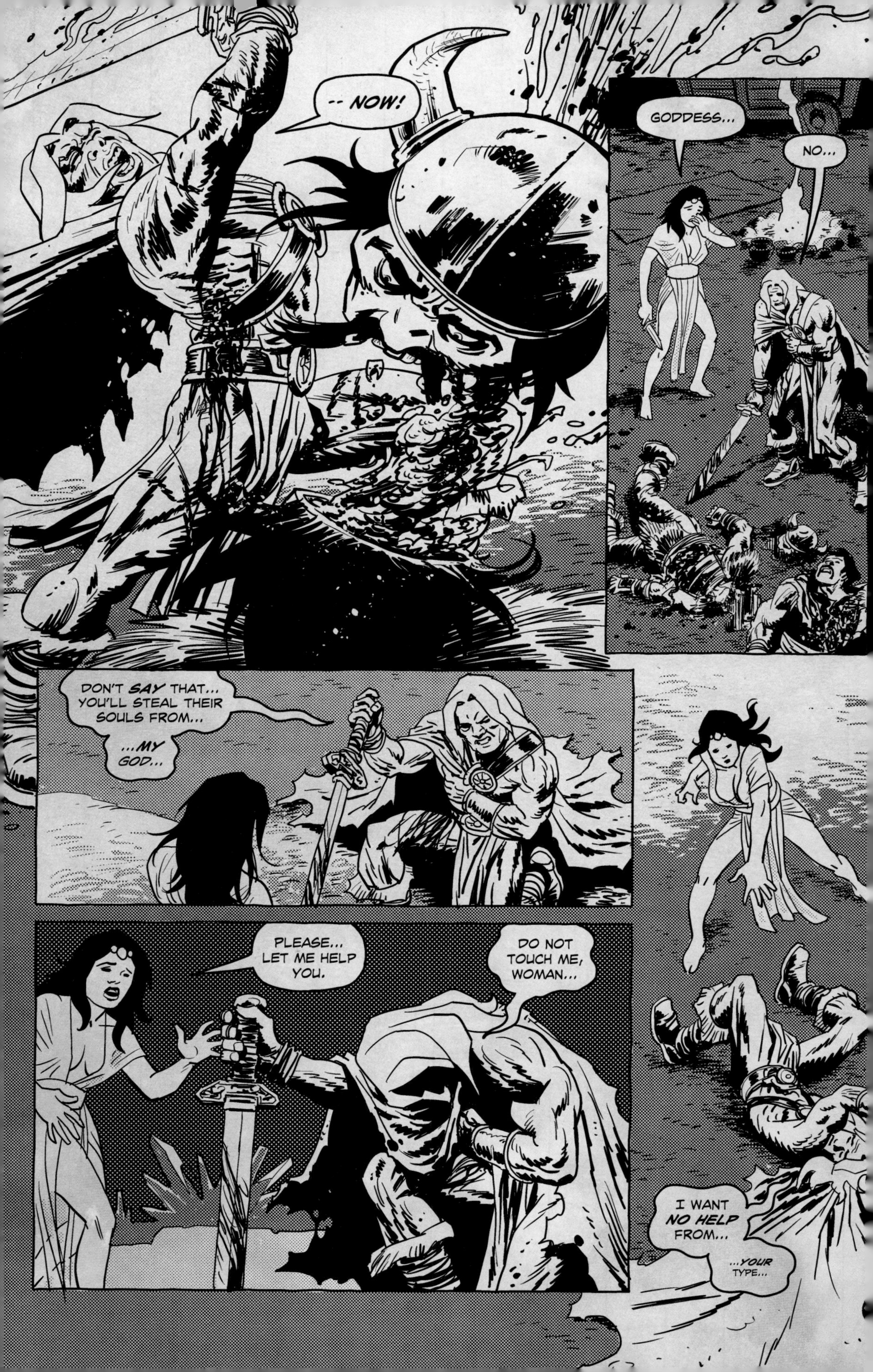

-- NOW!
GODDESS...
NO...
DON'T SAY THAT... YOU'LL STEAL THEIR SOULS FROM...
...MY GOD...
PLEASE... LET ME HELP YOU.
DO NOT TOUCH ME, WOMAN...
I WANT NO HELP FROM...
...YOUR TYPE...

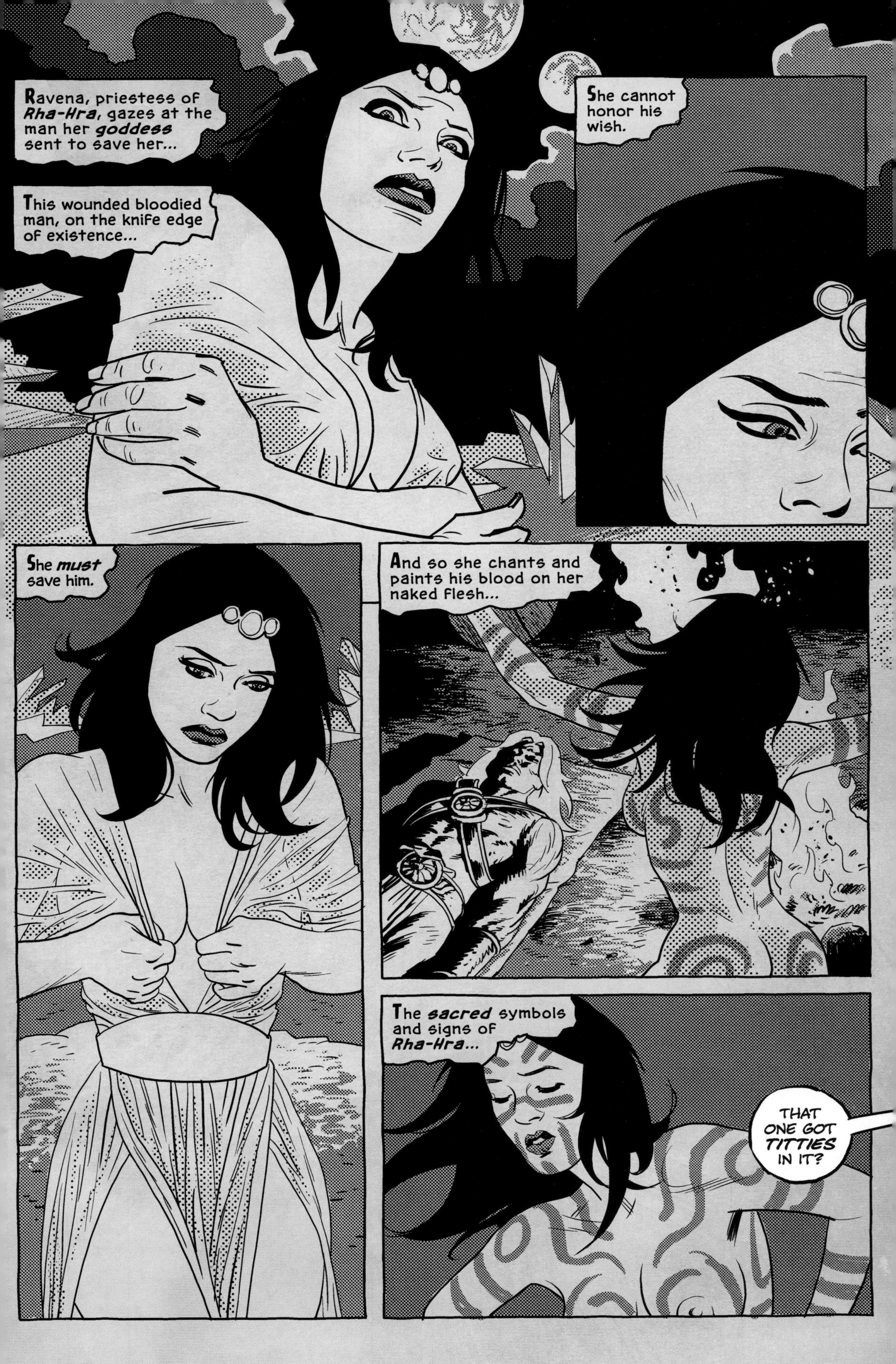
Ravena, priestess of *Rha-Hra*, gazes at the man her ***goddess*** sent to save her...
This wounded bloodied man, on the knife edge of existence...
She cannot honor his wish.
She ***must*** save him.
And so she chants and paints his blood on her naked flesh...
The ***sacred*** symbols and signs of *Rha-Hra*...
THAT ONE GOT ***TITTIES*** IN IT?

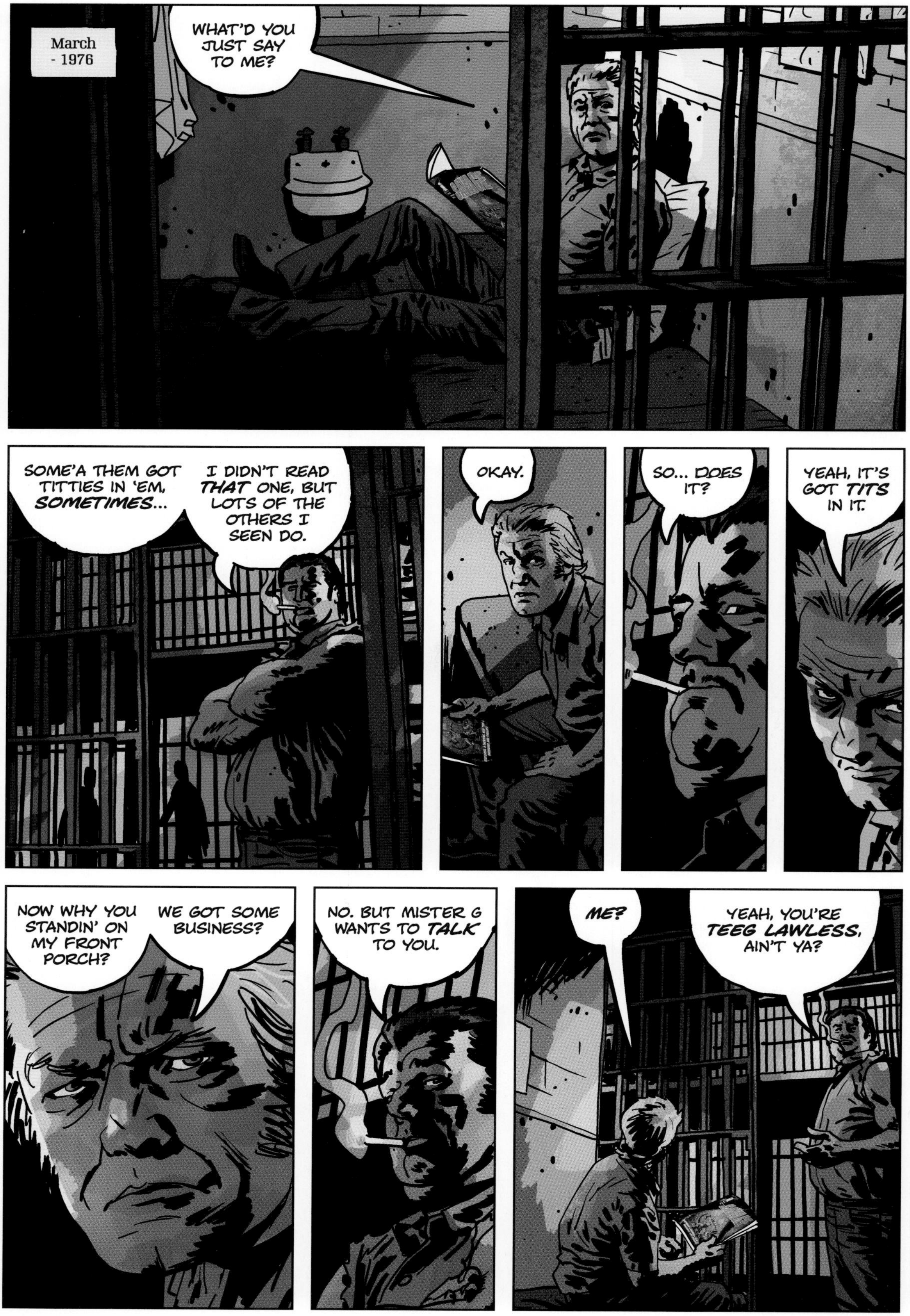
March - 1976
WHAT'D YOU JUST SAY TO ME?
SOME'A THEM GOT TITTIES IN 'EM, SOMETIMES...
I DIDN'T READ THAT ONE, BUT LOTS OF THE OTHERS I SEEN DO.
OKAY.
SO... DOES IT?
YEAH, IT'S GOT TITS IN IT.
NOW WHY YOU STANDIN' ON MY FRONT PORCH?
WE GOT SOME BUSINESS?
NO. BUT MISTER G WANTS TO TALK TO YOU.
ME?
YEAH, YOU'RE TEEG LAWLESS, AIN'T YA?

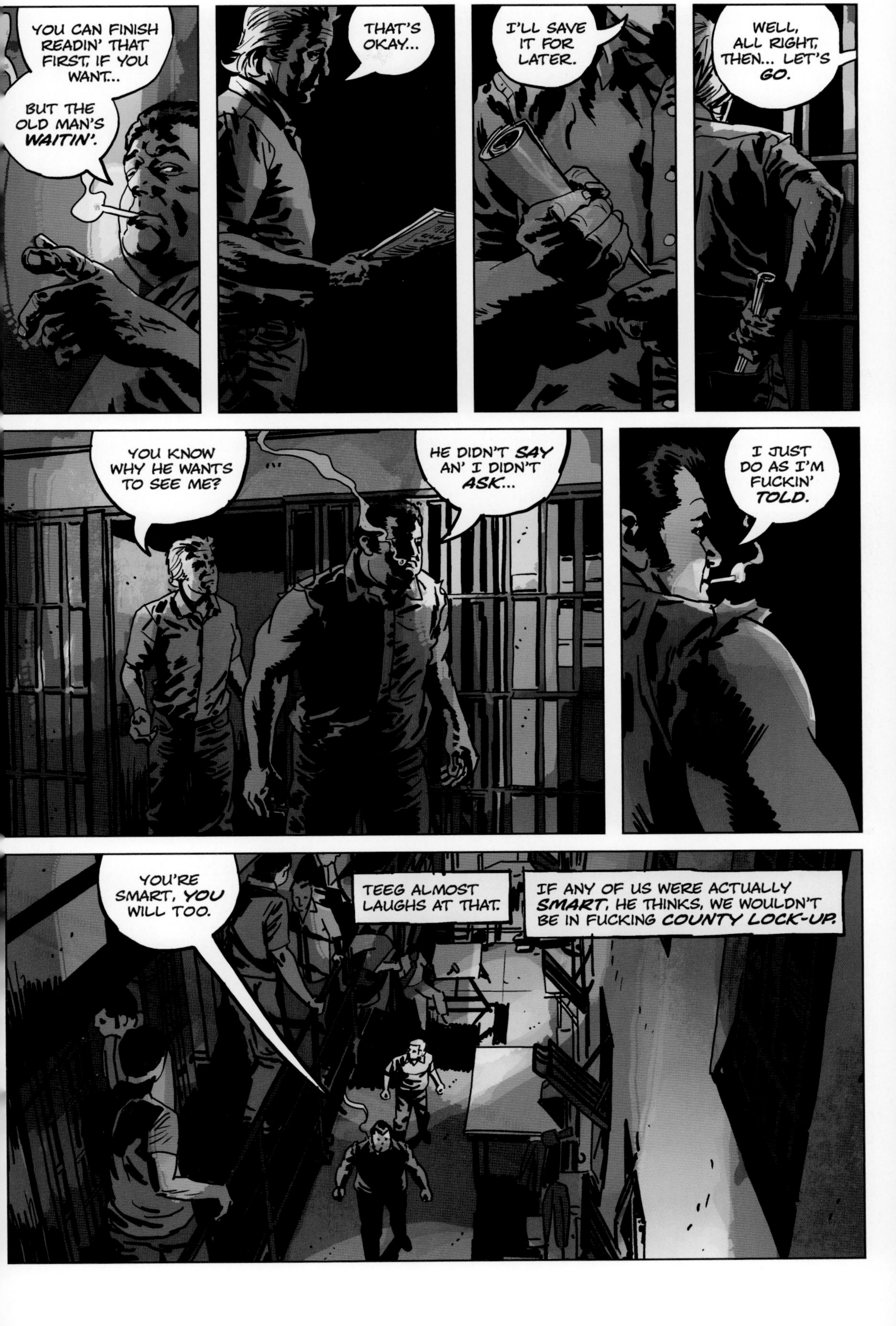

YOU CAN FINISH READIN' THAT FIRST, IF YOU WANT...
BUT THE OLD MAN'S *WAITIN'*.
THAT'S OKAY...
I'LL SAVE IT FOR LATER.
WELL, ALL RIGHT, THEN... LET'S *GO*.
YOU KNOW WHY HE WANTS TO SEE ME?
HE DIDN'T *SAY* AN' I DIDN'T *ASK*...
I JUST DO AS I'M FUCKIN' *TOLD*.
YOU'RE SMART, *YOU* WILL TOO.
TEEG ALMOST LAUGHS AT THAT.
IF ANY OF US WERE ACTUALLY *SMART*, HE THINKS, WE WOULDN'T BE IN FUCKING *COUNTY LOCK-UP*.

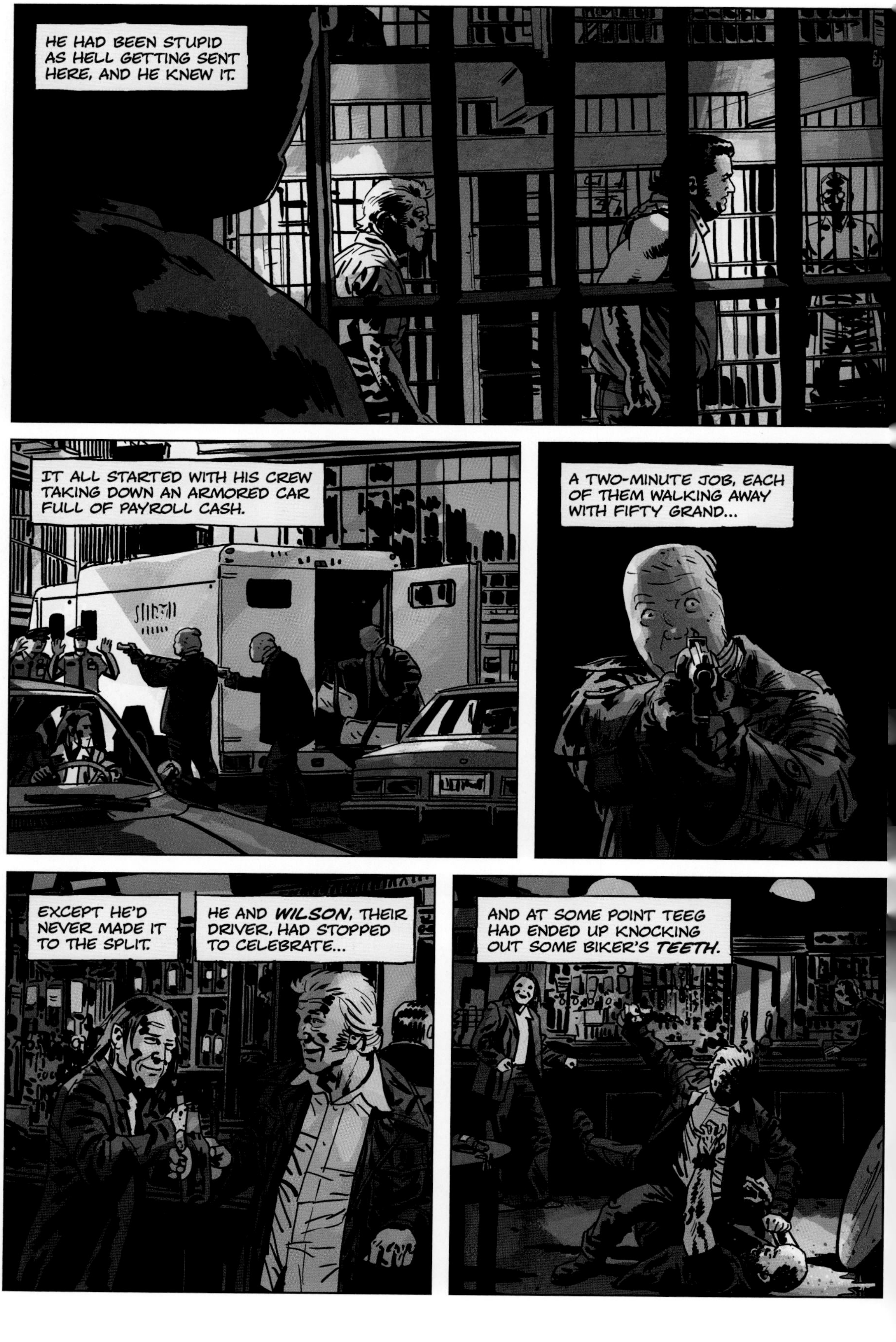
HE HAD BEEN STUPID AS HELL GETTING SENT HERE, AND HE KNEW IT.
IT ALL STARTED WITH HIS CREW TAKING DOWN AN ARMORED CAR FULL OF PAYROLL CASH.
A TWO-MINUTE JOB, EACH OF THEM WALKING AWAY WITH FIFTY GRAND...
EXCEPT HE'D NEVER MADE IT TO THE SPLIT.
HE AND *WILSON*, THEIR DRIVER, HAD STOPPED TO CELEBRATE...
AND AT SOME POINT TEEG HAD ENDED UP KNOCKING OUT SOME BIKER'S *TEETH*.

DIDN'T EVEN REMEMBER WHAT STARTED IT.

JUST WOKE UP IN THE BACK OF A SQUAD CAR.

THE BIKER *WASN'T* PRESSING CHARGES.

NO. TEEG HAD BEEN POPPED FOR A BENCH WARRANT.

FAILURE TO APPEAR, IN FUCKING *TRAFFIC COURT.*

SO NOW HE WAS *TWO WEEKS* INTO A 30-DAY JOLT FOR *CONTEMPT.*

HE'D BEEN RIDING IT OUT QUIETLY...

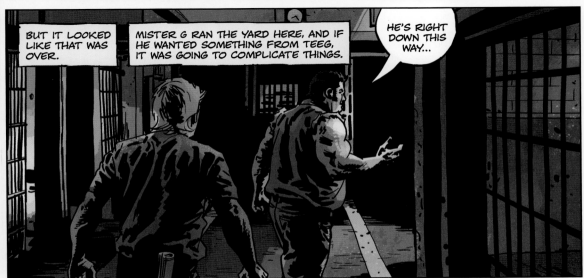

BUT IT LOOKED LIKE THAT WAS OVER.

MISTER G RAN THE YARD HERE, AND IF HE WANTED SOMETHING FROM TEEG, IT WAS GOING TO COMPLICATE THINGS.

HE'S RIGHT DOWN THIS WAY...

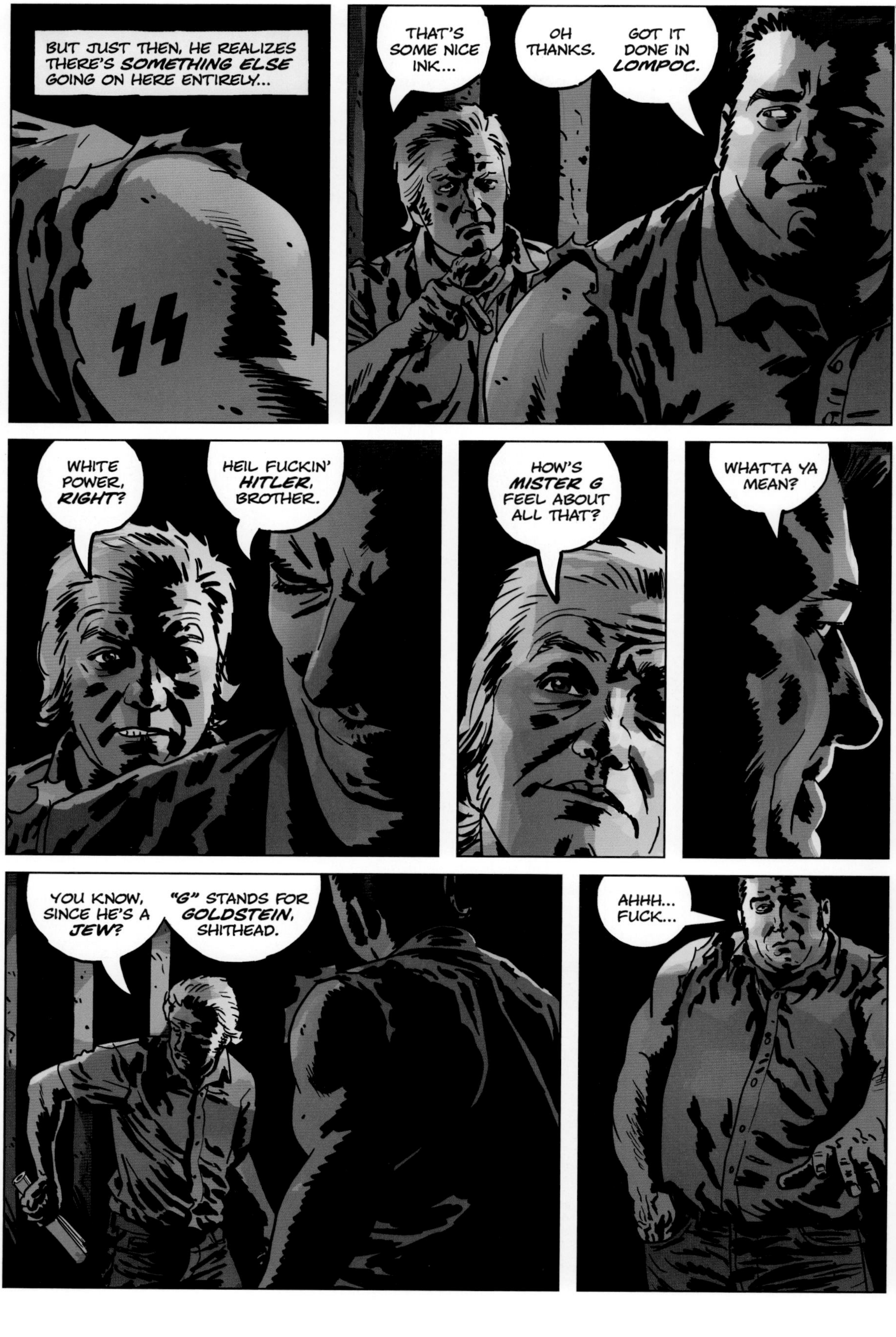
BUT JUST THEN, HE REALIZES THERE'S SOMETHING ELSE GOING ON HERE ENTIRELY...
THAT'S SOME NICE INK...
OH THANKS.
GOT IT DONE IN LOMPOC.
WHITE POWER, RIGHT?
HEIL FUCKIN' HITLER, BROTHER.
HOW'S MISTER G FEEL ABOUT ALL THAT?
WHATTA YA MEAN?
YOU KNOW, SINCE HE'S A JEW?
"G" STANDS FOR GOLDSTEIN, SHITHEAD.
AHHH... FUCK...

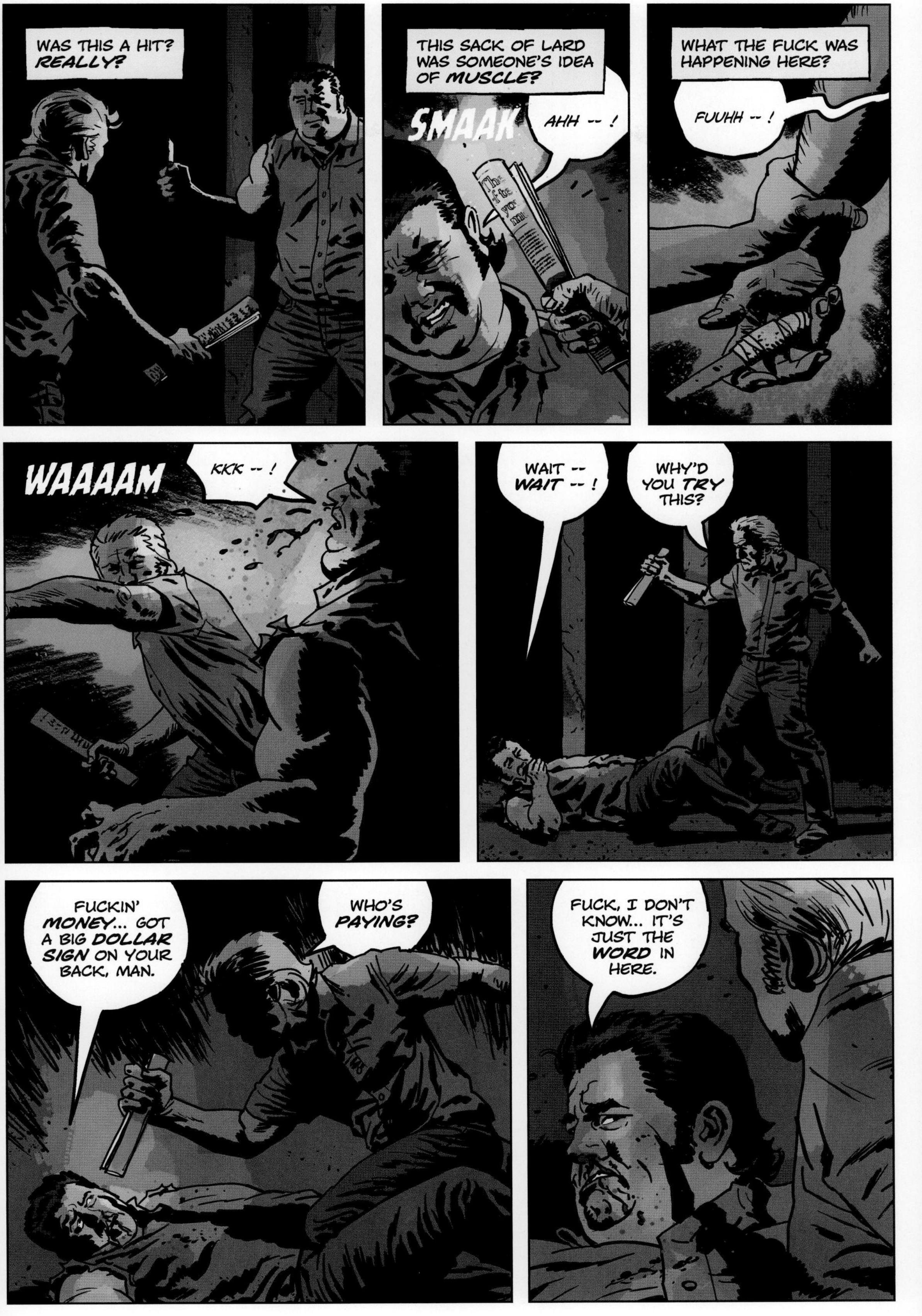
WAS THIS A HIT? REALLY?
THIS SACK OF LARD WAS SOMEONE'S IDEA OF MUSCLE?
SMAAK
AHH -- !
WHAT THE FUCK WAS HAPPENING HERE?
FUUHH -- !
WAAAAM
KKK -- !
WAIT -- WAIT -- !
WHY'D YOU TRY THIS?
FUCKIN' MONEY... GOT A BIG DOLLAR SIGN ON YOUR BACK, MAN.
WHO'S PAYING?
FUCK, I DON'T KNOW... IT'S JUST THE WORD IN HERE.

THAT'S ALL I KNOW -- I SWEAR, MAN. I SWEAR.
YEAH...
...I BELIEVE YOU.
GYAAA -- !
KILLING HAD ALWAYS COME TOO EASILY TO TEEG.
HE DID IT ALMOST WITHOUT THINKING...
...GGH...
...OR HE'D HAVE USED THIS ASSHOLE'S SHIV INSTEAD.
AH, SHIT...
NOW HE HAD TO GET RID OF THE EVIDENCE.
I WASN'T DONE READING THAT YET, YOU FAT FUCK...

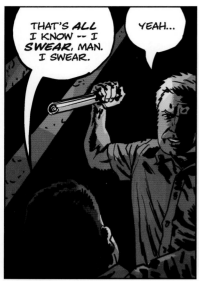

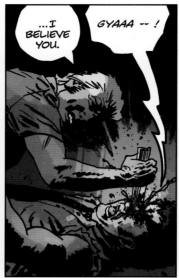

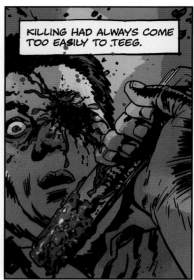

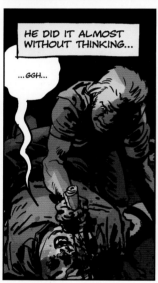

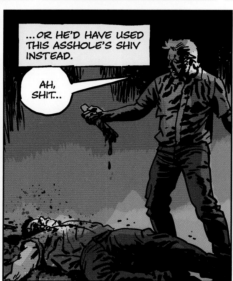

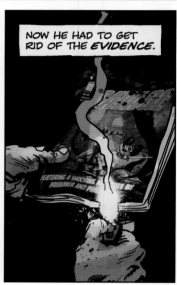

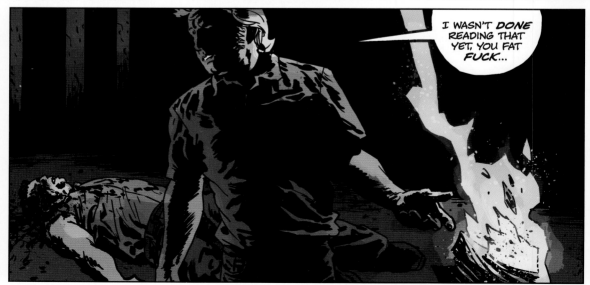

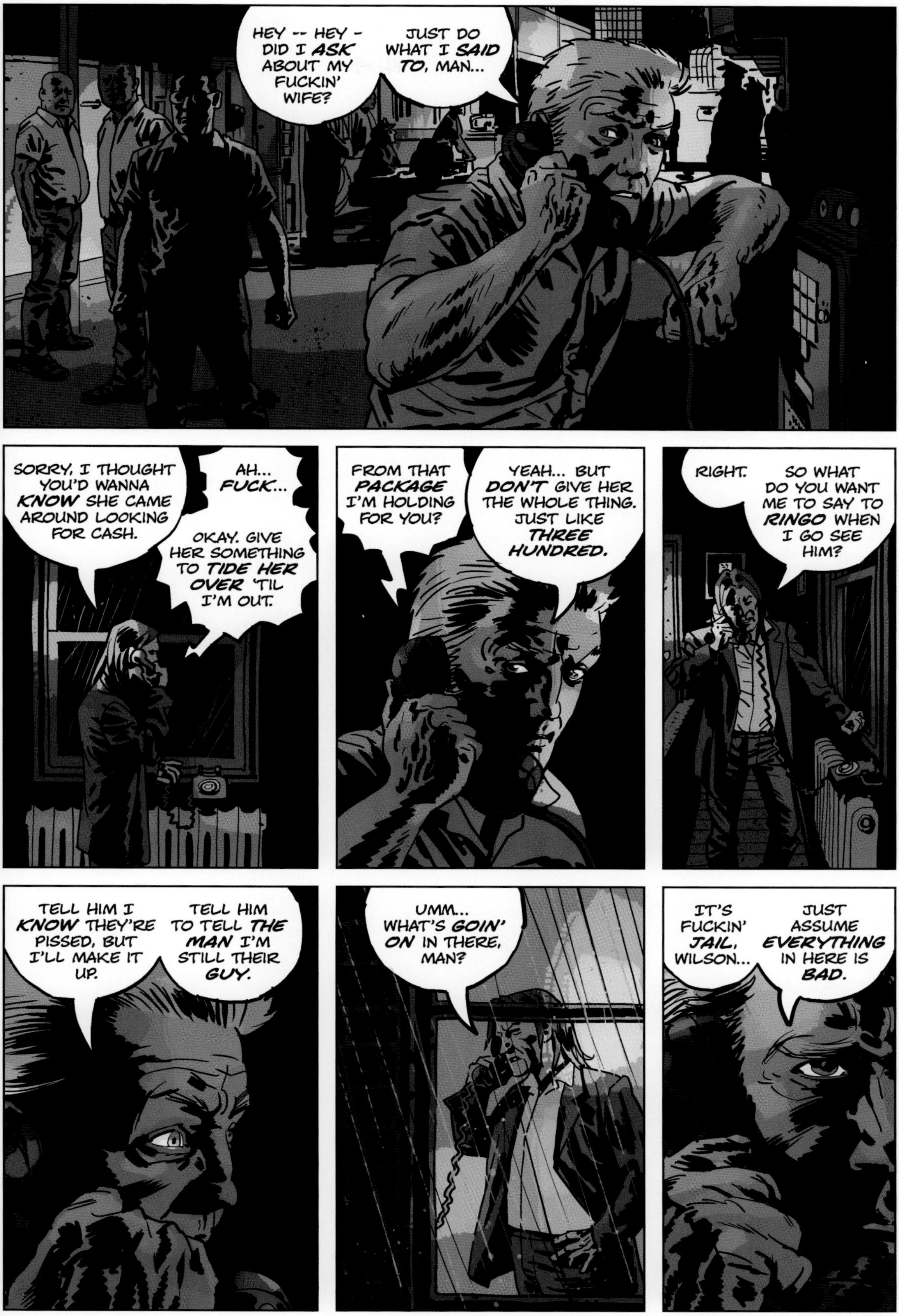
HEY -- HEY - DID I ASK ABOUT MY FUCKIN' WIFE?
JUST DO WHAT I SAID TO, MAN...
SORRY, I THOUGHT YOU'D WANNA KNOW SHE CAME AROUND LOOKING FOR CASH.
AH... FUCK...
OKAY. GIVE HER SOMETHING TO TIDE HER OVER 'TIL I'M OUT.
FROM THAT PACKAGE I'M HOLDING FOR YOU?
YEAH... BUT DON'T GIVE HER THE WHOLE THING. JUST LIKE THREE HUNDRED.
RIGHT.
SO WHAT DO YOU WANT ME TO SAY TO RINGO WHEN I GO SEE HIM?
TELL HIM I KNOW THEY'RE PISSED, BUT I'LL MAKE IT UP.
TELL HIM TO TELL THE MAN I'M STILL THEIR GUY.
UMM... WHAT'S GOIN' ON IN THERE, MAN?
IT'S FUCKIN' JAIL, WILSON...
JUST ASSUME EVERYTHING IN HERE IS BAD.

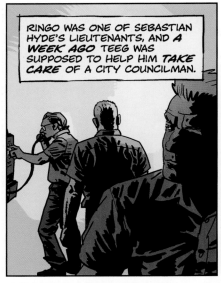

RINGO WAS ONE OF SEBASTIAN HYDE'S LIEUTENANTS, AND *A WEEK AGO* TEEG WAS SUPPOSED TO HELP HIM *TAKE CARE* OF A CITY COUNCILMAN.

THE GUY WAS BLOCKING A CONSTRUCTION CONTRACT HYDE NEEDED... OR *WANTED*, AT LEAST.

BUT TEEG HADN'T *BEEN THERE* A WEEK AGO, BECAUSE HE WAS IN *HERE*.

AND THAT COUNCILMAN WAS STILL WALKING AROUND TOWN, LIKE HE *OWNED* THE PLACE.

STILL, WOULD THAT BE REASON ENOUGH FOR HYDE TO WANT TEEG *DEAD*?

AND IF IT *WAS*, WOULDN'T HE HAVE SENT SOMEONE WHO COULD ACTUALLY PULL IT OFF?

AN *OPEN CONTRACT* WASN'T EXACTLY HIS STYLE...

EVEN IF KILLING PEOPLE FOR INCONVENIENCING HIM *WAS*.

PRETTY SURE YOU ALREADY READ ALL *THOSE ONES*, LAWLESS...

YEAH, MOST OF 'EM...

YOU GOT ANOTHER COPY OF LAST MONTH'S ISSUE?
WHAT HAPPENED TO THE ONE YOU CHECKED OUT YESTERDAY?
AH... FUCKIN' GUARD TOOK IT OFF ME IN THE LUNCHROOM.
SAID I LOOKED AT HIM WRONG.
CHRIST... YOU EVER THINK OF KEEPIN' YOUR HEAD DOWN ONCE IN A WHILE?
I THOUGHT I WAS.
THAT AIN'T WHAT I'M HEARIN'...
WHAT ARE YOU HEARING?
THAT YOU PROB'LY WON'T BE RETURNIN' ANYTHING YOU CHECK OUTTA HERE.
I'LL BE FINE... JUST FIND ME THE GODDAMN MAGAZINE.

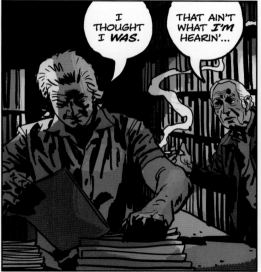

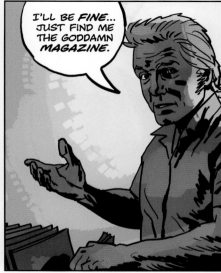

ALL RIGHT, HOLD YOUR HORSES...

OH YEAH, THIS IS A *GOOD* ONE.

SAVAGE

THERE'S THIS PART WHERE *ZANGAR* RIPS THIS GUY'S HEART OUT WHILE HE --

C'MON, *GIFF* -- I HAVEN'T *GOT* TO THAT YET.

I'M NOT *RUININ'* IT. YOU *KNOW* HE'S GONNA KILL EVERYONE...

IT'S *ZANGAR*. THAT'S WHAT HE *DOES.*

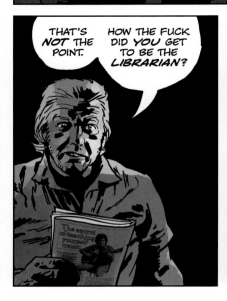

THAT'S *NOT* THE POINT.

HOW THE FUCK DID *YOU* GET TO BE THE *LIBRARIAN?*

AUTOEROTIC ASPHYXIATION.

WHAT?

SAVAGE

LAST GUY WHO HAD THIS GIG ACCIDENTLY *HUNG HIMSELF* WHILE *JERKIN' OFF*...

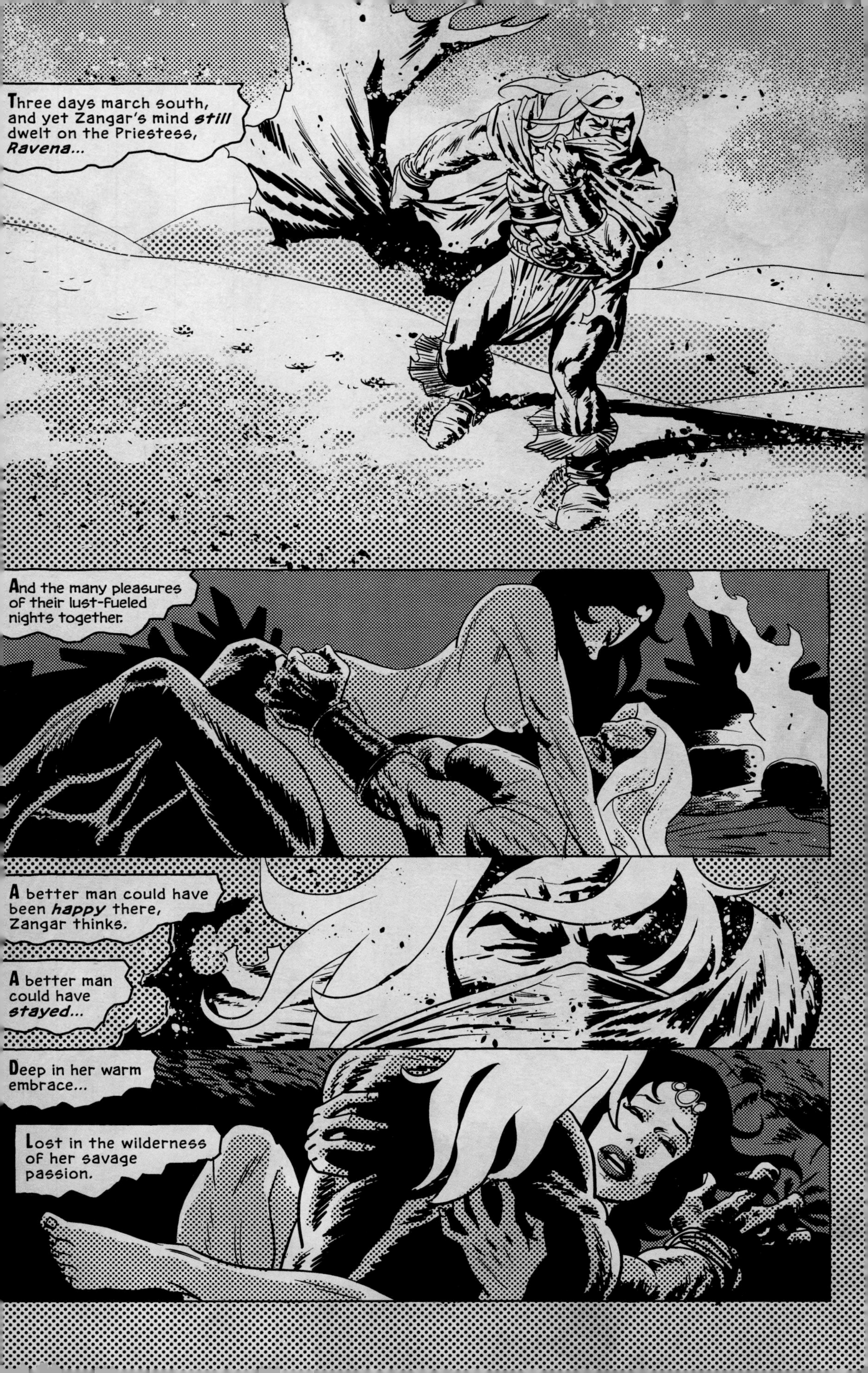
Three days march south, and yet Zangar's mind *still* dwelt on the Priestess, *Ravena*...
And the many pleasures of their lust-fueled nights together.
A better man could have been *happy* there, Zangar thinks.
A better man could have *stayed*...
Deep in her warm embrace...
Lost in the wilderness of her savage passion.

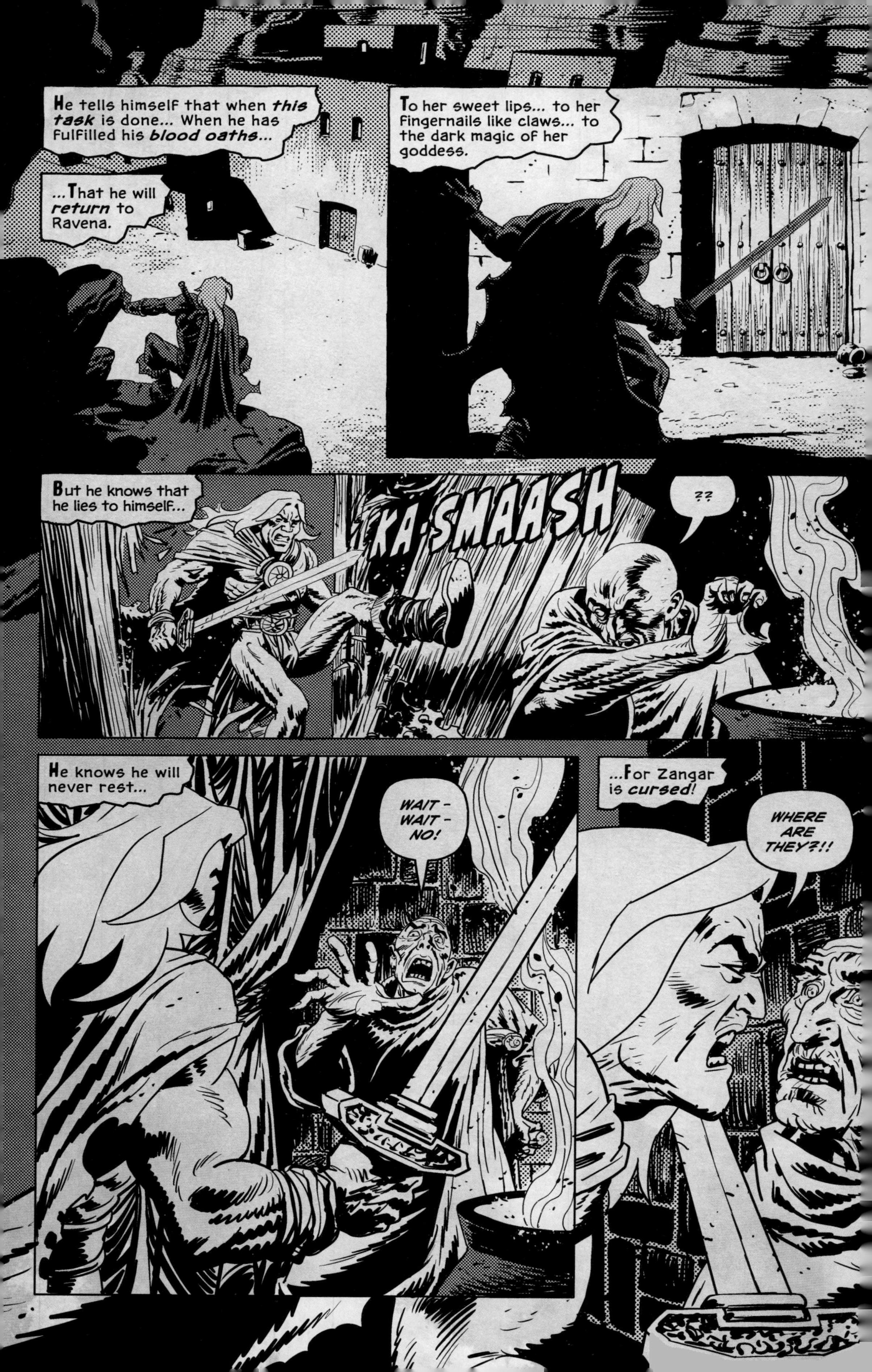
He tells himself that when this task is done... When he has fulfilled his blood oaths...
...That he will return to Ravena.
To her sweet lips... to her fingernails like claws... to the dark magic of her goddess.
But he knows that he lies to himself...
KA-SMAASH
??
He knows he will never rest...
WAIT - WAIT - NO!
...For Zangar is cursed!
WHERE ARE THEY?!!

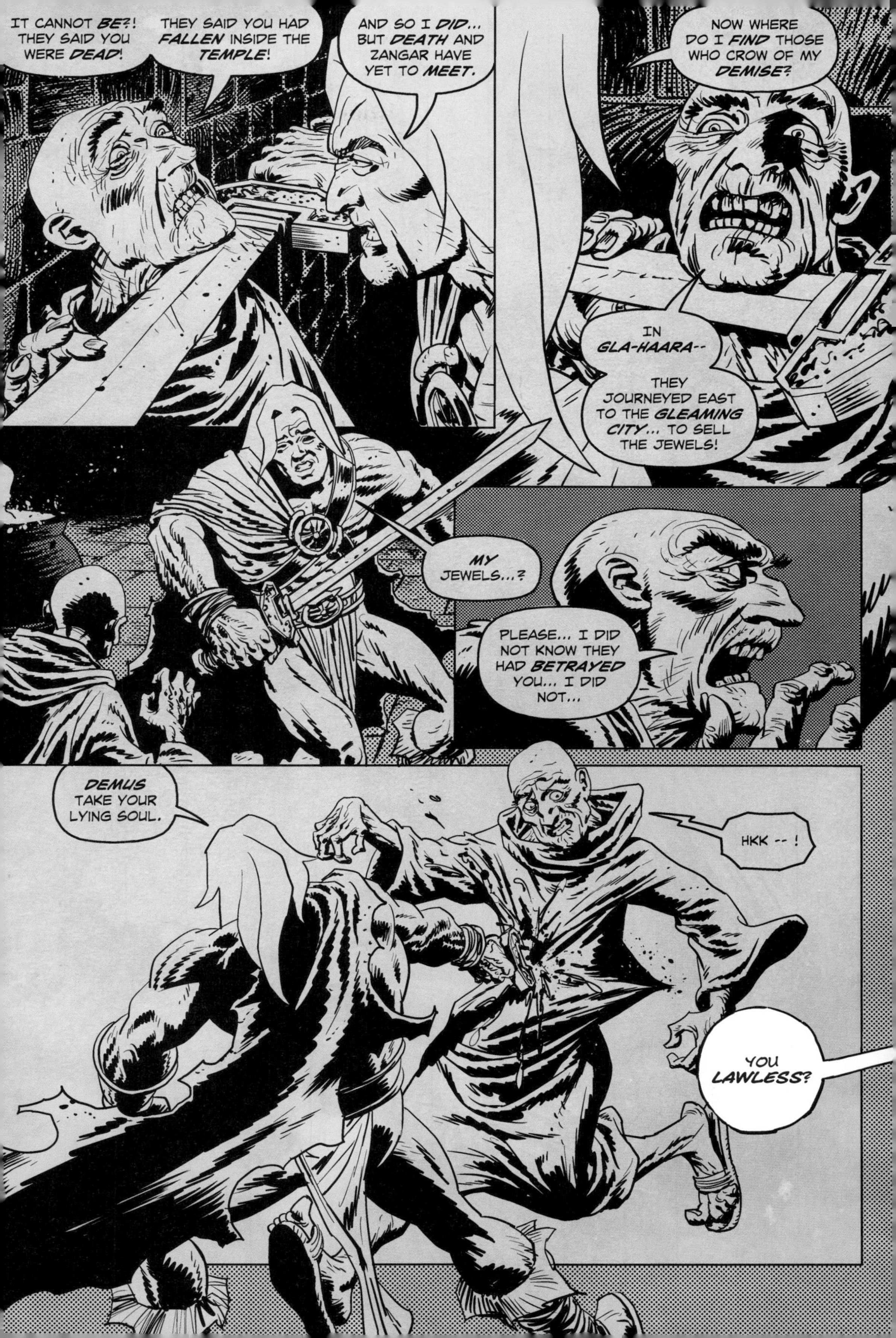
IT CANNOT BE?! THEY SAID YOU WERE DEAD!
THEY SAID YOU HAD FALLEN INSIDE THE TEMPLE!
AND SO I DID... BUT DEATH AND ZANGAR HAVE YET TO MEET.
NOW WHERE DO I FIND THOSE WHO CROW OF MY DEMISE?
IN GLA-HAARA--
THEY JOURNEYED EAST TO THE GLEAMING CITY... TO SELL THE JEWELS!
MY JEWELS...?
PLEASE... I DID NOT KNOW THEY HAD BETRAYED YOU... I DID NOT...
DEMUS TAKE YOUR LYING SOUL.
HKK -- !
YOU LAWLESS?

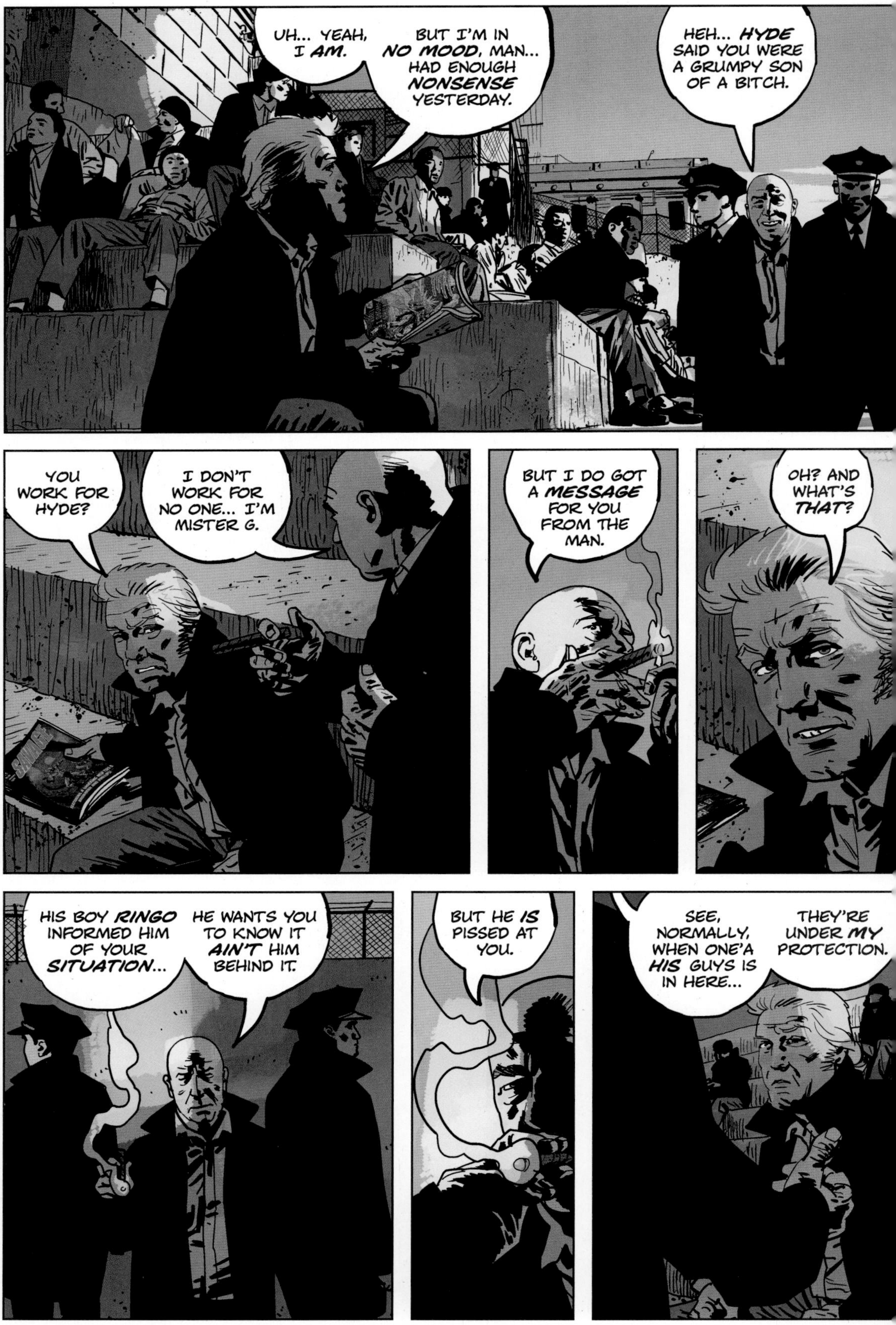
UH... YEAH, I AM.
BUT I'M IN NO MOOD, MAN... HAD ENOUGH NONSENSE YESTERDAY.
HEH... HYDE SAID YOU WERE A GRUMPY SON OF A BITCH.
YOU WORK FOR HYDE?
I DON'T WORK FOR NO ONE... I'M MISTER G.
BUT I DO GOT A MESSAGE FOR YOU FROM THE MAN.
OH? AND WHAT'S THAT?
HIS BOY RINGO INFORMED HIM OF YOUR SITUATION...
HE WANTS YOU TO KNOW IT AIN'T HIM BEHIND IT.
BUT HE IS PISSED AT YOU.
SEE, NORMALLY, WHEN ONE'A HIS GUYS IS IN HERE...
THEY'RE UNDER MY PROTECTION.

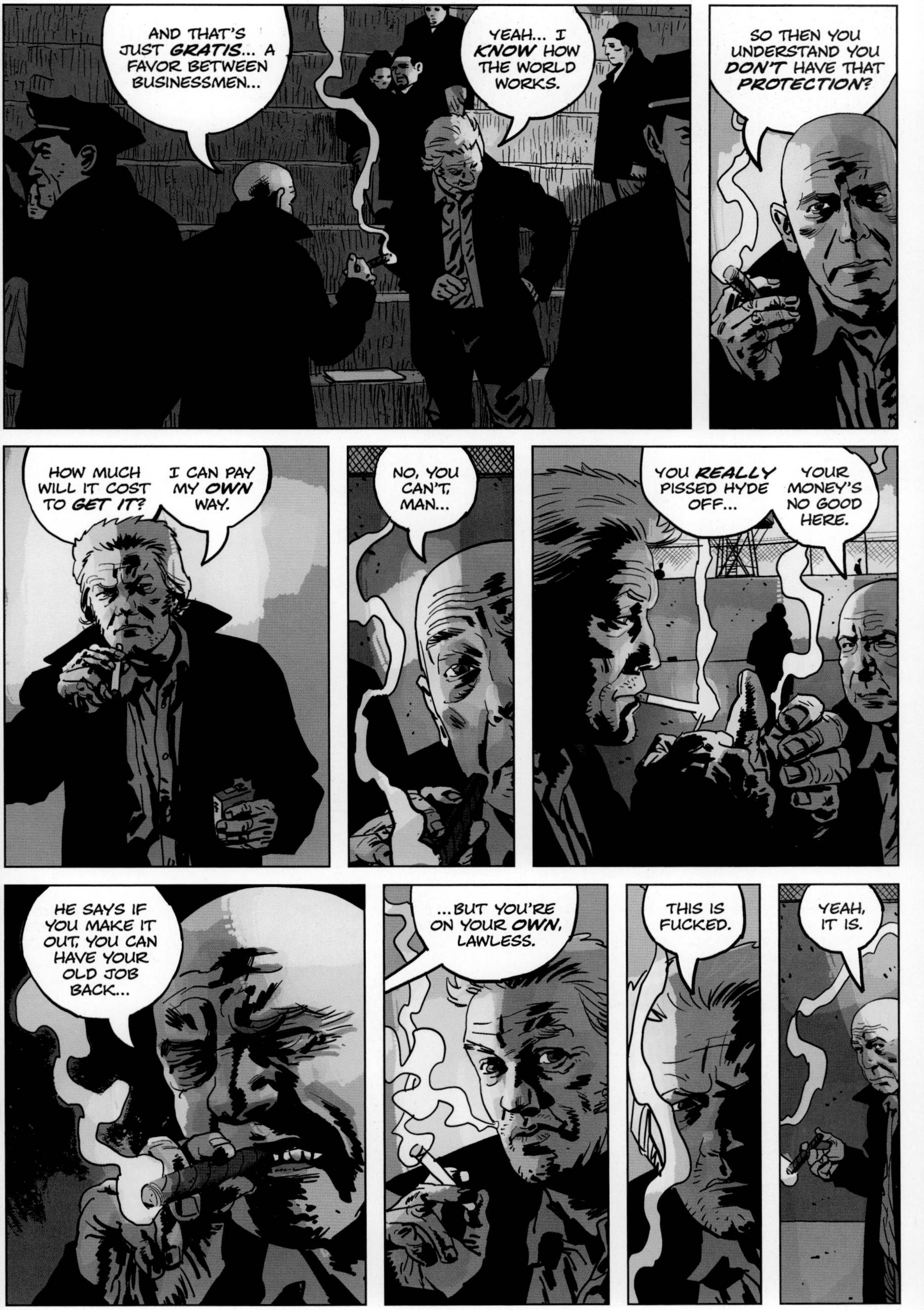
AND THAT'S JUST GRATIS... A FAVOR BETWEEN BUSINESSMEN...
YEAH... I KNOW HOW THE WORLD WORKS.
SO THEN YOU UNDERSTAND YOU DON'T HAVE THAT PROTECTION?
HOW MUCH WILL IT COST TO GET IT?
I CAN PAY MY OWN WAY.
NO, YOU CAN'T, MAN...
YOU REALLY PISSED HYDE OFF...
YOUR MONEY'S NO GOOD HERE.
HE SAYS IF YOU MAKE IT OUT, YOU CAN HAVE YOUR OLD JOB BACK...
...BUT YOU'RE ON YOUR OWN, LAWLESS.
THIS IS FUCKED.
YEAH, IT IS.

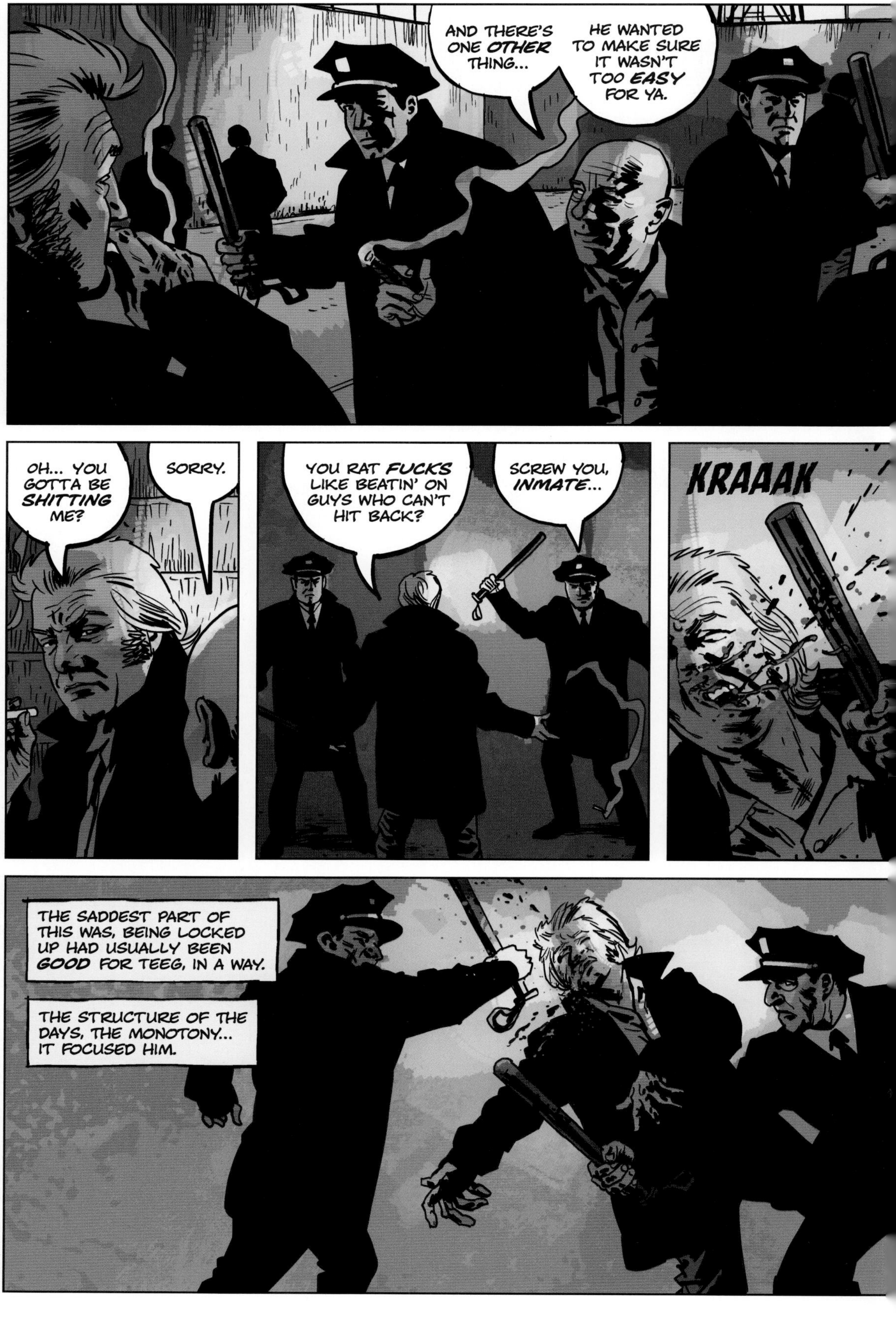
AND THERE'S ONE OTHER THING...
HE WANTED TO MAKE SURE IT WASN'T TOO EASY FOR YA.
OH... YOU GOTTA BE SHITTING ME?
SORRY.
YOU RAT FUCKS LIKE BEATIN' ON GUYS WHO CAN'T HIT BACK?
SCREW YOU, INMATE...
KRAAAK
THE SADDEST PART OF THIS WAS, BEING LOCKED UP HAD USUALLY BEEN GOOD FOR TEEG, IN A WAY.
THE STRUCTURE OF THE DAYS, THE MONOTONY... IT FOCUSED HIM.

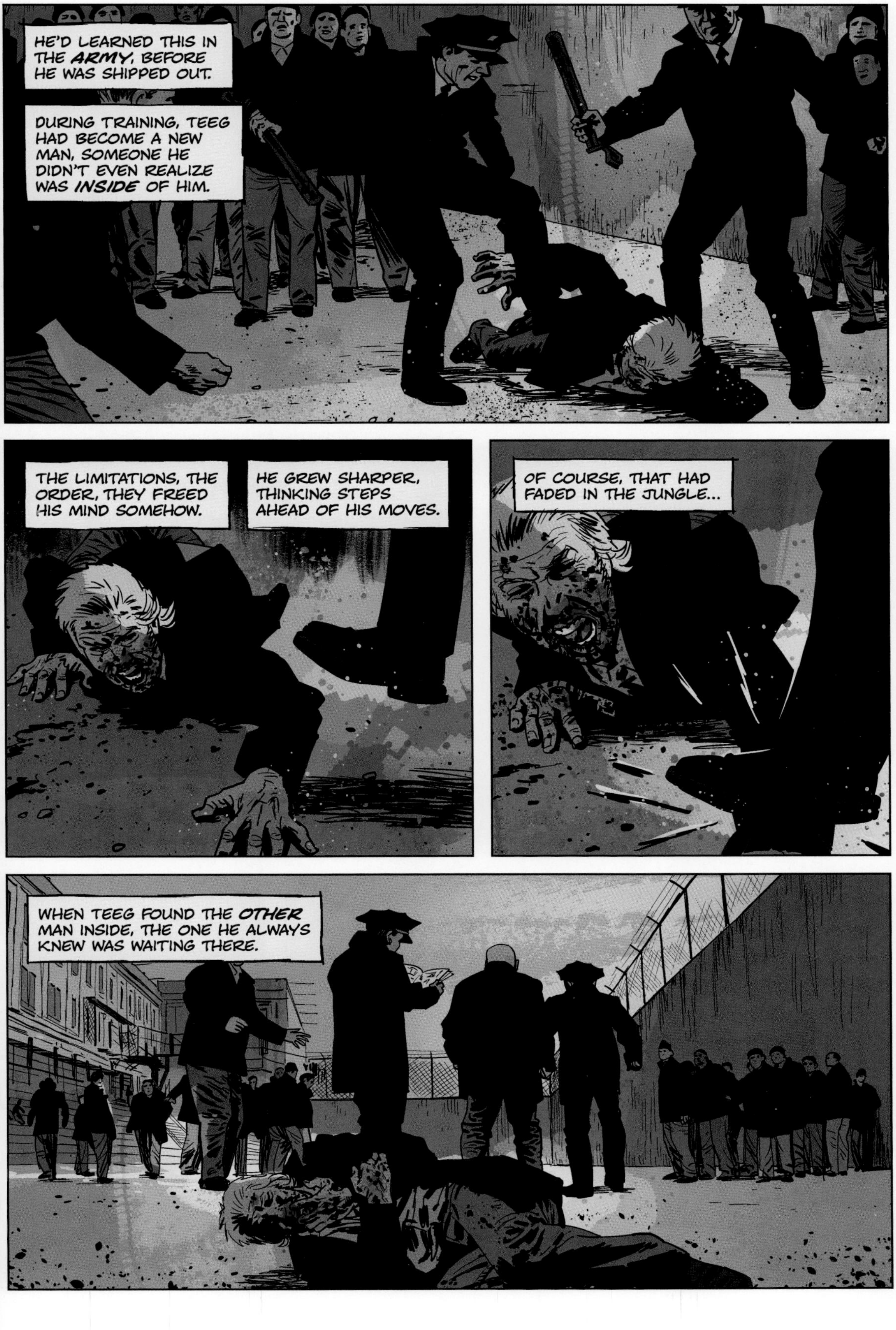
HE'D LEARNED THIS IN THE ARMY, BEFORE HE WAS SHIPPED OUT.
DURING TRAINING, TEEG HAD BECOME A NEW MAN, SOMEONE HE DIDN'T EVEN REALIZE WAS INSIDE OF HIM.
THE LIMITATIONS, THE ORDER, THEY FREED HIS MIND SOMEHOW.
HE GREW SHARPER, THINKING STEPS AHEAD OF HIS MOVES.
OF COURSE, THAT HAD FADED IN THE JUNGLE...
WHEN TEEG FOUND THE OTHER MAN INSIDE, THE ONE HE ALWAYS KNEW WAS WAITING THERE.

THAT WAS THE MAN HE WAS *OUTSIDE*, IN THE REAL WORLD...

WHERE HE ONLY MADE *BAD* DECISIONS.

FREEDOM JUST GAVE HIM TOO DAMN MANY *CHOICES*.

TOO MANY WAYS TO SELF-DESTRUCT.

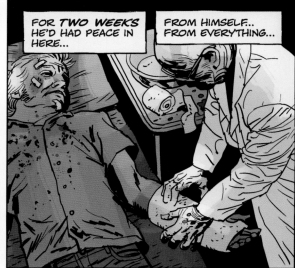

FOR *TWO WEEKS* HE'D HAD PEACE IN HERE...

FROM HIMSELF... FROM EVERYTHING...

BUT NOW SOMEONE'S SENT THE OUTSIDE WORLD IN *AFTER* HIM.

AND HE DOESN'T EVEN KNOW *WHO*... OR WHY...

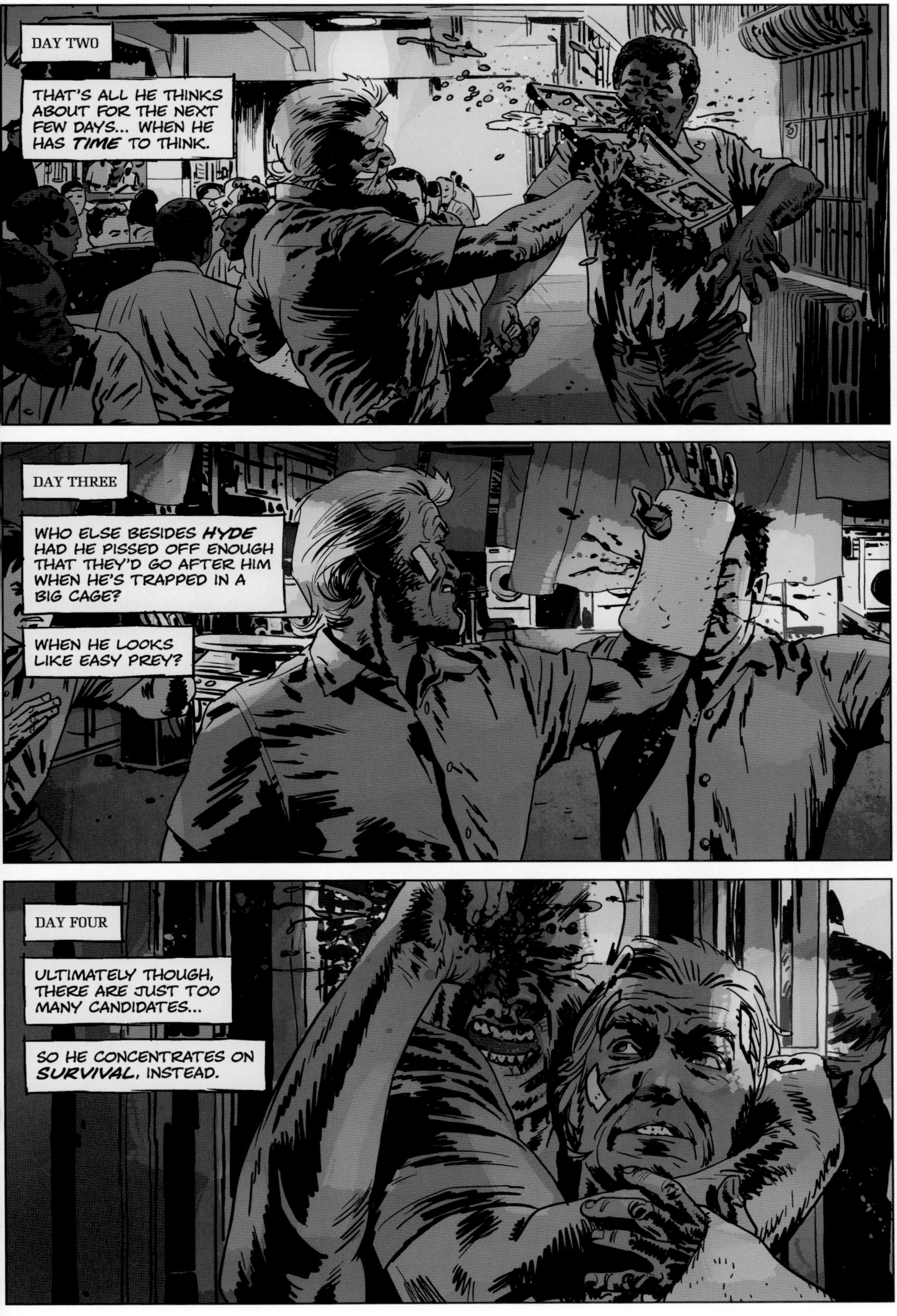
DAY TWO
THAT'S ALL HE THINKS ABOUT FOR THE NEXT FEW DAYS... WHEN HE HAS TIME TO THINK.
DAY THREE
WHO ELSE BESIDES HYDE HAD HE PISSED OFF ENOUGH THAT THEY'D GO AFTER HIM WHEN HE'S TRAPPED IN A BIG CAGE?
WHEN HE LOOKS LIKE EASY PREY?
DAY FOUR
ULTIMATELY THOUGH, THERE ARE JUST TOO MANY CANDIDATES...
SO HE CONCENTRATES ON SURVIVAL, INSTEAD.

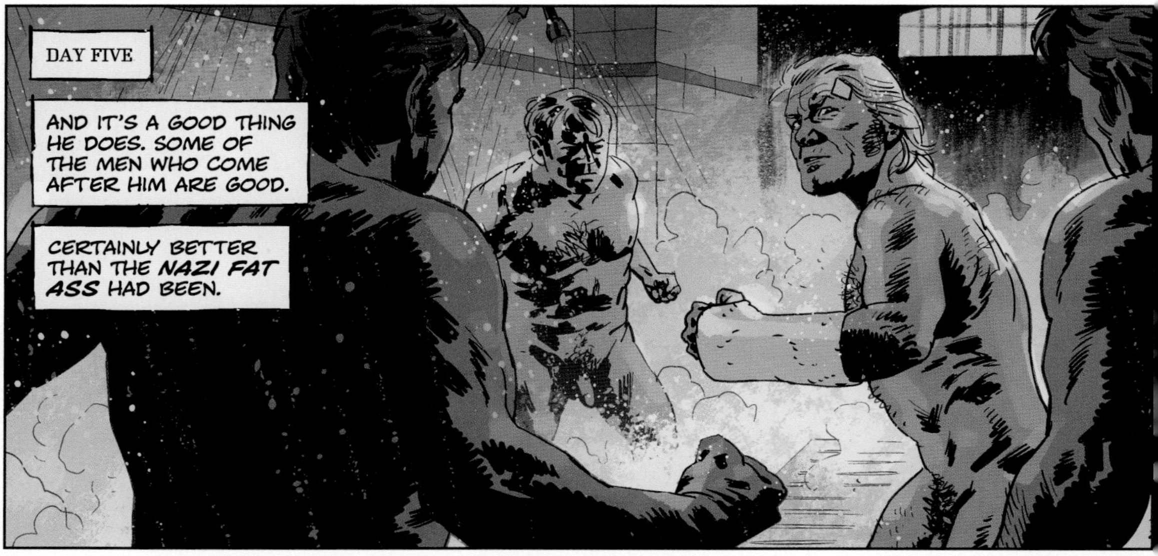
DAY FIVE
AND IT'S A GOOD THING HE DOES. SOME OF THE MEN WHO COME AFTER HIM ARE GOOD.
CERTAINLY BETTER THAN THE NAZI FAT ASS HAD BEEN.

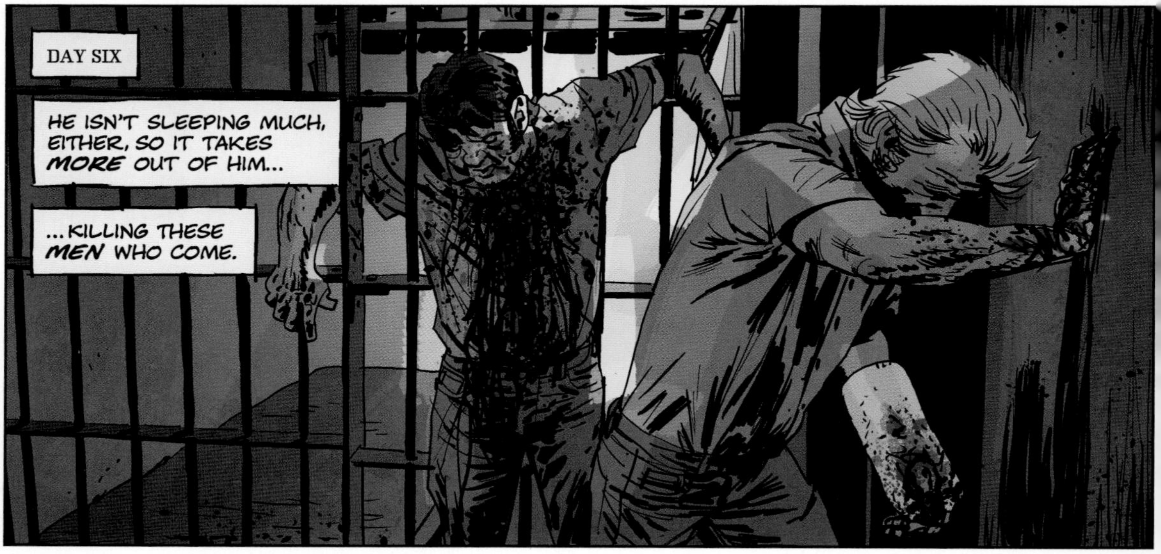
DAY SIX
HE ISN'T SLEEPING MUCH, EITHER, SO IT TAKES MORE OUT OF HIM...
...KILLING THESE MEN WHO COME.

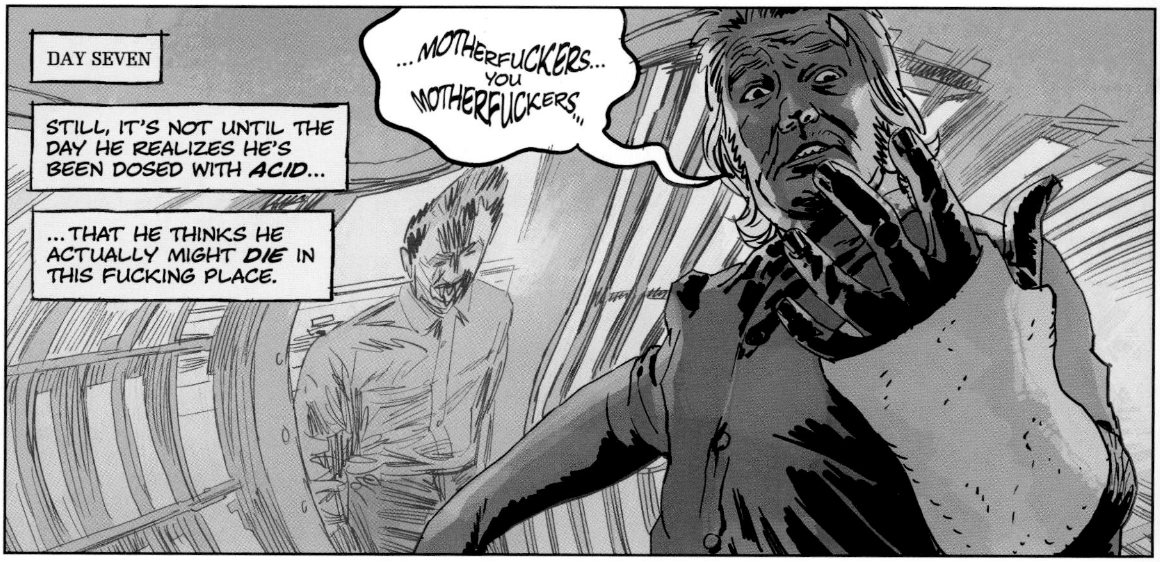
DAY SEVEN
STILL, IT'S NOT UNTIL THE DAY HE REALIZES HE'S BEEN DOSED WITH ACID...
...THAT HE THINKS HE ACTUALLY MIGHT DIE IN THIS FUCKING PLACE.
...MOTHERFUCKERS... YOU MOTHERFUCKERS...

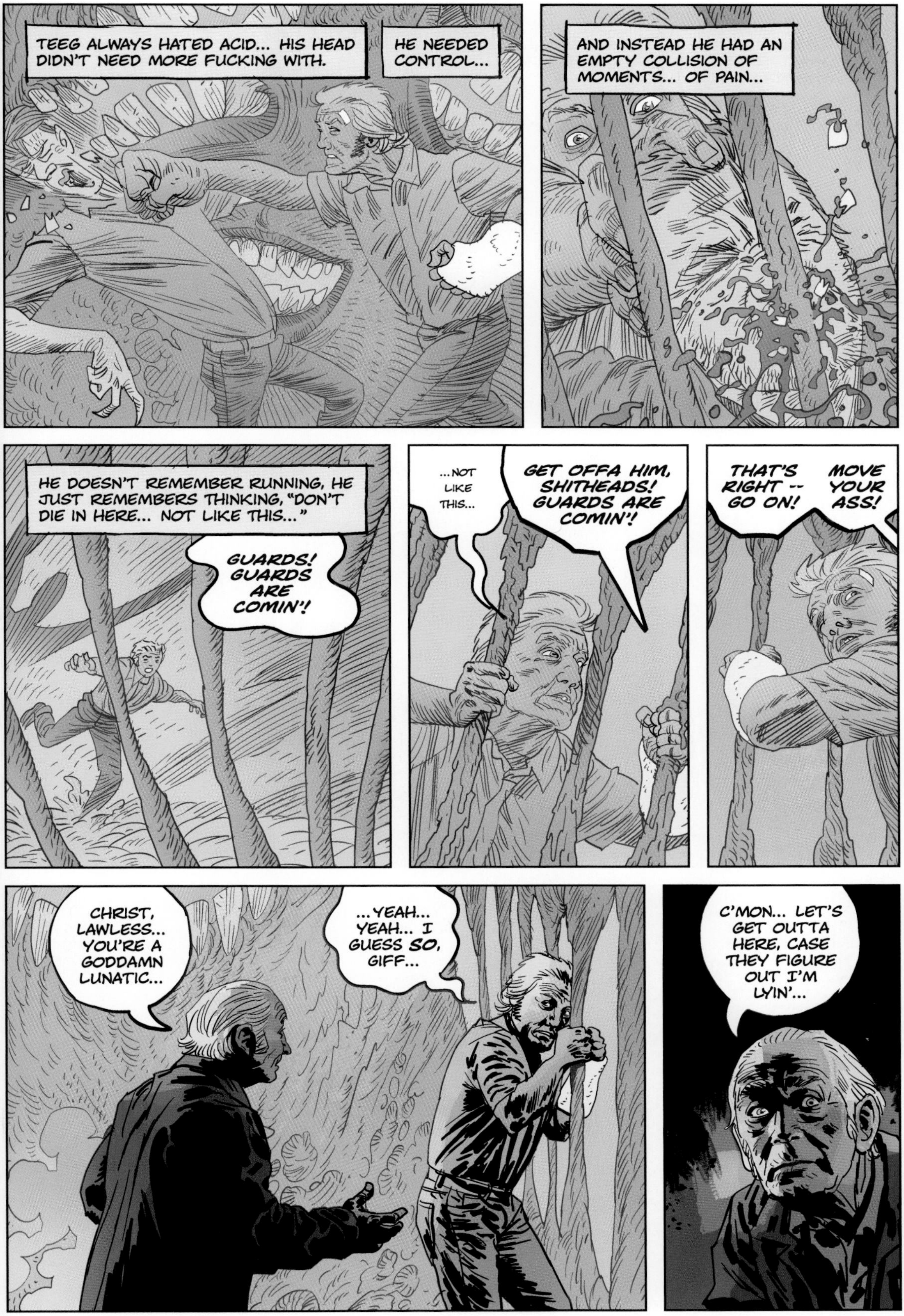
TEEG ALWAYS HATED ACID... HIS HEAD DIDN'T NEED MORE FUCKING WITH.
HE NEEDED CONTROL...
AND INSTEAD HE HAD AN EMPTY COLLISION OF MOMENTS... OF PAIN...
HE DOESN'T REMEMBER RUNNING, HE JUST REMEMBERS THINKING, "DON'T DIE IN HERE... NOT LIKE THIS..."
GUARDS! GUARDS ARE COMIN'!
...NOT LIKE THIS...
GET OFFA HIM, SHITHEADS! GUARDS ARE COMIN'!
THAT'S RIGHT -- GO ON!
MOVE YOUR ASS!
CHRIST, LAWLESS... YOU'RE A GODDAMN LUNATIC...
...YEAH... YEAH... I GUESS SO, GIFF...
C'MON... LET'S GET OUTTA HERE, CASE THEY FIGURE OUT I'M LYIN'...

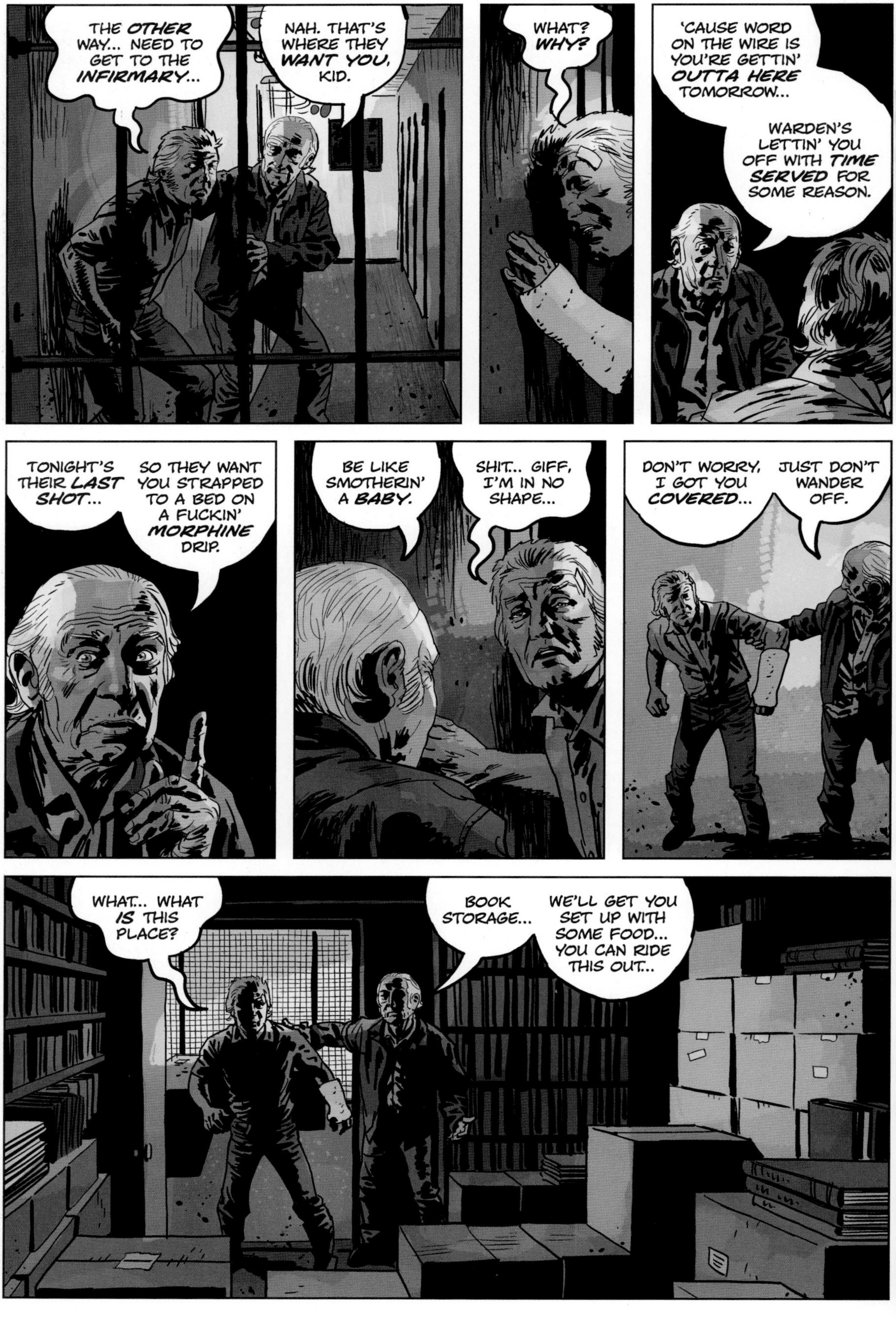
THE OTHER WAY... NEED TO GET TO THE INFIRMARY...
NAH. THAT'S WHERE THEY WANT YOU, KID.
WHAT? WHY?
'CAUSE WORD ON THE WIRE IS YOU'RE GETTIN' OUTTA HERE TOMORROW...
WARDEN'S LETTIN' YOU OFF WITH TIME SERVED FOR SOME REASON.
TONIGHT'S THEIR LAST SHOT...
SO THEY WANT YOU STRAPPED TO A BED ON A FUCKIN' MORPHINE DRIP.
BE LIKE SMOTHERIN' A BABY.
SHIT... GIFF, I'M IN NO SHAPE...
DON'T WORRY, I GOT YOU COVERED...
JUST DON'T WANDER OFF.
WHAT... WHAT IS THIS PLACE?
BOOK STORAGE...
WE'LL GET YOU SET UP WITH SOME FOOD... YOU CAN RIDE THIS OUT...

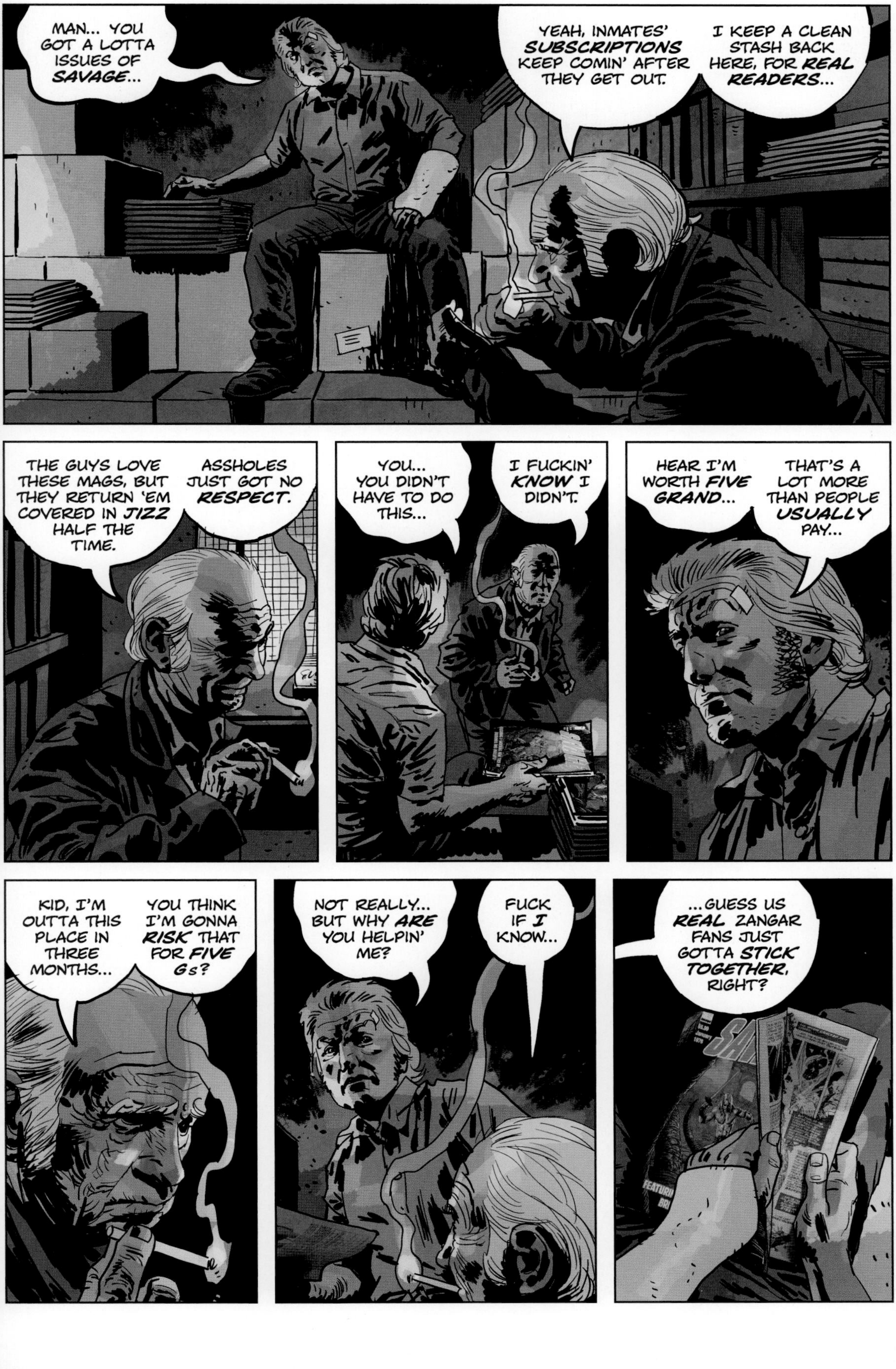
MAN... YOU GOT A LOTTA ISSUES OF SAVAGE...
YEAH, INMATES' SUBSCRIPTIONS KEEP COMIN' AFTER THEY GET OUT.
I KEEP A CLEAN STASH BACK HERE, FOR REAL READERS...
THE GUYS LOVE THESE MAGS, BUT THEY RETURN 'EM COVERED IN JIZZ HALF THE TIME.
ASSHOLES JUST GOT NO RESPECT.
YOU... YOU DIDN'T HAVE TO DO THIS...
I FUCKIN' KNOW I DIDN'T.
HEAR I'M WORTH FIVE GRAND...
THAT'S A LOT MORE THAN PEOPLE USUALLY PAY...
KID, I'M OUTTA THIS PLACE IN THREE MONTHS...
YOU THINK I'M GONNA RISK THAT FOR FIVE Gs?
NOT REALLY... BUT WHY ARE YOU HELPIN' ME?
FUCK IF I KNOW...
...GUESS US REAL ZANGAR FANS JUST GOTTA STICK TOGETHER, RIGHT?

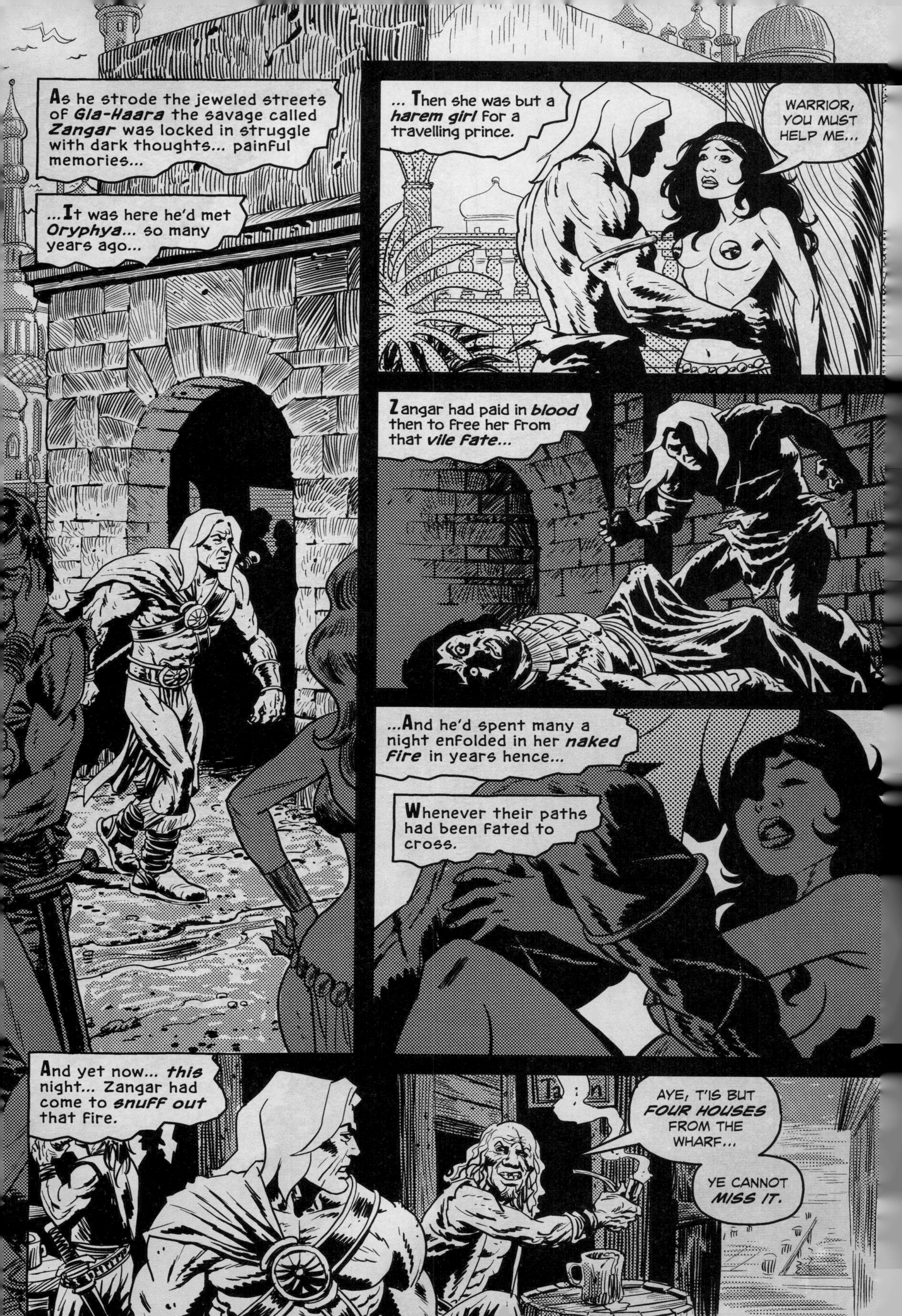
As he strode the jeweled streets of Gia-Haara the savage called Zangar was locked in struggle with dark thoughts... painful memories...
...It was here he'd met Oryphya... so many years ago...
... Then she was but a harem girl for a travelling prince.
WARRIOR, YOU MUST HELP ME...
Zangar had paid in blood then to free her from that vile fate...
...And he'd spent many a night enfolded in her naked fire in years hence...
Whenever their paths had been fated to cross.
And yet now... this night... Zangar had come to snuff out that fire.
AYE, T'IS BUT FOUR HOUSES FROM THE WHARF...
YE CANNOT MISS IT.

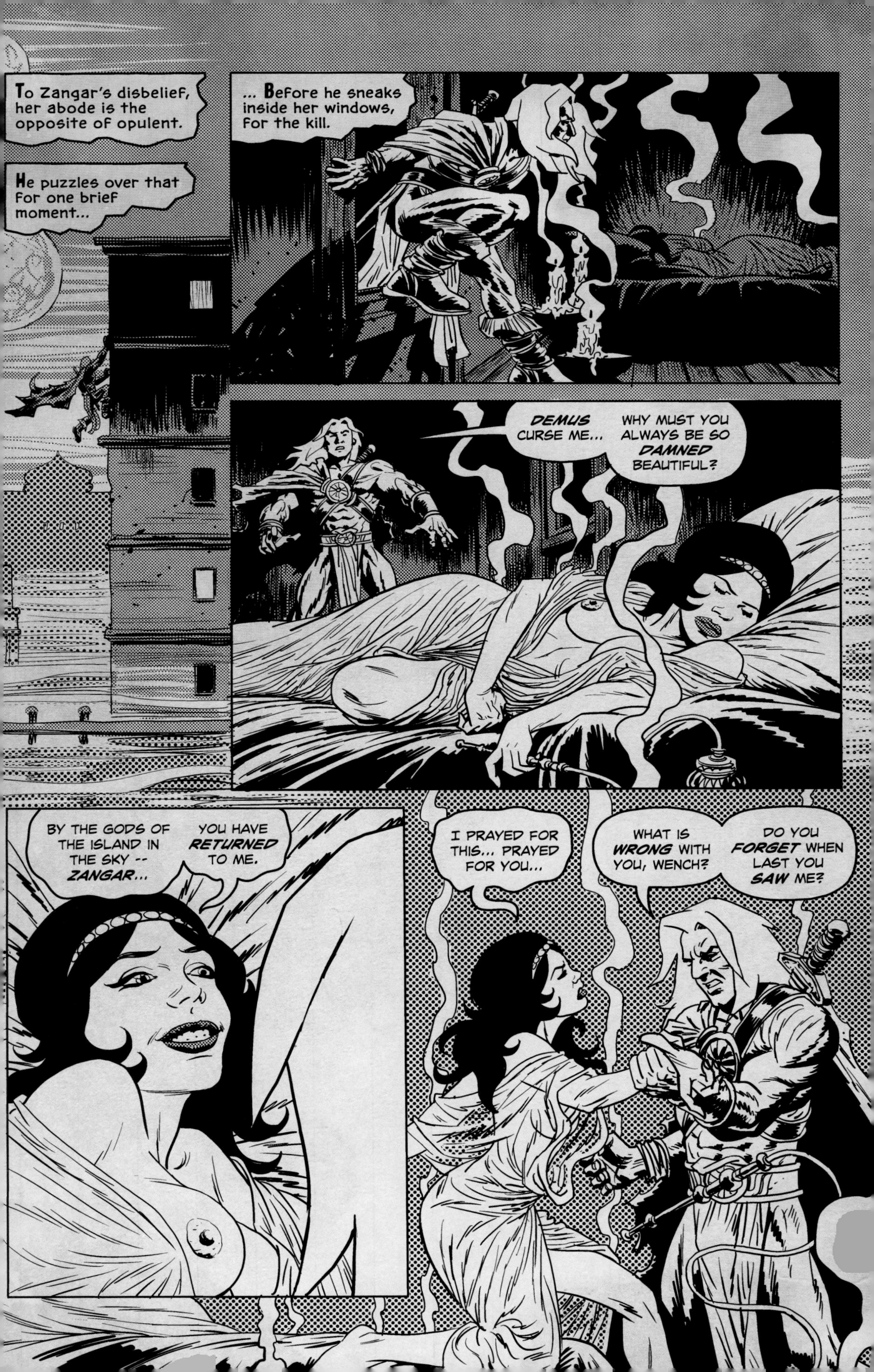
To Zangar's disbelief, her abode is the opposite of opulent.
He puzzles over that for one brief moment...
... Before he sneaks inside her windows, for the kill.
DEMUS CURSE ME...
WHY MUST YOU ALWAYS BE SO DAMNED BEAUTIFUL?
BY THE GODS OF THE ISLAND IN THE SKY -- ZANGAR...
YOU HAVE RETURNED TO ME.
I PRAYED FOR THIS... PRAYED FOR YOU...
WHAT IS WRONG WITH YOU, WENCH?
DO YOU FORGET WHEN LAST YOU SAW ME?

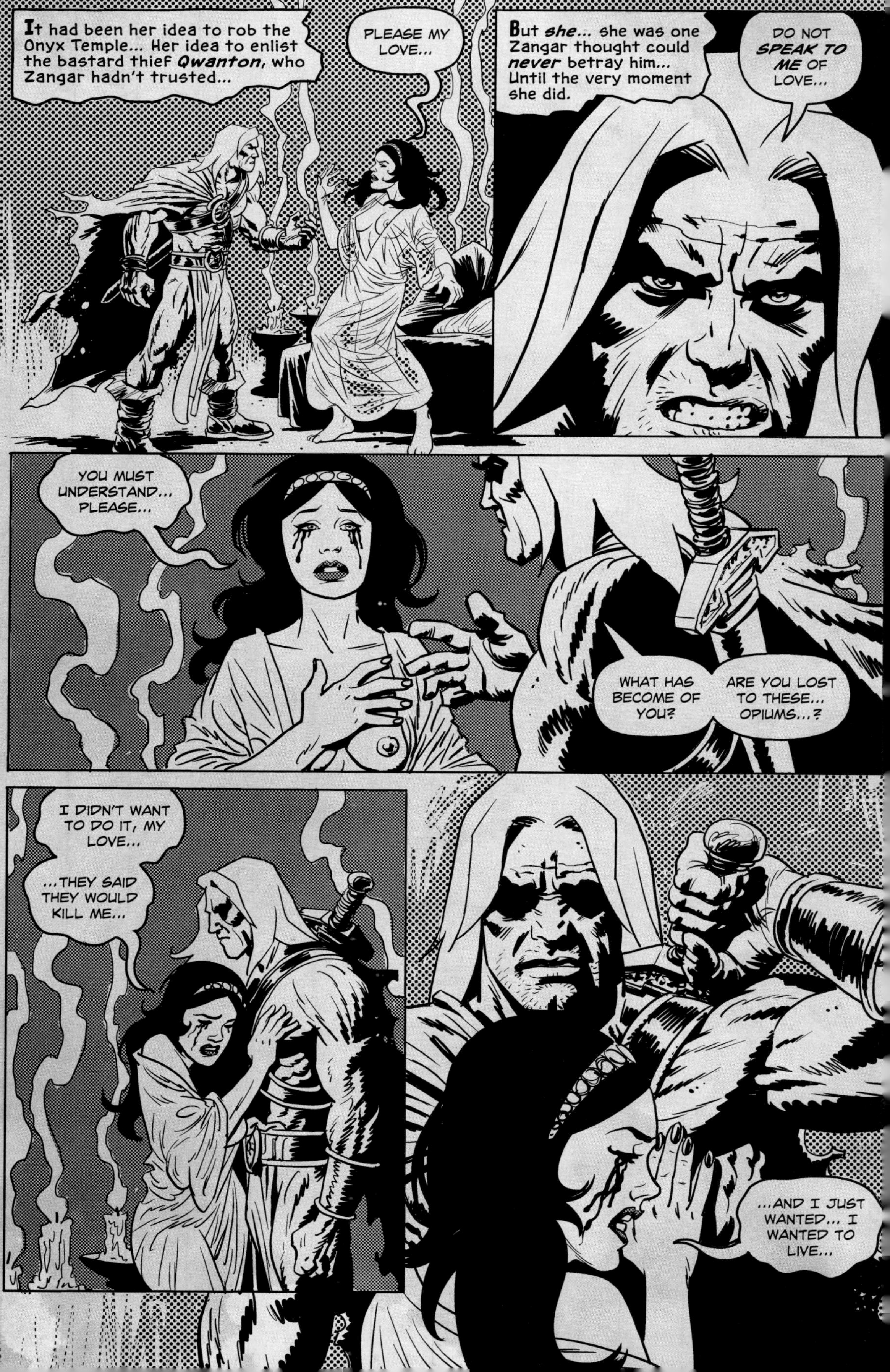

It had been her idea to rob the Onyx Temple... Her idea to enlist the bastard thief *Qwanton*, who Zangar hadn't trusted...
PLEASE MY LOVE...
But *she*... she was one Zangar thought could *never* betray him... Until the very moment she did.
DO NOT *SPEAK TO ME* OF LOVE...
YOU MUST UNDERSTAND... PLEASE...
WHAT HAS BECOME OF YOU?
ARE YOU LOST TO THESE... OPIUMS...?
I DIDN'T WANT TO DO IT, MY LOVE...
...THEY SAID THEY WOULD KILL ME...
...AND I JUST WANTED... I WANTED TO LIVE...

RINGO WAS WAITING THE NEXT MORNING WHEN THEY LET TEEG OUT.

YO, LAWLESS... OVER HERE...

TOP –
REARMS
YOND
POINT
CK ALL
ONS WITH
TOWER

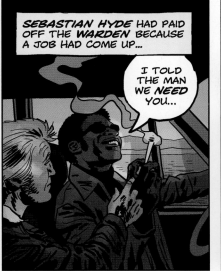

SEBASTIAN HYDE HAD PAID OFF THE WARDEN BECAUSE A JOB HAD COME UP...

I TOLD THE MAN WE NEED YOU...

BUT THE MOTHERFUCKIN' WARDEN WAS HAPPY TO GET RID'A YOUR ASS...

YOU BEEN MESSIN' UP HIS STATS.

I WASN'T AWARE HE GAVE A FUCK.

MAN, I DON'T EVEN WANNA START THE LIST OF SHIT YOU AIN'T AWARE OF, LAWLESS.

RINGO WAS JOKING, BUT THE ONLY THING ON THAT LIST TEEG CARED ABOUT WAS: WHO THE FUCK HAD TAKEN THE HIT OUT ON HIM?

WE MEET TOMORROW AT THE UNDERTOW. DON'T MISS IT THIS TIME.

I'LL TRY MY BEST...

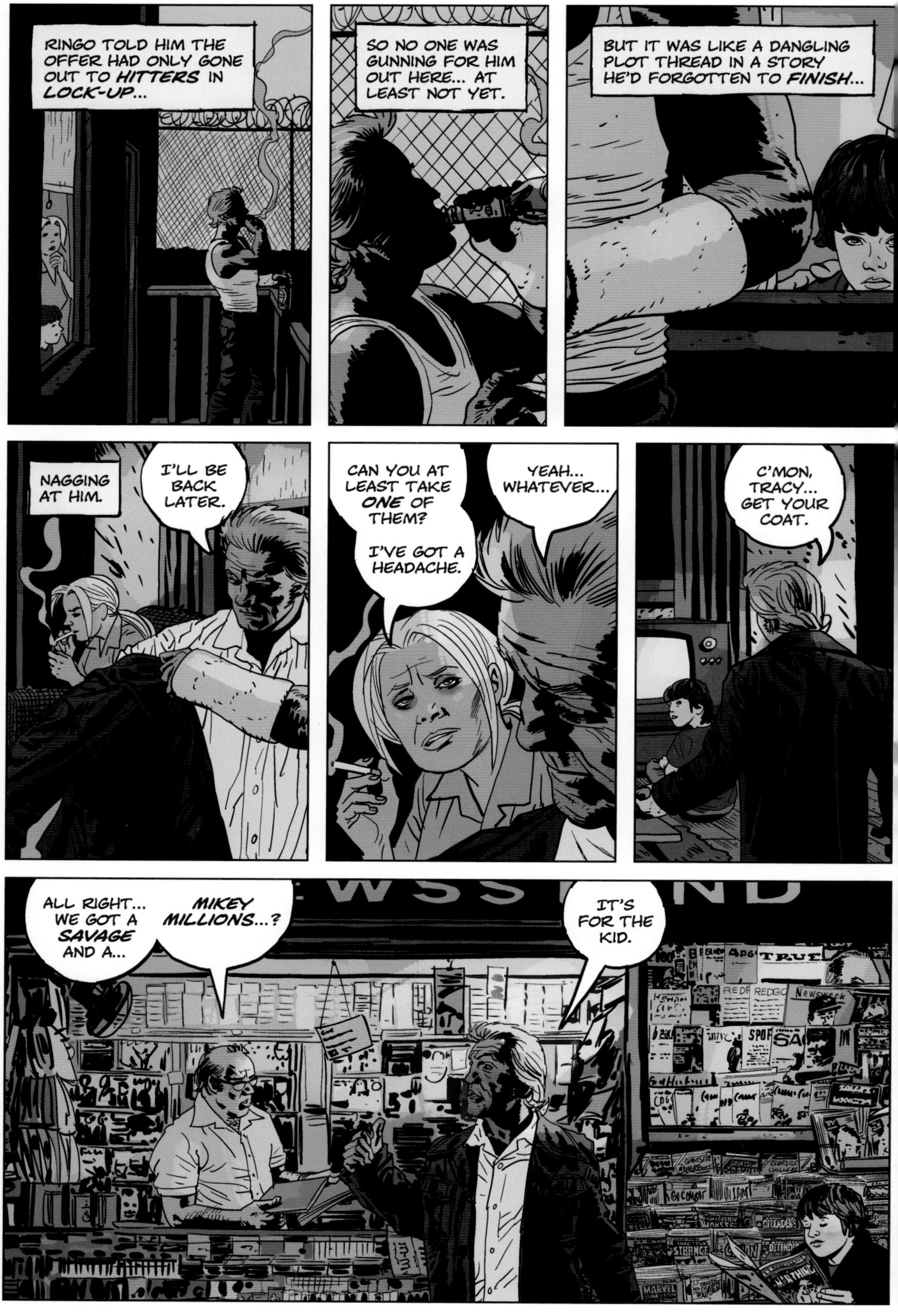
RINGO TOLD HIM THE OFFER HAD ONLY GONE OUT TO *HITTERS* IN *LOCK-UP*...
SO NO ONE WAS GUNNING FOR HIM OUT HERE... AT LEAST NOT YET.
BUT IT WAS LIKE A DANGLING PLOT THREAD IN A STORY HE'D FORGOTTEN TO *FINISH*...
NAGGING AT HIM.
I'LL BE BACK LATER.
CAN YOU AT LEAST TAKE *ONE* OF THEM?
I'VE GOT A HEADACHE.
YEAH... WHATEVER...
C'MON, TRACY... GET YOUR COAT.
ALL RIGHT... WE GOT A *SAVAGE* AND A...
MIKEY MILLIONS...?
IT'S FOR THE KID.

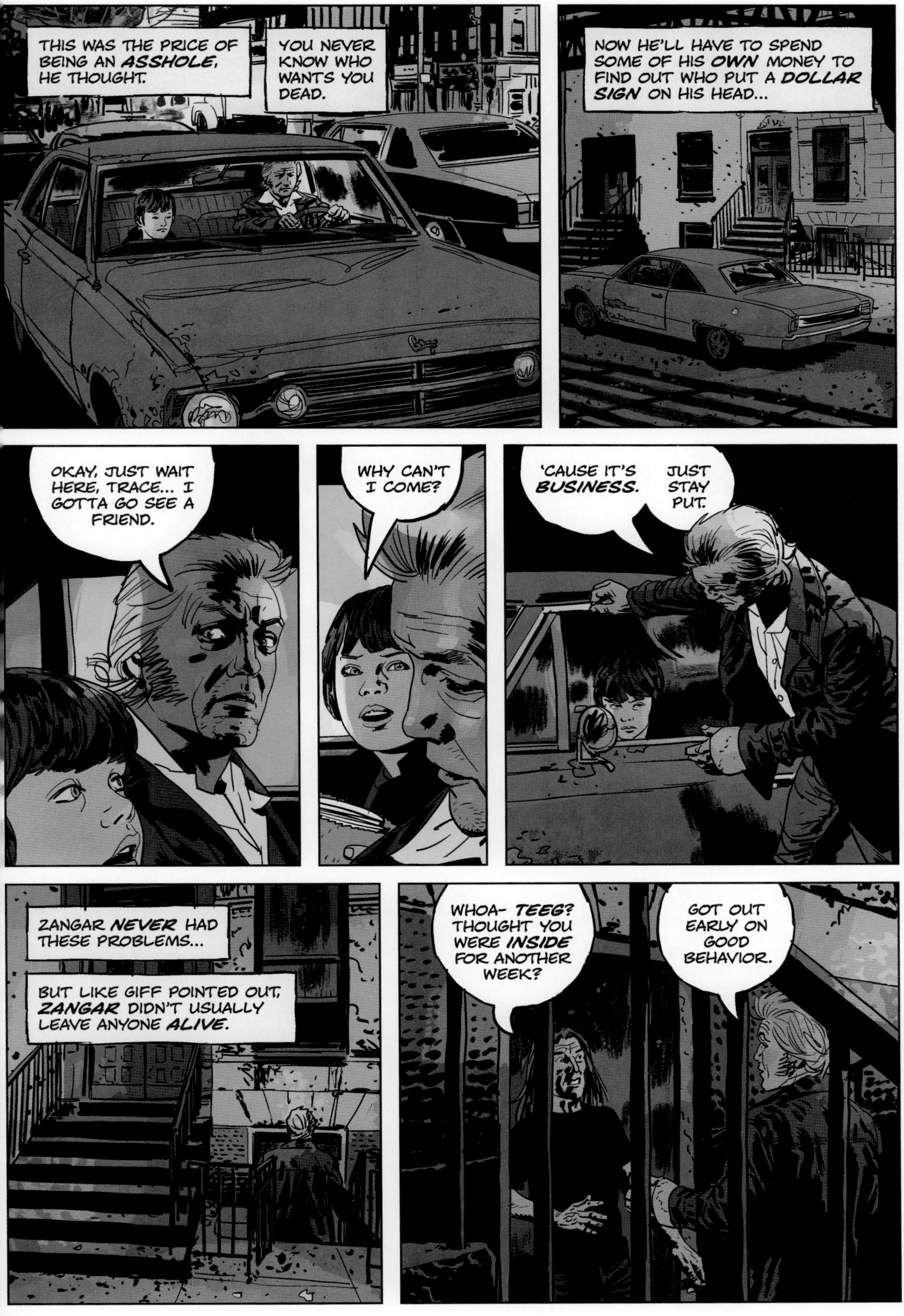
THIS WAS THE PRICE OF BEING AN ASSHOLE, HE THOUGHT.
YOU NEVER KNOW WHO WANTS YOU DEAD.
NOW HE'LL HAVE TO SPEND SOME OF HIS OWN MONEY TO FIND OUT WHO PUT A DOLLAR SIGN ON HIS HEAD...
OKAY, JUST WAIT HERE, TRACE... I GOTTA GO SEE A FRIEND.
WHY CAN'T I COME?
'CAUSE IT'S BUSINESS.
JUST STAY PUT.
ZANGAR NEVER HAD THESE PROBLEMS...
BUT LIKE GIFF POINTED OUT, ZANGAR DIDN'T USUALLY LEAVE ANYONE ALIVE.
WHOA- TEEG? THOUGHT YOU WERE INSIDE FOR ANOTHER WEEK?
GOT OUT EARLY ON GOOD BEHAVIOR.

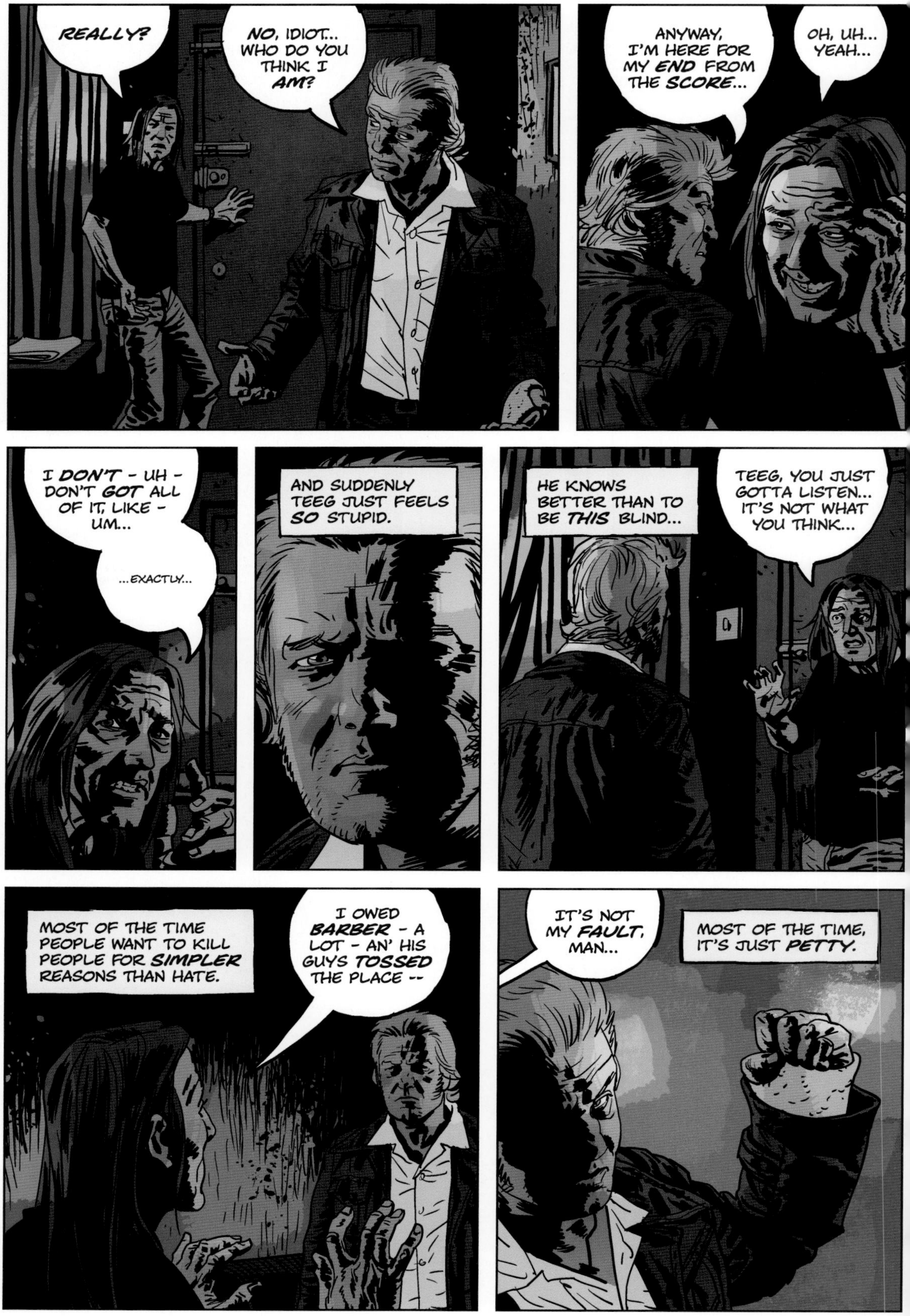
REALLY?
NO, IDIOT... WHO DO YOU THINK I AM?
ANYWAY, I'M HERE FOR MY END FROM THE SCORE...
OH, UH... YEAH...
I DON'T - UH - DON'T GOT ALL OF IT, LIKE - UM...
...EXACTLY...
AND SUDDENLY TEEG JUST FEELS SO STUPID.
HE KNOWS BETTER THAN TO BE THIS BLIND...
TEEG, YOU JUST GOTTA LISTEN... IT'S NOT WHAT YOU THINK...
MOST OF THE TIME PEOPLE WANT TO KILL PEOPLE FOR SIMPLER REASONS THAN HATE.
I OWED BARBER - A LOT - AN' HIS GUYS TOSSED THE PLACE --
IT'S NOT MY FAULT, MAN...
MOST OF THE TIME, IT'S JUST PETTY.

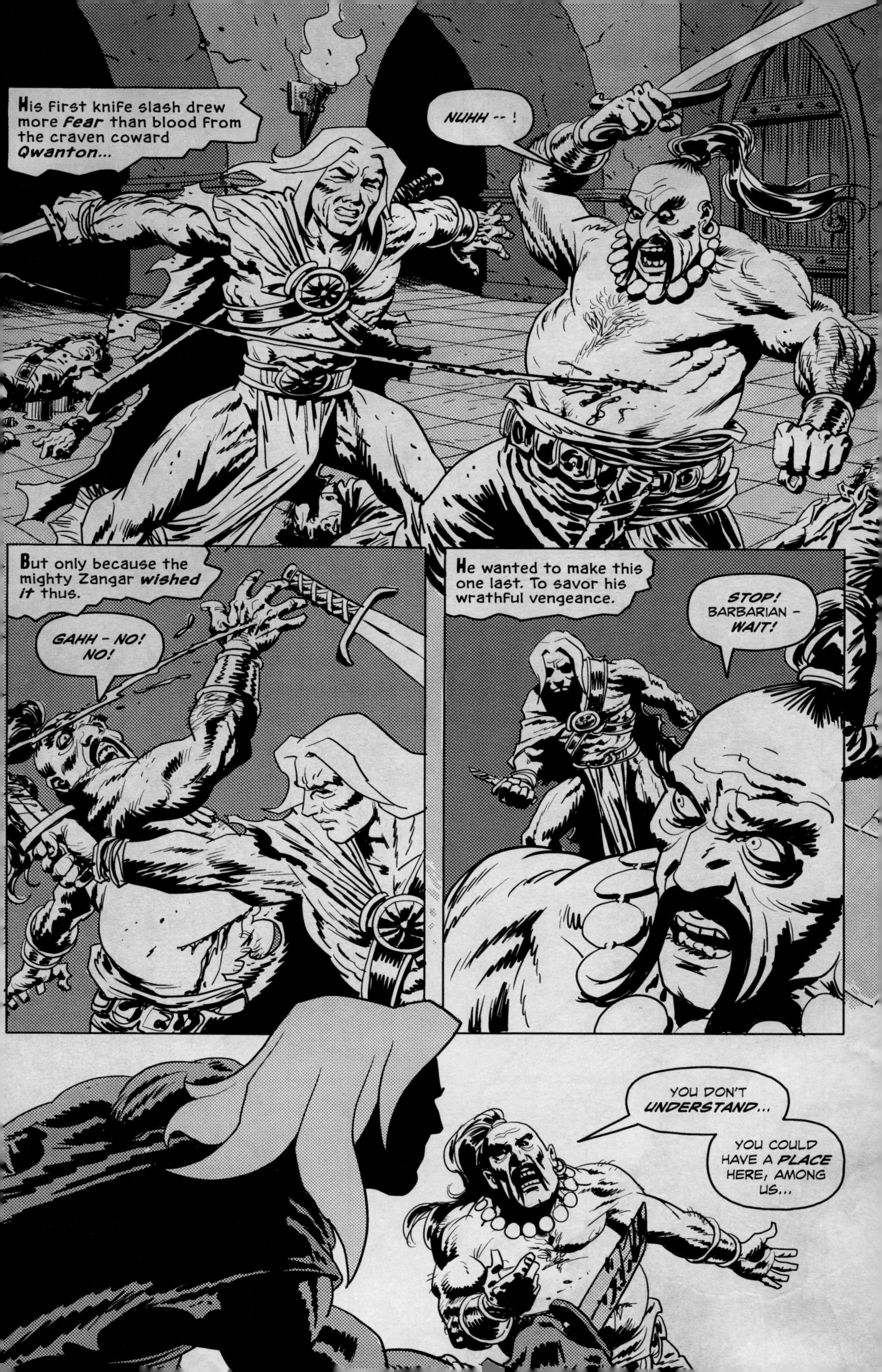
His first knife slash drew more *fear* than blood from the craven coward *Qwanton...*
NUHH -- !
But only because the mighty Zangar *wished it* thus.
GAHH - NO! NO!
He wanted to make this one last. To savor his wrathful vengeance.
STOP! BARBARIAN - *WAIT!*
YOU DON'T *UNDERSTAND...*
YOU COULD HAVE A *PLACE* HERE, AMONG US...

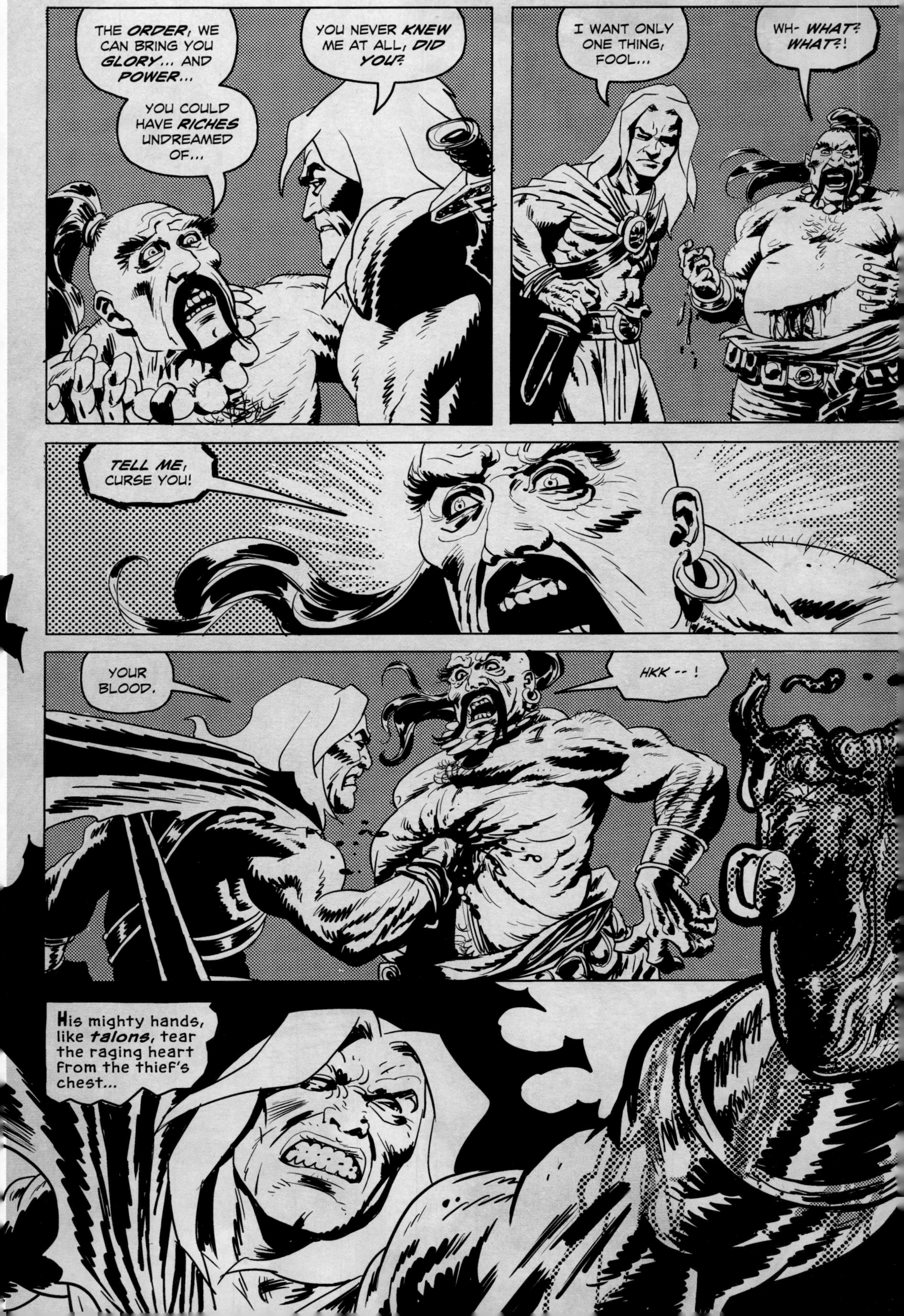
THE ORDER, WE CAN BRING YOU GLORY... AND POWER...
YOU COULD HAVE RICHES UNDREAMED OF...
YOU NEVER KNEW ME AT ALL, DID YOU?
I WANT ONLY ONE THING, FOOL...
WH- WHAT? WHAT?!
TELL ME, CURSE YOU!
YOUR BLOOD.
HKK -- !
His mighty hands, like talons, tear the raging heart from the thief's chest...

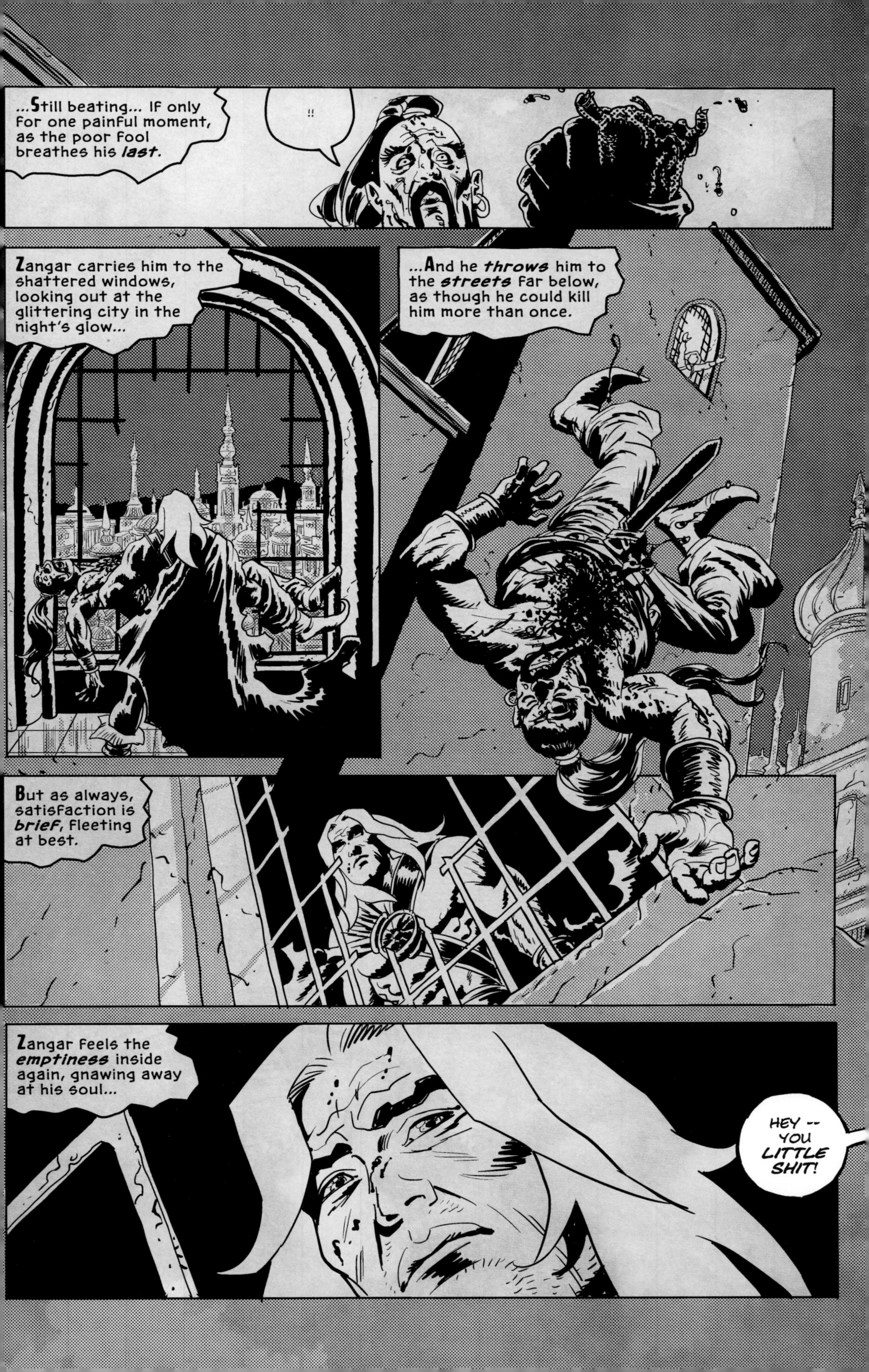
...Still beating... If only for one painful moment, as the poor fool breathes his *last*.
!!
Zangar carries him to the shattered windows, looking out at the glittering city in the night's glow...
...And he *throws* him to the *streets* far below, as though he could kill him more than once.
But as always, satisfaction is *brief*, fleeting at best.
Zangar feels the *emptiness* inside again, gnawing away at his soul...
HEY -- YOU LITTLE SHIT!

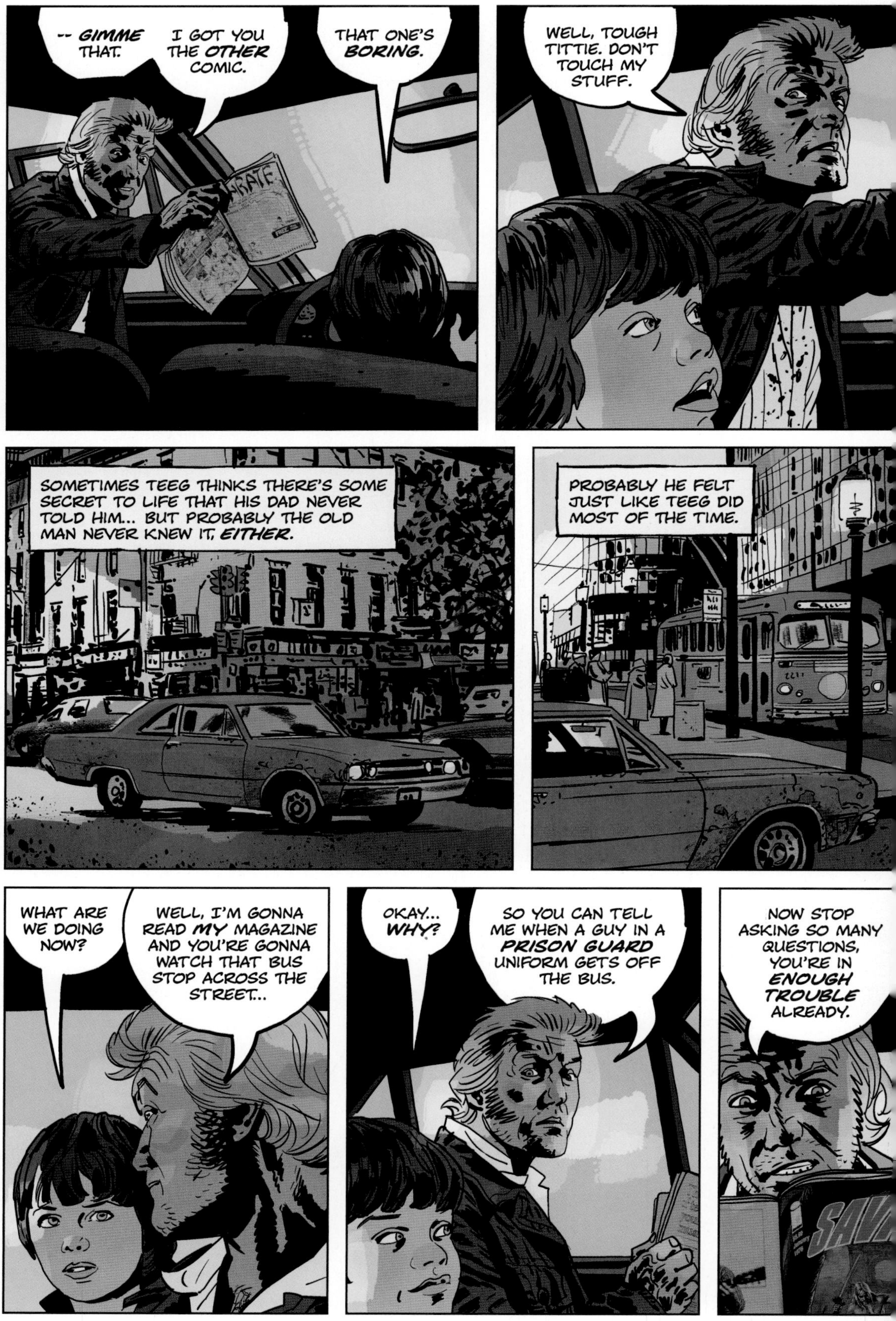
-- GIMME THAT.
I GOT YOU THE OTHER COMIC.
THAT ONE'S BORING.
WELL, TOUGH TITTIE. DON'T TOUCH MY STUFF.
SOMETIMES TEEG THINKS THERE'S SOME SECRET TO LIFE THAT HIS DAD NEVER TOLD HIM... BUT PROBABLY THE OLD MAN NEVER KNEW IT, EITHER.
PROBABLY HE FELT JUST LIKE TEEG DID MOST OF THE TIME.
WHAT ARE WE DOING NOW?
WELL, I'M GONNA READ MY MAGAZINE AND YOU'RE GONNA WATCH THAT BUS STOP ACROSS THE STREET...
OKAY... WHY?
SO YOU CAN TELL ME WHEN A GUY IN A PRISON GUARD UNIFORM GETS OFF THE BUS.
NOW STOP ASKING SO MANY QUESTIONS, YOU'RE IN ENOUGH TROUBLE ALREADY.

Wrong
Place

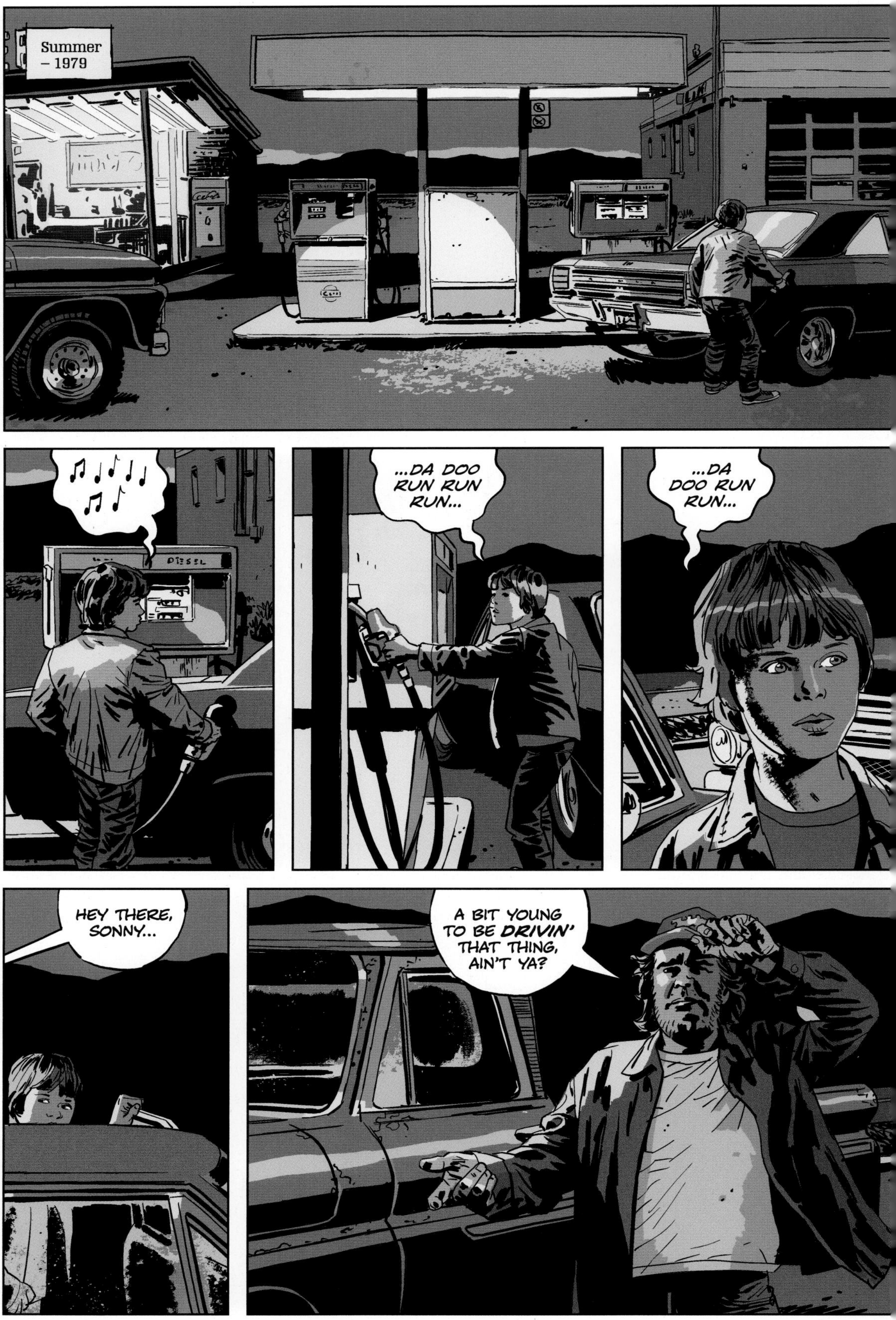
Summer
– 1979
...DA DOO
RUN RUN
RUN...
...DA
DOO RUN
RUN...
HEY THERE,
SONNY...
A BIT YOUNG
TO BE DRIVIN'
THAT THING,
AIN'T YA?

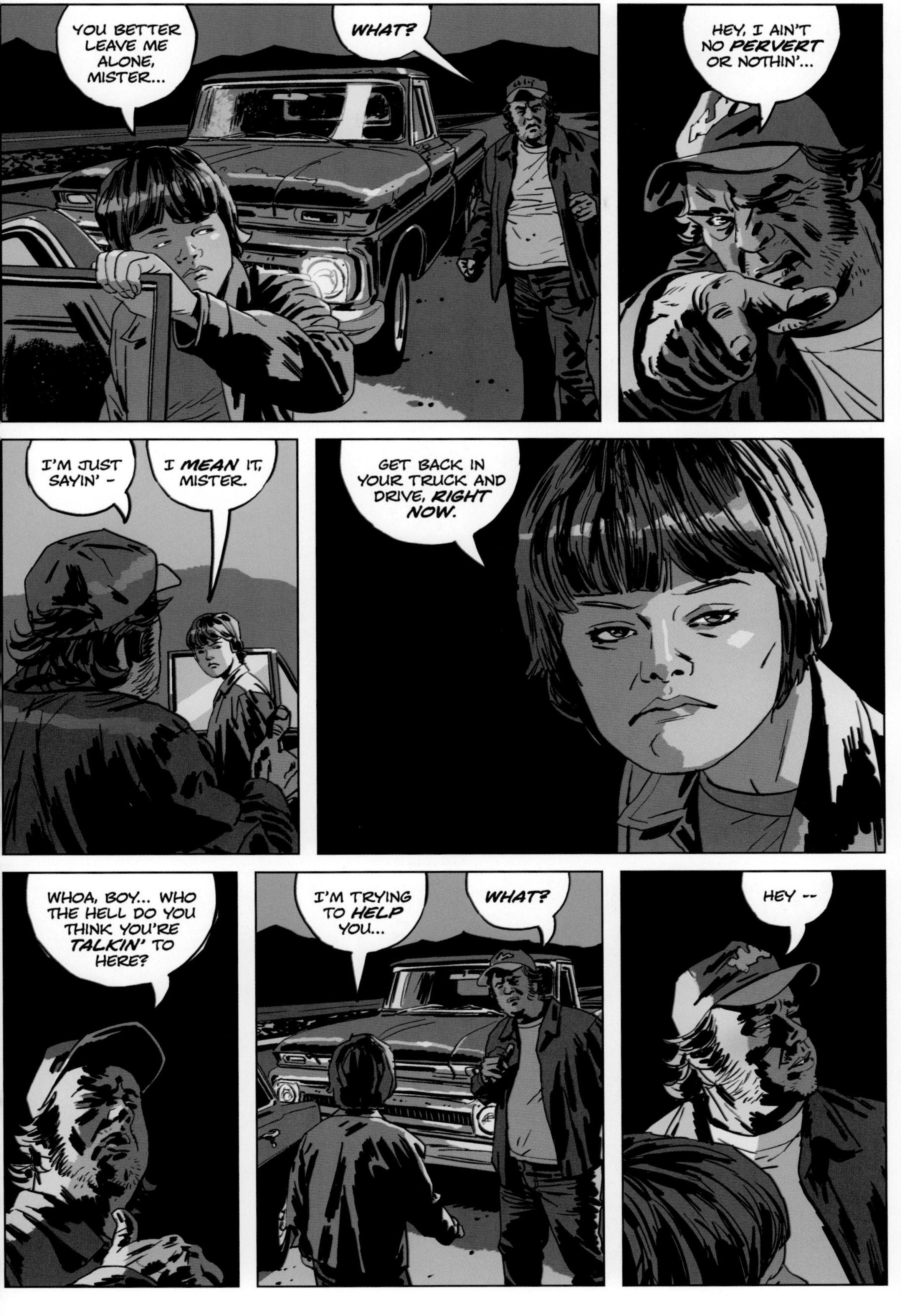
YOU BETTER LEAVE ME ALONE, MISTER...
WHAT?
HEY, I AIN'T NO PERVERT OR NOTHIN'...
I'M JUST SAYIN' -
I MEAN IT, MISTER.
GET BACK IN YOUR TRUCK AND DRIVE, RIGHT NOW.
WHOA, BOY... WHO THE HELL DO YOU THINK YOU'RE TALKIN' TO HERE?
I'M TRYING TO HELP YOU...
WHAT?
HEY --

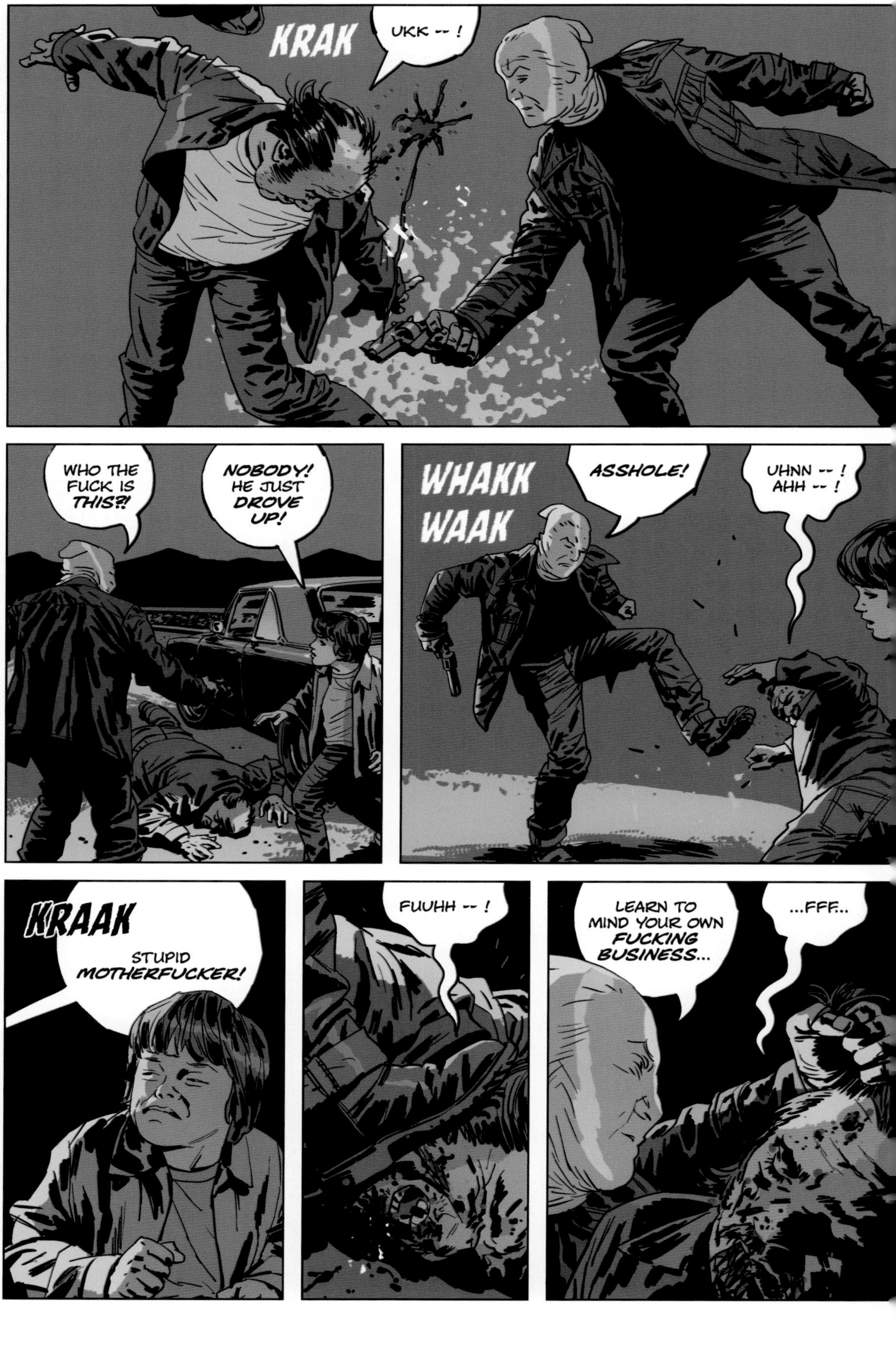
KRAK
UKK -- !
WHO THE FUCK IS THIS?!
NOBODY! HE JUST DROVE UP!
WHAKK
WAAK
ASSHOLE!
UHNN -- ! AHH -- !
KRAAK
STUPID MOTHERFUCKER!
FUUHH -- !
LEARN TO MIND YOUR OWN FUCKING BUSINESS...
...FFF..

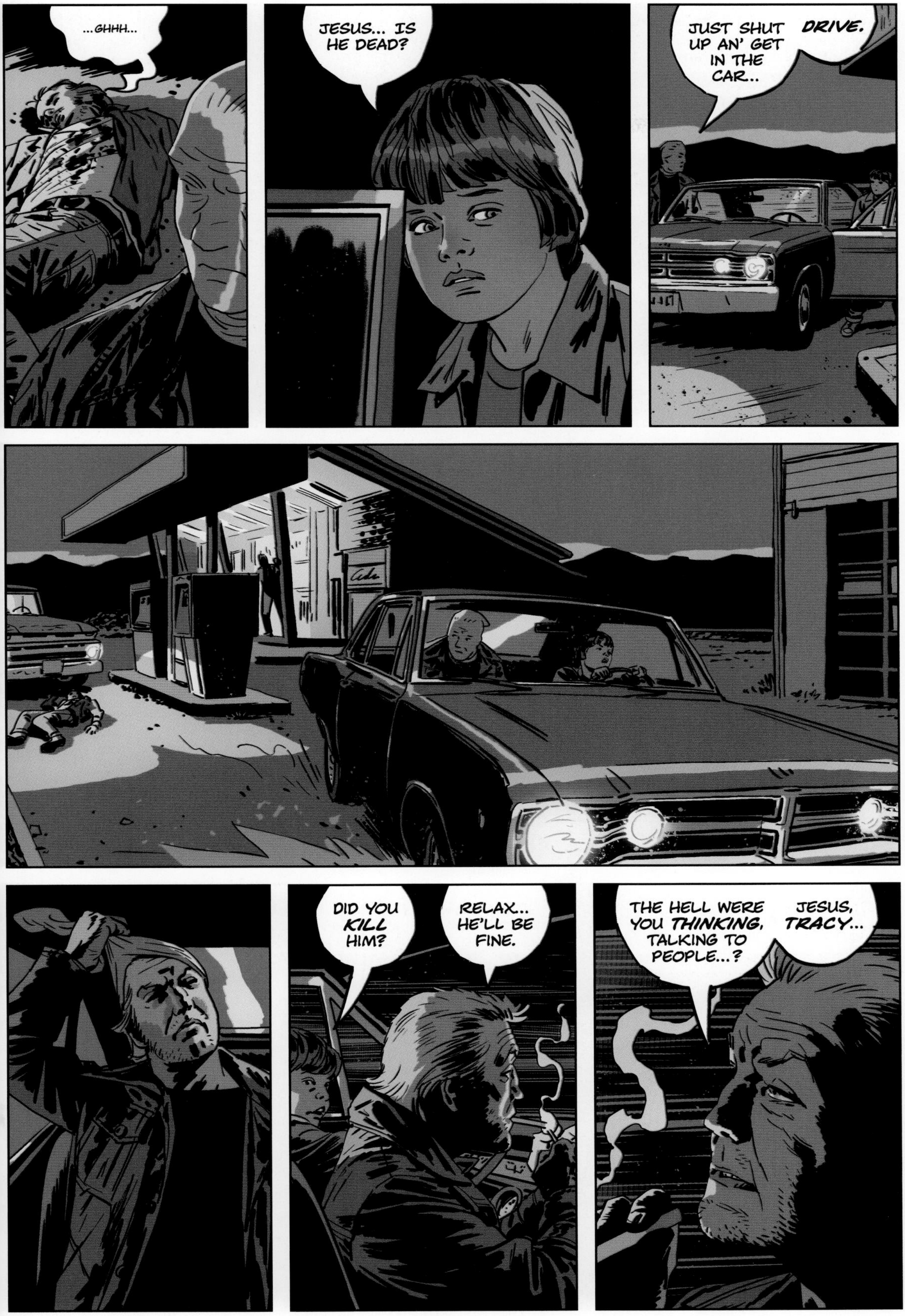
...GHHH...
JESUS... IS HE DEAD?
JUST SHUT UP AN' GET IN THE CAR...
DRIVE.
DID YOU KILL HIM?
RELAX... HE'LL BE FINE.
THE HELL WERE YOU THINKING, TALKING TO PEOPLE...?
JESUS, TRACY...

A week ago my Dad got a phone call during dinner.

It was one of those calls where he just listens, except this time he said "*shit*" like five times, too.

Half an hour later we were on our way out of town.

Dad says a man with a son attracts less attention on the road...

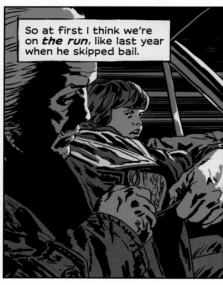

So at first I think we're on *the run*, like last year when he skipped bail.

That's when he taught me to drive... Back when I was just a kid.

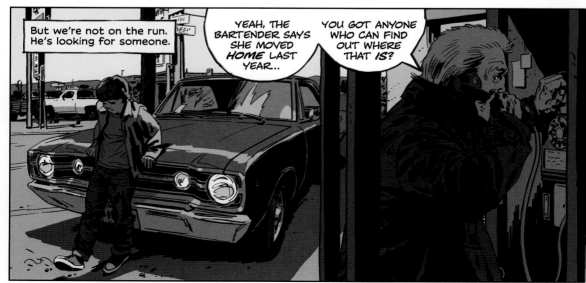

But we're not on the run. He's looking for someone.

YEAH, THE BARTENDER SAYS SHE MOVED *HOME* LAST YEAR...

YOU GOT ANYONE WHO CAN FIND OUT WHERE THAT *IS*?

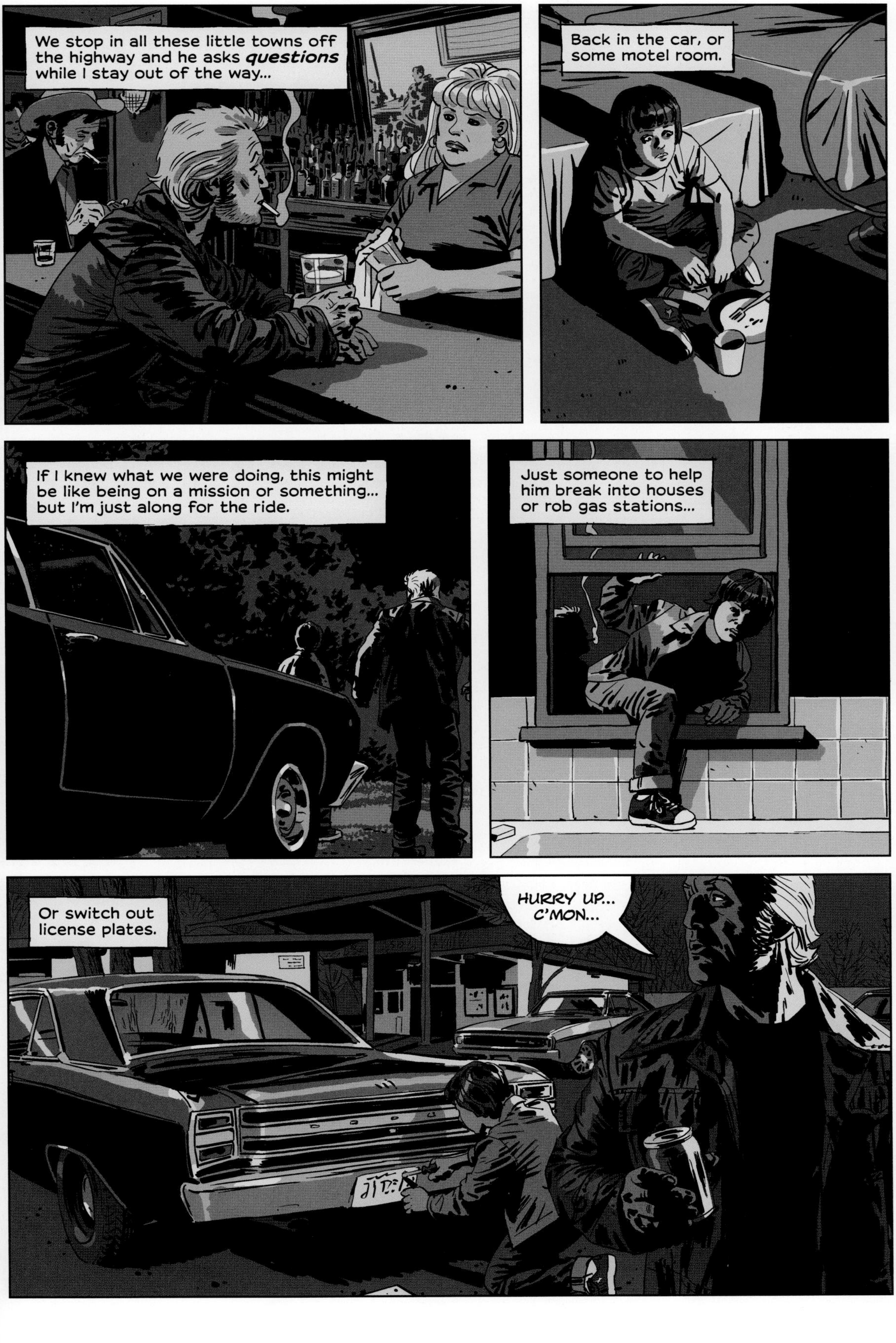
We stop in all these little towns off the highway and he asks *questions* while I stay out of the way...
Back in the car, or some motel room.
If I knew what we were doing, this might be like being on a mission or something... but I'm just along for the ride.
Just someone to help him break into houses or rob gas stations...
Or switch out license plates.
HURRY UP... C'MON...

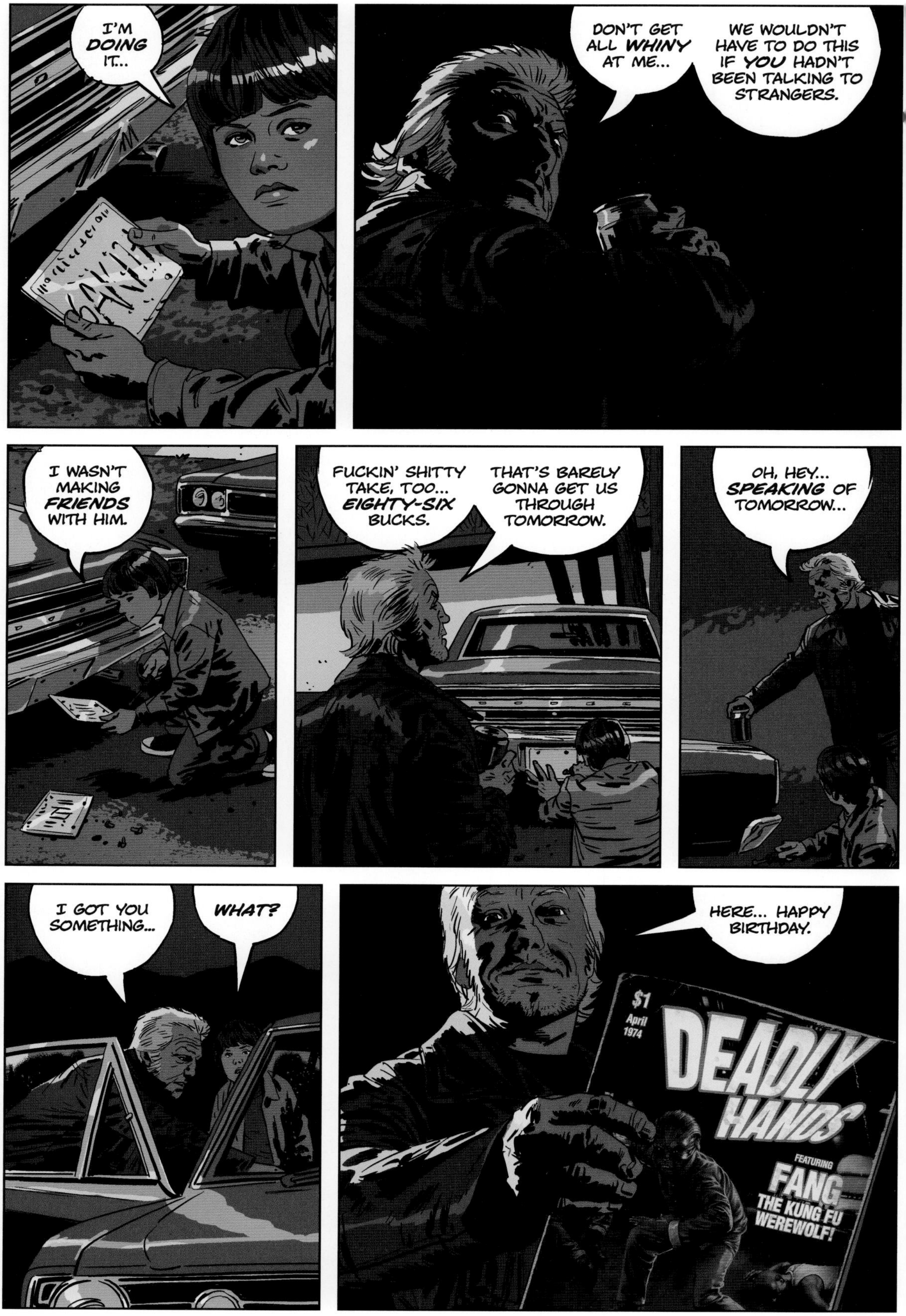
I'M DOING IT...
DON'T GET ALL WHINY AT ME...
WE WOULDN'T HAVE TO DO THIS IF YOU HADN'T BEEN TALKING TO STRANGERS.
I WASN'T MAKING FRIENDS WITH HIM.
FUCKIN' SHITTY TAKE, TOO... EIGHTY-SIX BUCKS.
THAT'S BARELY GONNA GET US THROUGH TOMORROW.
OH, HEY... SPEAKING OF TOMORROW...
I GOT YOU SOMETHING...
WHAT?
HERE... HAPPY BIRTHDAY.
$1
April 1974
DEADLY HANDS
FEATURING
FANG
THE KUNG FU WEREWOLF!

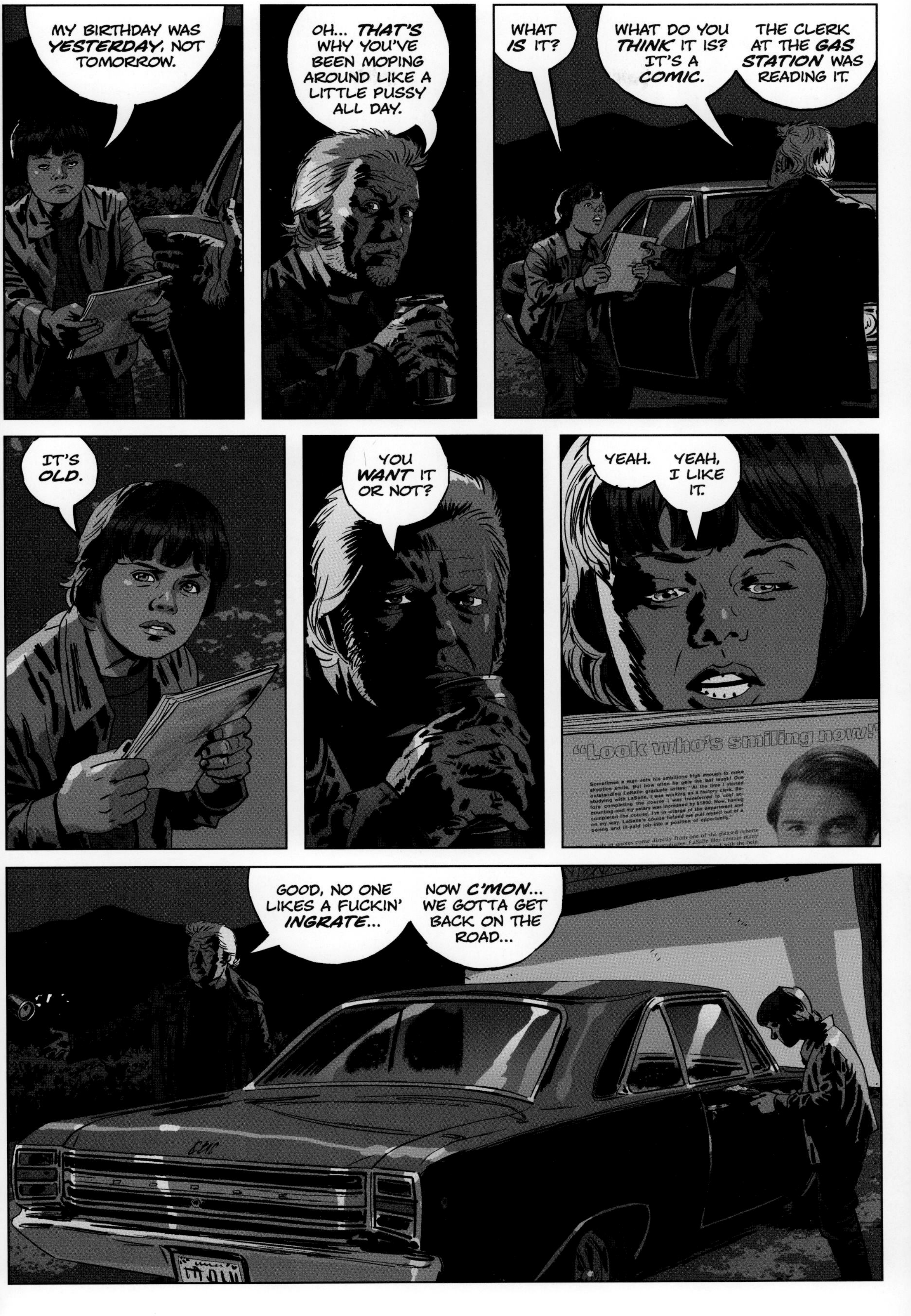
MY BIRTHDAY WAS YESTERDAY, NOT TOMORROW.
OH... THAT'S WHY YOU'VE BEEN MOPING AROUND LIKE A LITTLE PUSSY ALL DAY.
WHAT IS IT?
WHAT DO YOU THINK IT IS? IT'S A COMIC.
THE CLERK AT THE GAS STATION WAS READING IT.
IT'S OLD.
YOU WANT IT OR NOT?
YEAH.
YEAH, I LIKE IT.
"Look who's smiling now!"
Sometimes a man sets his ambitions high enough to make skeptics smile. But how often he gets the last laugh! One outstanding LaSalle graduate writes: "At the time I started studying with LaSalle, I was working as a factory clerk. Before completing the course I was transferred to cost accounting and my salary was increased by $1800. Now, having completed the course, I'm in charge of the department and on my way. LaSalle's course helped me pull myself out of a boring and ill-paid job into a position of opportunity."
GOOD, NO ONE LIKES A FUCKIN' INGRATE...
NOW C'MON... WE GOTTA GET BACK ON THE ROAD...

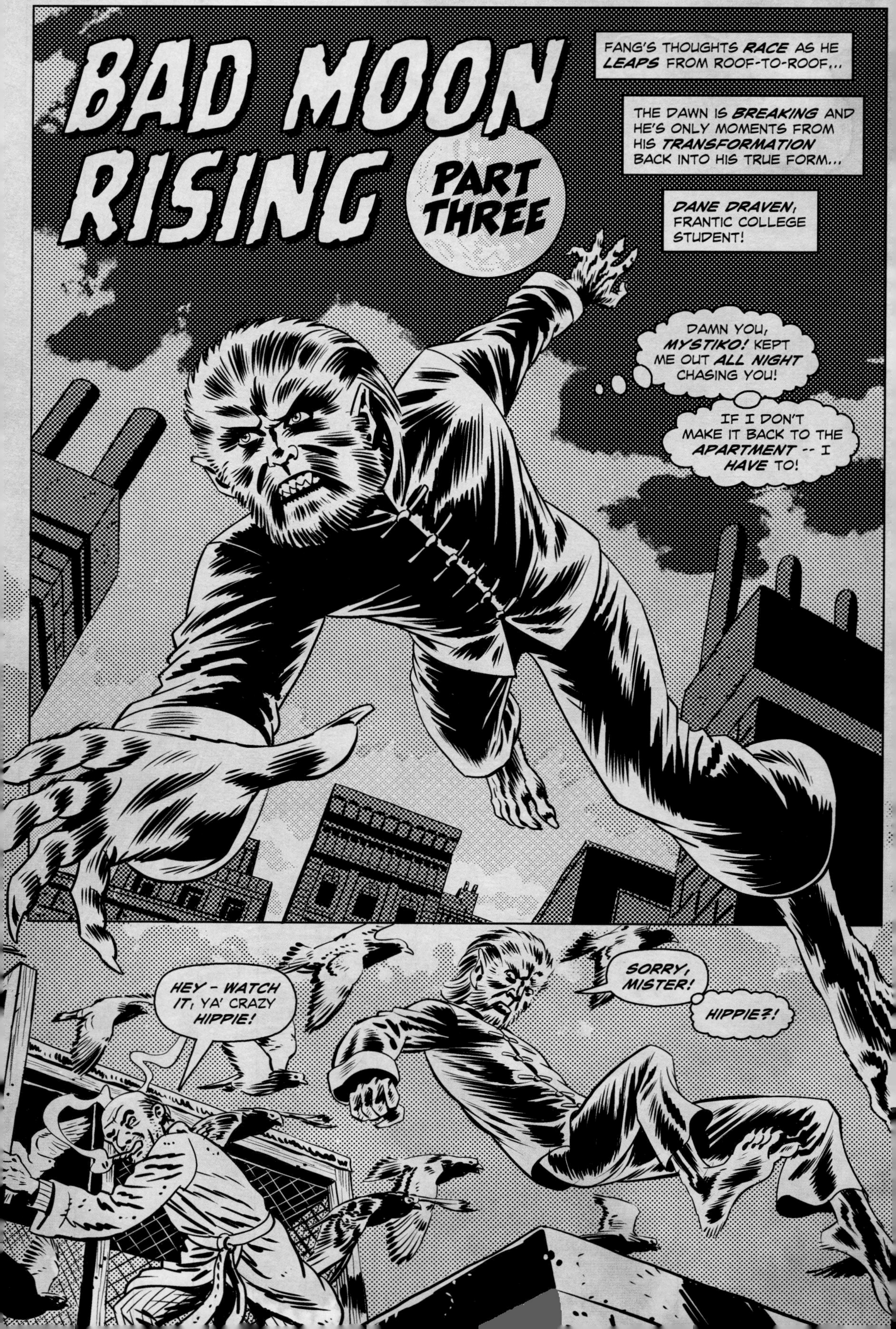
BAD MOON RISING
PART THREE
FANG'S THOUGHTS RACE AS HE LEAPS FROM ROOF-TO-ROOF...
THE DAWN IS BREAKING AND HE'S ONLY MOMENTS FROM HIS TRANSFORMATION BACK INTO HIS TRUE FORM...
DANE DRAVEN, FRANTIC COLLEGE STUDENT!
DAMN YOU, MYSTIKO! KEPT ME OUT ALL NIGHT CHASING YOU!
IF I DON'T MAKE IT BACK TO THE APARTMENT -- I HAVE TO!
HEY - WATCH IT, YA' CRAZY HIPPIE!
SORRY, MISTER!
HIPPIE?!

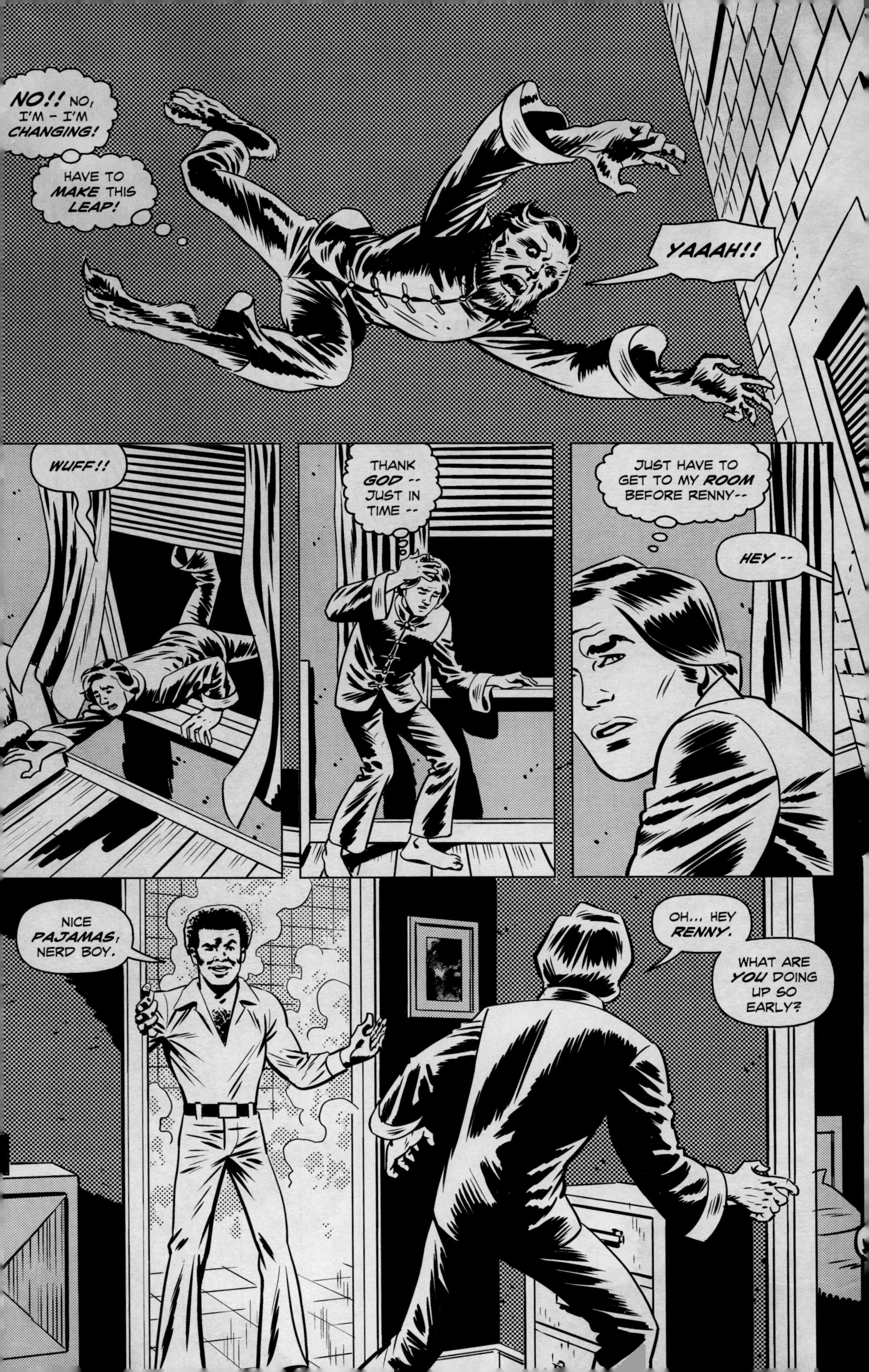
NO!! NO, I'M - I'M CHANGING!
HAVE TO MAKE THIS LEAP!
YAAAH!!
WUFF!!
THANK GOD -- JUST IN TIME --
JUST HAVE TO GET TO MY ROOM BEFORE RENNY--
HEY --
NICE PAJAMAS, NERD BOY.
OH... HEY RENNY.
WHAT ARE YOU DOING UP SO EARLY?

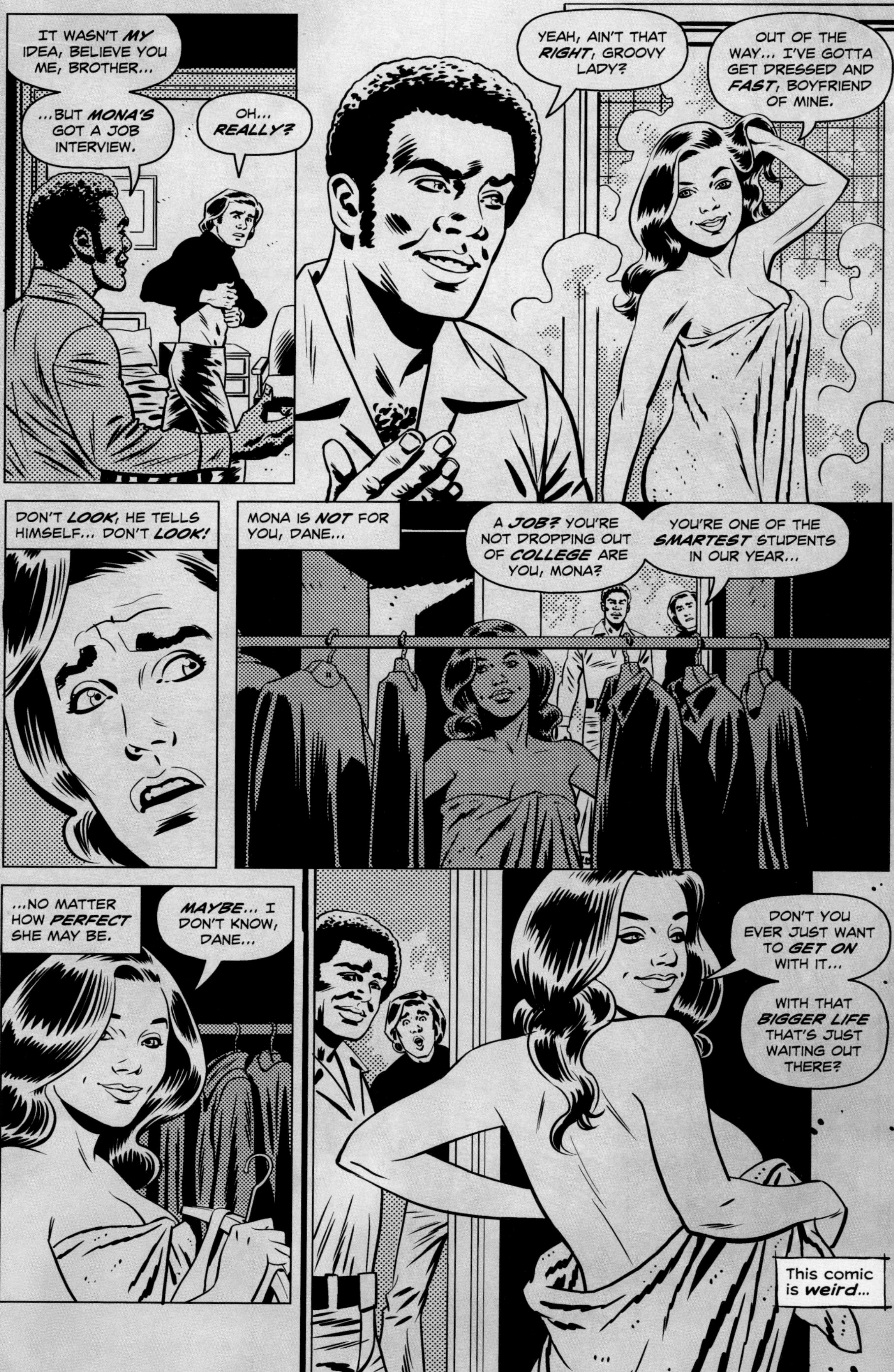
IT WASN'T MY IDEA, BELIEVE YOU ME, BROTHER...
...BUT MONA'S GOT A JOB INTERVIEW.
OH... REALLY?
YEAH, AIN'T THAT RIGHT, GROOVY LADY?
OUT OF THE WAY... I'VE GOTTA GET DRESSED AND FAST, BOYFRIEND OF MINE.
DON'T LOOK, HE TELLS HIMSELF... DON'T LOOK!
MONA IS NOT FOR YOU, DANE...
A JOB? YOU'RE NOT DROPPING OUT OF COLLEGE ARE YOU, MONA?
YOU'RE ONE OF THE SMARTEST STUDENTS IN OUR YEAR...
...NO MATTER HOW PERFECT SHE MAY BE.
MAYBE... I DON'T KNOW, DANE...
DON'T YOU EVER JUST WANT TO GET ON WITH IT...
WITH THAT BIGGER LIFE THAT'S JUST WAITING OUT THERE?
This comic is weird...

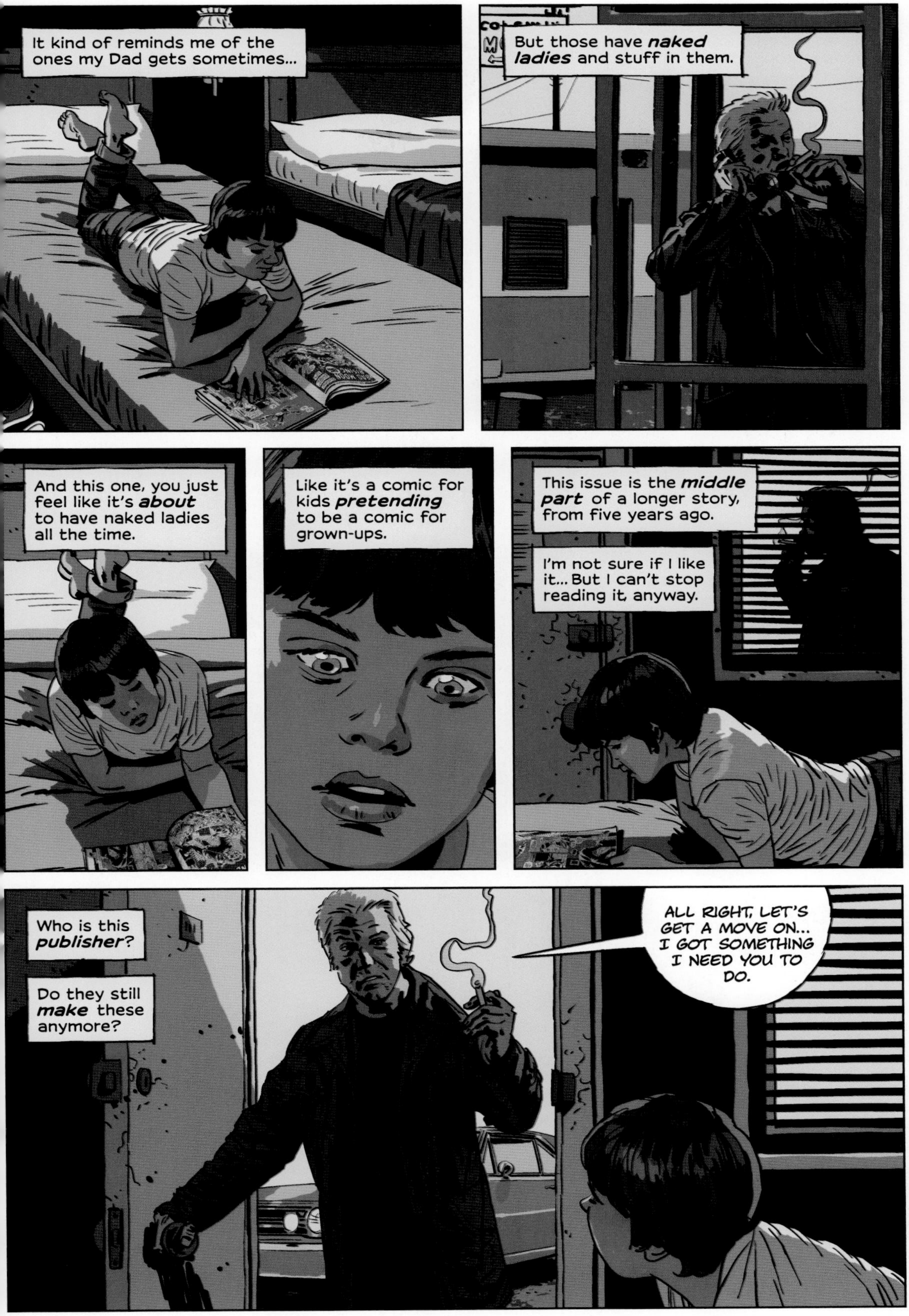

It kind of reminds me of the ones my Dad gets sometimes...
But those have *naked ladies* and stuff in them.
And this one, you just feel like it's *about* to have naked ladies all the time.
Like it's a comic for kids *pretending* to be a comic for grown-ups.
This issue is the *middle part* of a longer story, from five years ago.
I'm not sure if I like it... But I can't stop reading it, anyway.
Who is this *publisher*?
Do they still *make* these anymore?
ALL RIGHT, LET'S GET A MOVE ON... I GOT SOMETHING I NEED YOU TO DO.

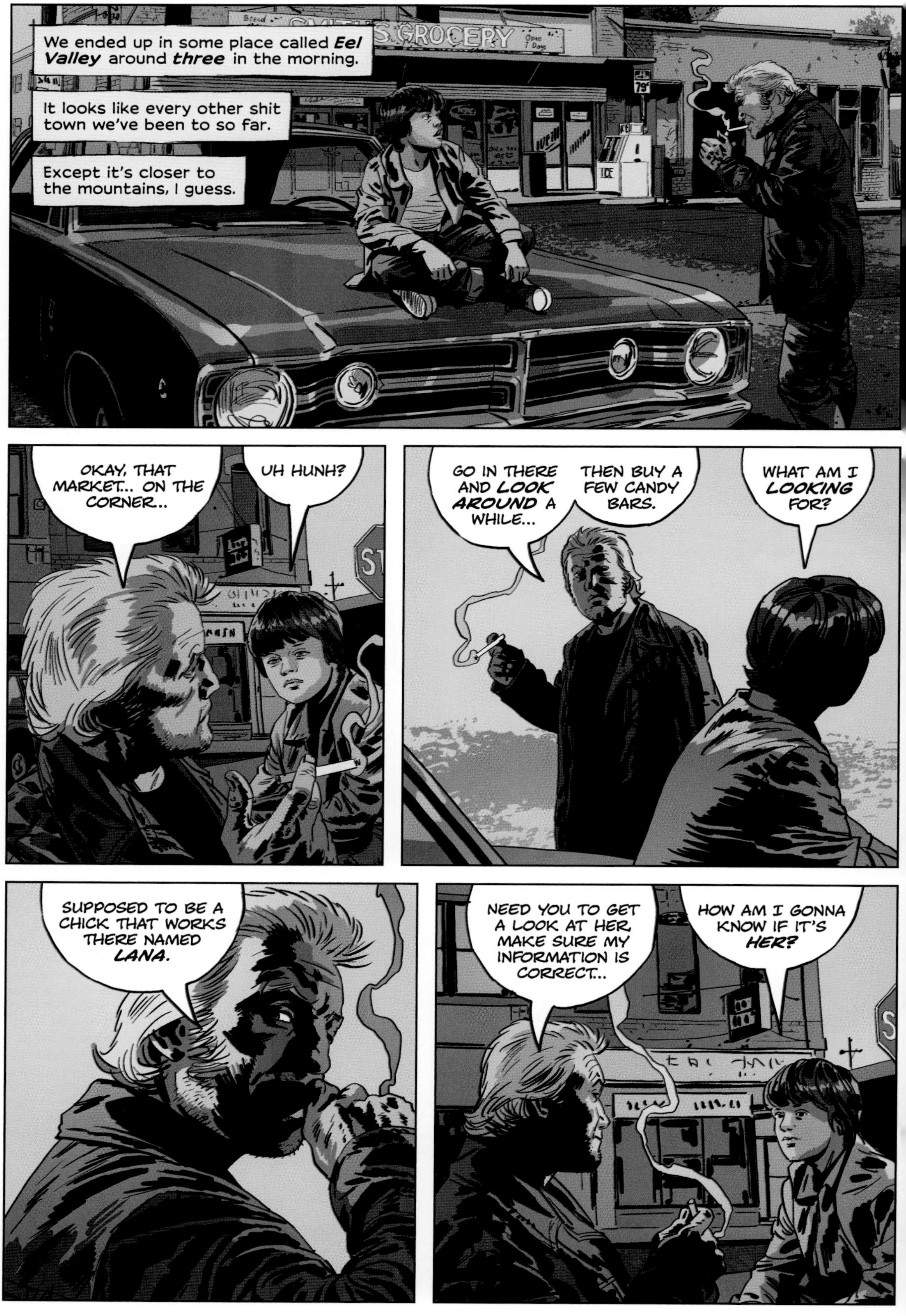

SMITH'S GROCERY
We ended up in some place called *Eel Valley* around *three* in the morning.
It looks like every other shit town we've been to so far.
Except it's closer to the mountains, I guess.
OKAY, THAT MARKET... ON THE CORNER..
UH HUNH?
GO IN THERE AND *LOOK AROUND* A WHILE...
THEN BUY A FEW CANDY BARS.
WHAT AM I *LOOKING* FOR?
SUPPOSED TO BE A CHICK THAT WORKS THERE NAMED *LANA.*
NEED YOU TO GET A LOOK AT HER, MAKE SURE MY INFORMATION IS CORRECT...
HOW AM I GONNA KNOW IF IT'S *HER?*

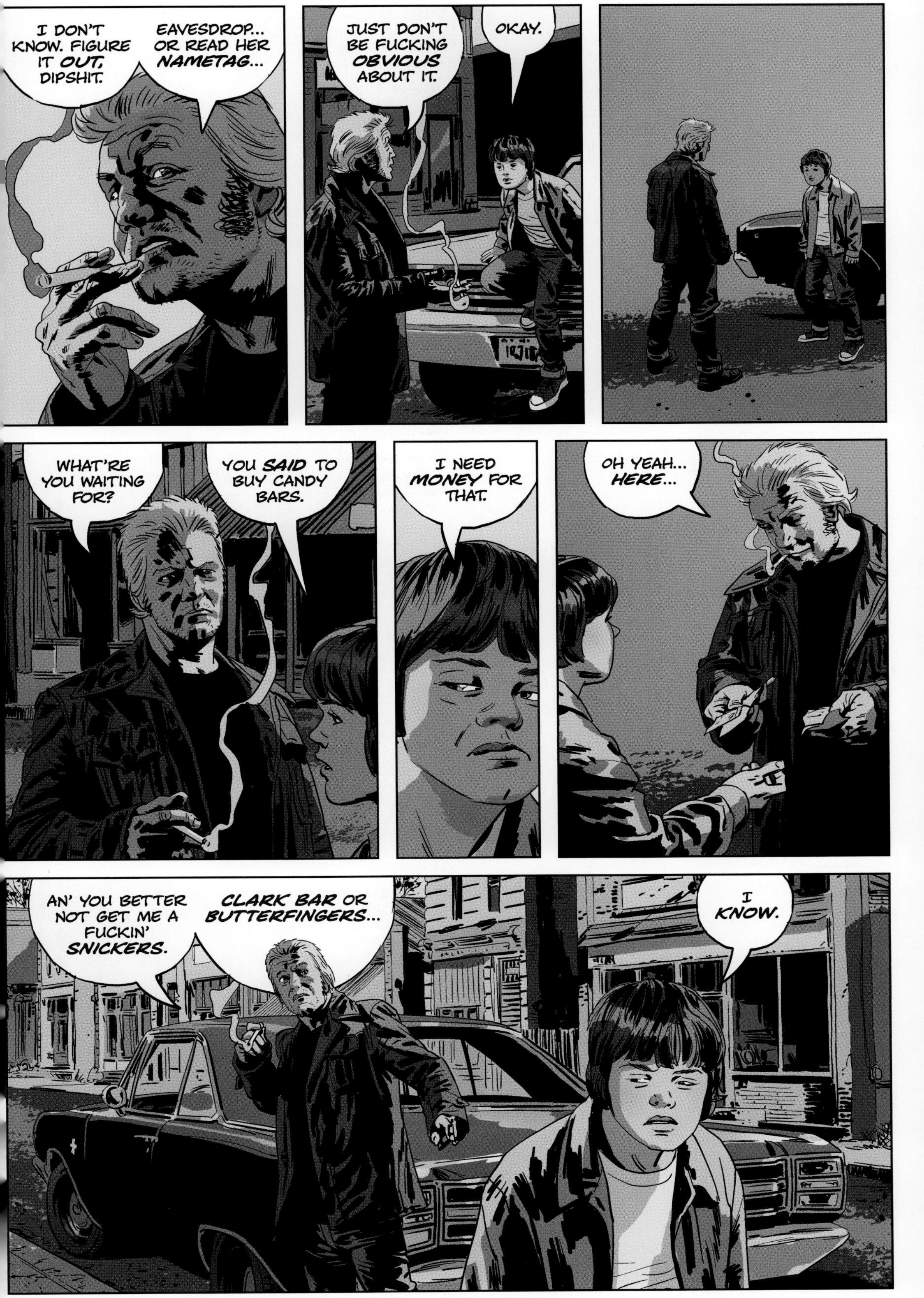
I DON'T KNOW. FIGURE IT OUT, DIPSHIT.
EAVESDROP... OR READ HER NAMETAG...
JUST DON'T BE FUCKING OBVIOUS ABOUT IT.
OKAY.
WHAT'RE YOU WAITING FOR?
YOU SAID TO BUY CANDY BARS.
I NEED MONEY FOR THAT.
OH YEAH... HERE...
AN' YOU BETTER NOT GET ME A FUCKIN' SNICKERS.
CLARK BAR OR BUTTERFINGERS...
I KNOW.

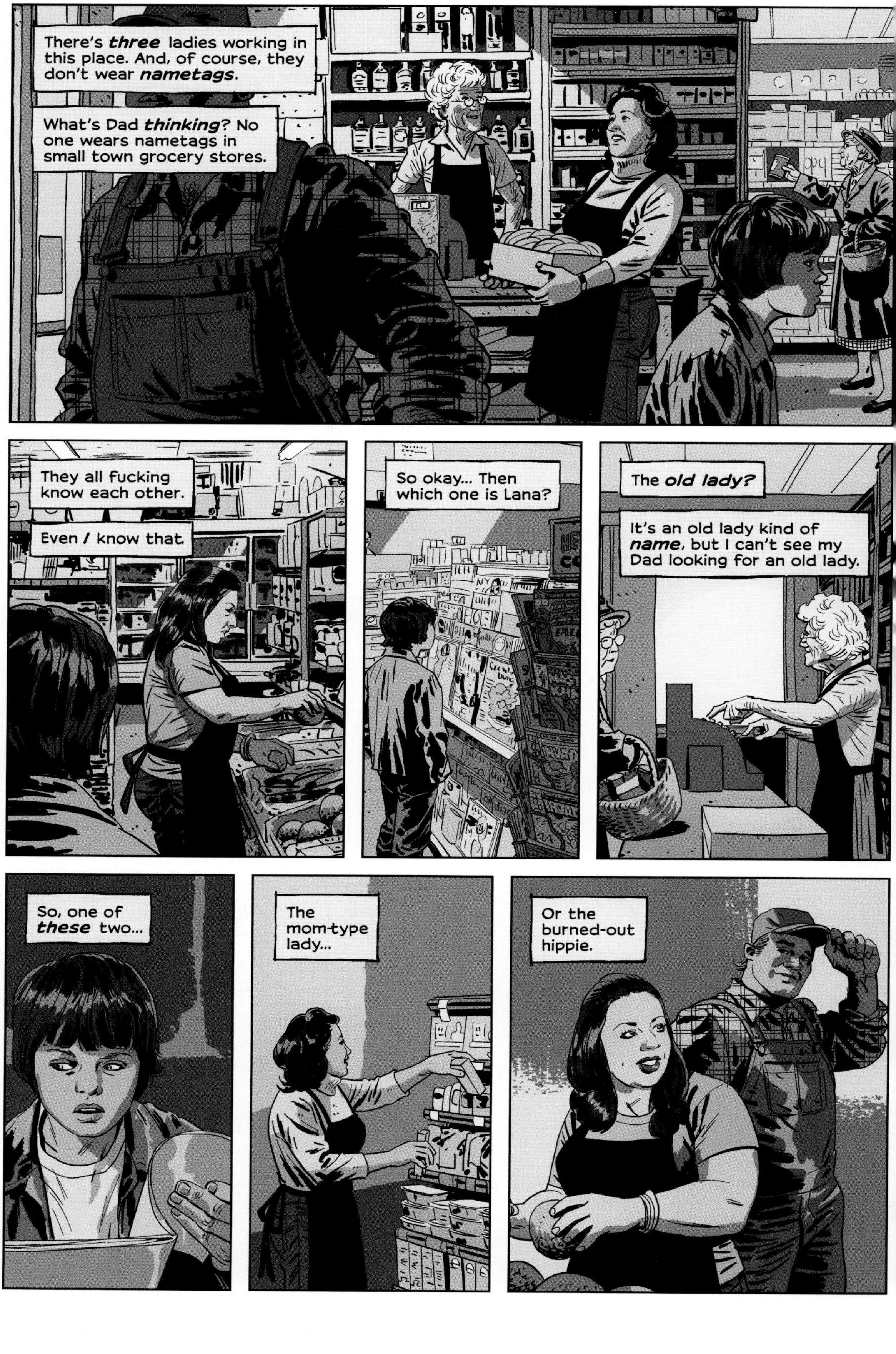
There's *three* ladies working in this place. And, of course, they don't wear *nametags*.
What's Dad *thinking*? No one wears nametags in small town grocery stores.
They all fucking know each other.
Even *I* know that.
So okay... Then which one is Lana?
The *old lady?*
It's an old lady kind of *name*, but I can't see my Dad looking for an old lady.
So, one of *these* two...
The mom-type lady...
Or the burned-out hippie.

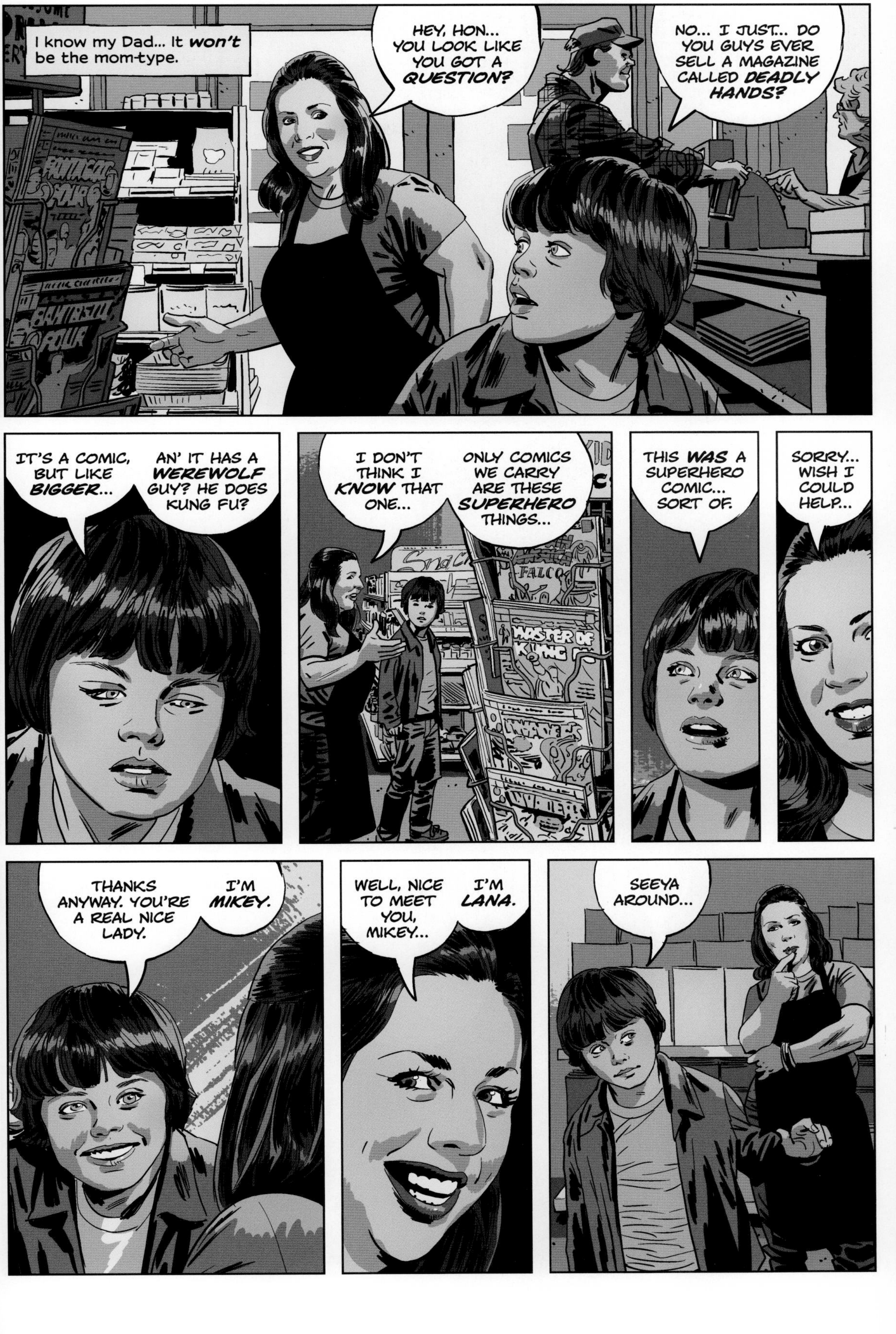
I know my Dad... It *won't* be the mom-type.
HEY, HON... YOU LOOK LIKE YOU GOT A *QUESTION?*
NO... I JUST... DO YOU GUYS EVER SELL A MAGAZINE CALLED *DEADLY HANDS?*
IT'S A COMIC, BUT LIKE *BIGGER*...
AN' IT HAS A *WEREWOLF* GUY? HE DOES KUNG FU?
I DON'T THINK I *KNOW* THAT ONE...
ONLY COMICS WE CARRY ARE THESE *SUPERHERO* THINGS...
MASTER OF KUNG
THIS *WAS* A SUPERHERO COMIC... SORT OF.
SORRY... WISH I COULD HELP...
THANKS ANYWAY. YOU'RE A REAL NICE LADY.
I'M *MIKEY.*
WELL, NICE TO MEET YOU, MIKEY...
I'M *LANA.*
SEEYA AROUND...

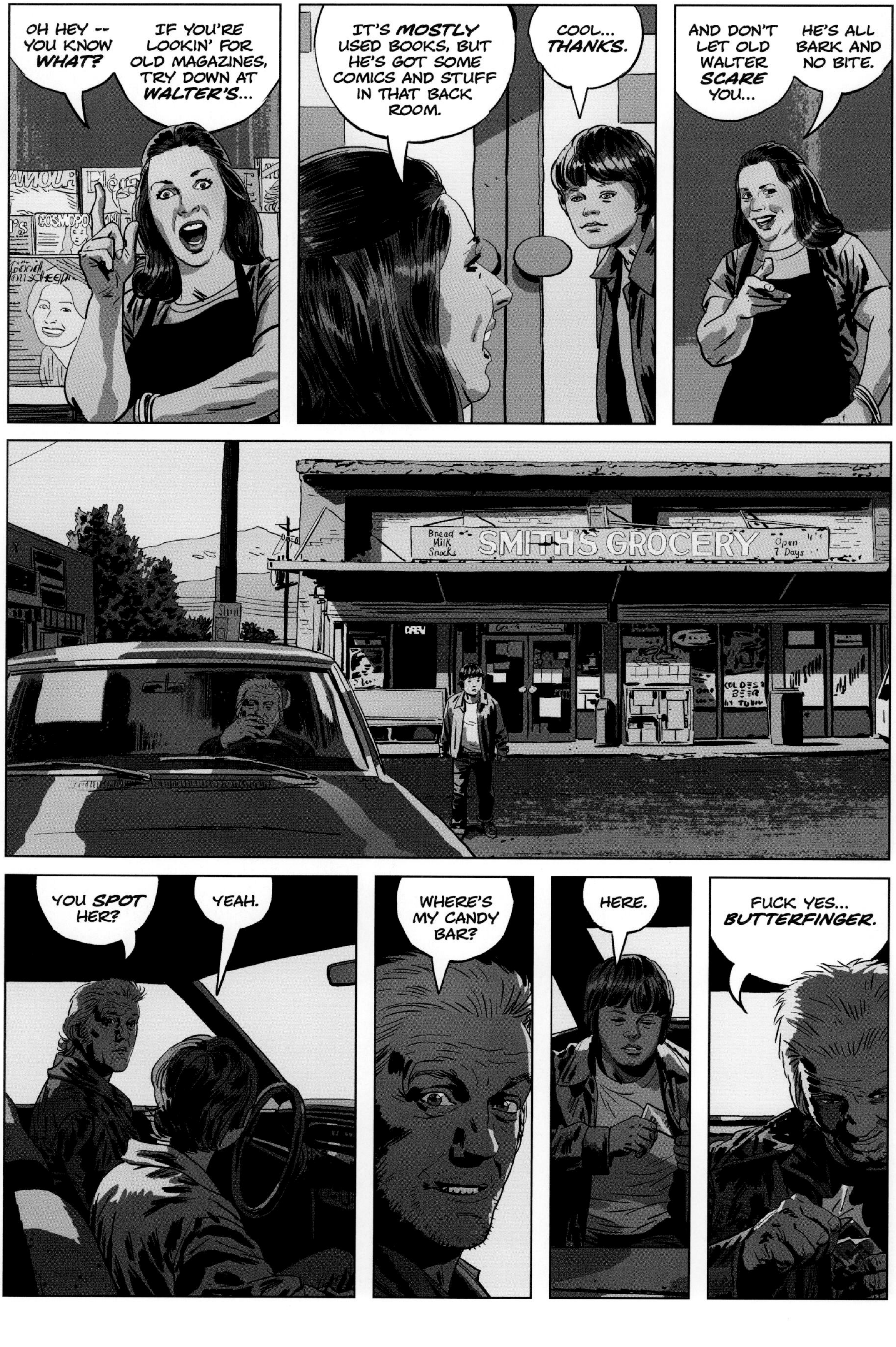
OH HEY -- YOU KNOW WHAT?
IF YOU'RE LOOKIN' FOR OLD MAGAZINES, TRY DOWN AT WALTER'S...
IT'S MOSTLY USED BOOKS, BUT HE'S GOT SOME COMICS AND STUFF IN THAT BACK ROOM.
COOL... THANKS.
AND DON'T LET OLD WALTER SCARE YOU...
HE'S ALL BARK AND NO BITE.
Bread Milk Snacks
SMITH'S GROCERY
Open 7 Days
YOU SPOT HER?
YEAH.
WHERE'S MY CANDY BAR?
HERE.
FUCK YES... BUTTERFINGER.

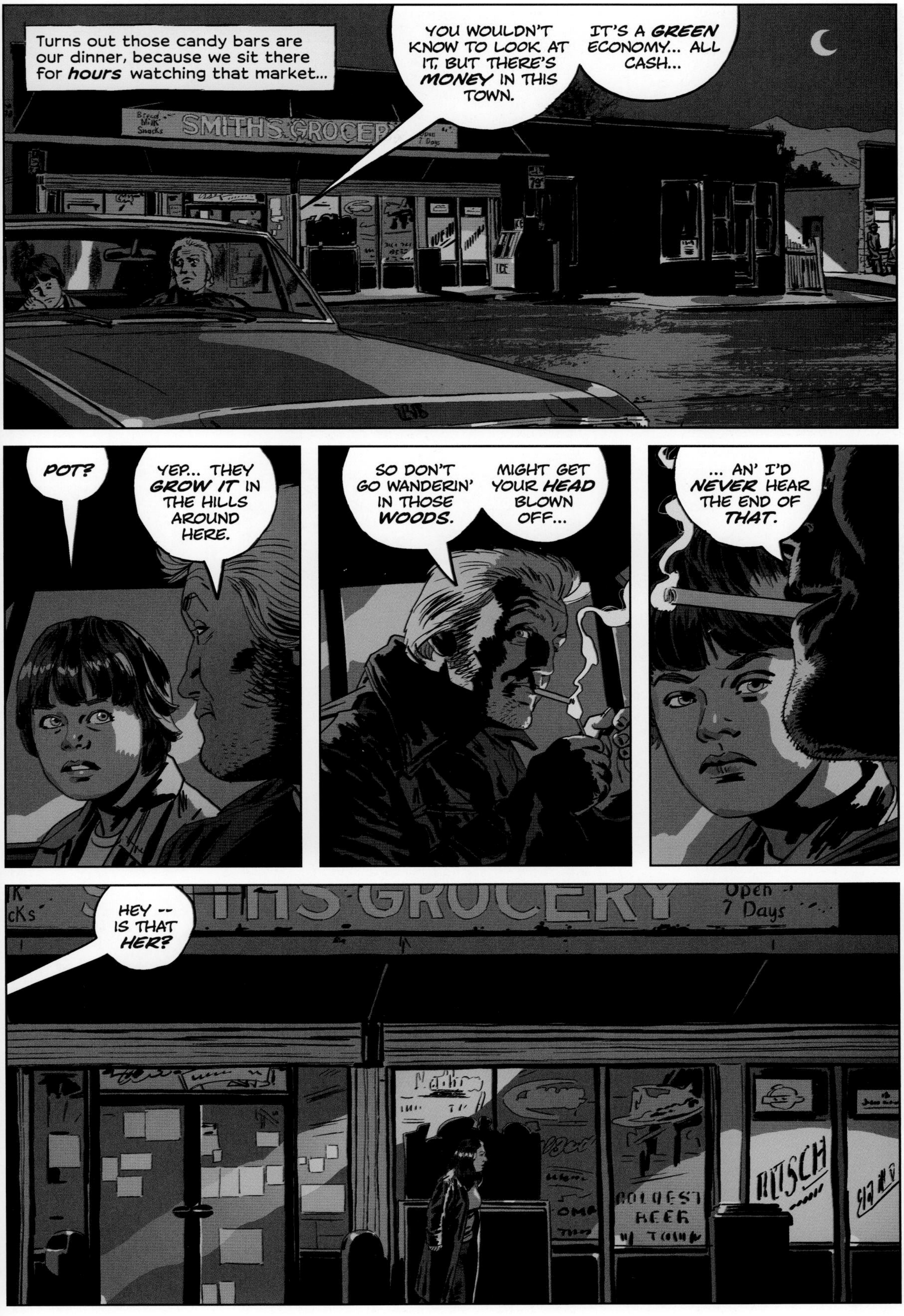

Turns out those candy bars are our dinner, because we sit there for **hours** watching that market...
YOU WOULDN'T KNOW TO LOOK AT IT, BUT THERE'S **MONEY** IN THIS TOWN.
IT'S A **GREEN** ECONOMY... ALL CASH...
SMITH'S GROCERY
Bread Milk Snacks
Open 7 Days
ICE
POT?
YEP... THEY **GROW IT** IN THE HILLS AROUND HERE.
SO DON'T GO WANDERIN' IN THOSE **WOODS.**
MIGHT GET YOUR **HEAD** BLOWN OFF...
... AN' I'D **NEVER** HEAR THE END OF **THAT.**
SMITHS GROCERY
Open 7 Days
HEY -- IS THAT **HER?**
COLDEST BEER IN TOWN

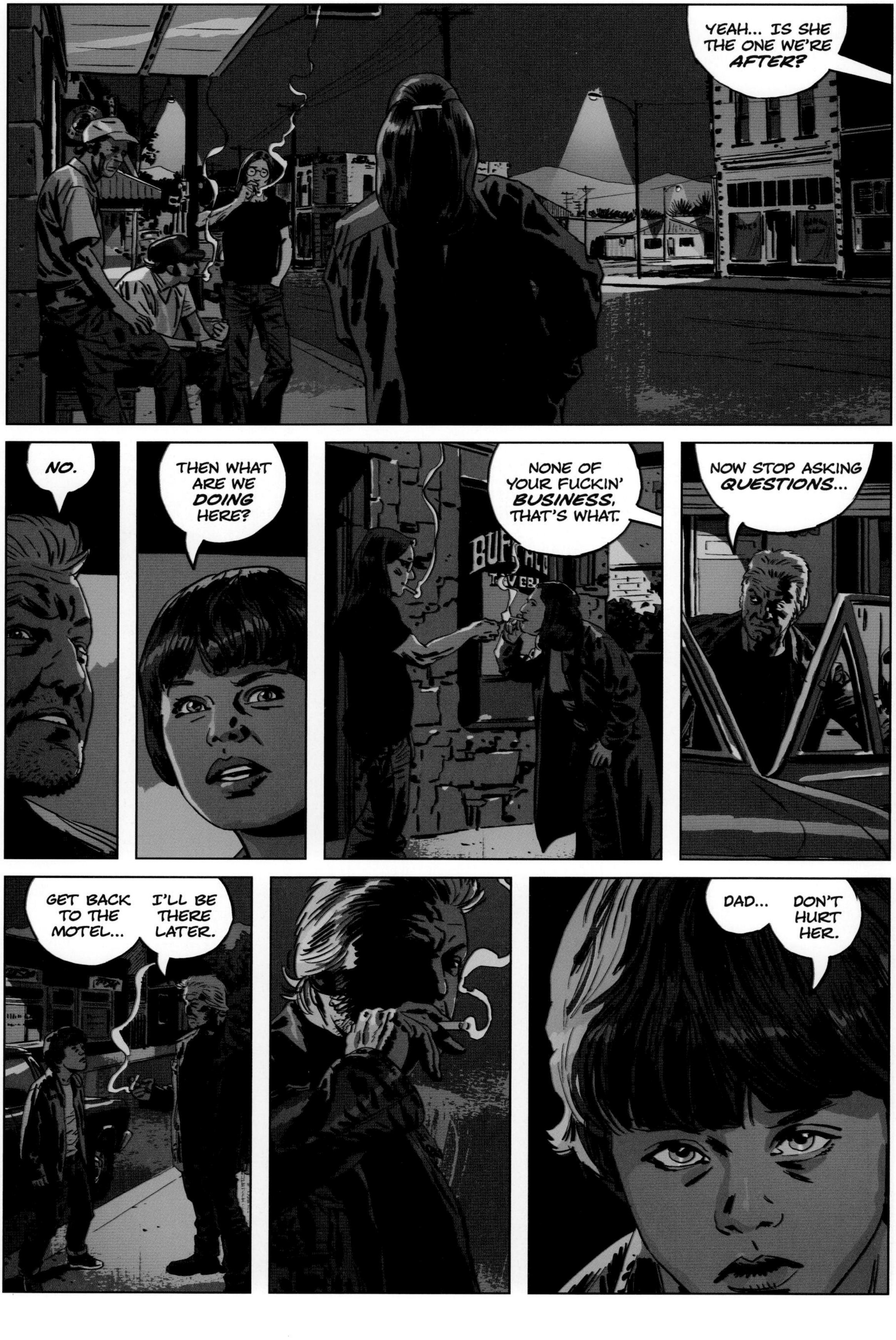
YEAH... IS SHE THE ONE WE'RE AFTER?
NO.
THEN WHAT ARE WE DOING HERE?
NONE OF YOUR FUCKIN' BUSINESS, THAT'S WHAT.
NOW STOP ASKING QUESTIONS...
GET BACK TO THE MOTEL...
I'LL BE THERE LATER.
DAD...
DON'T HURT HER.

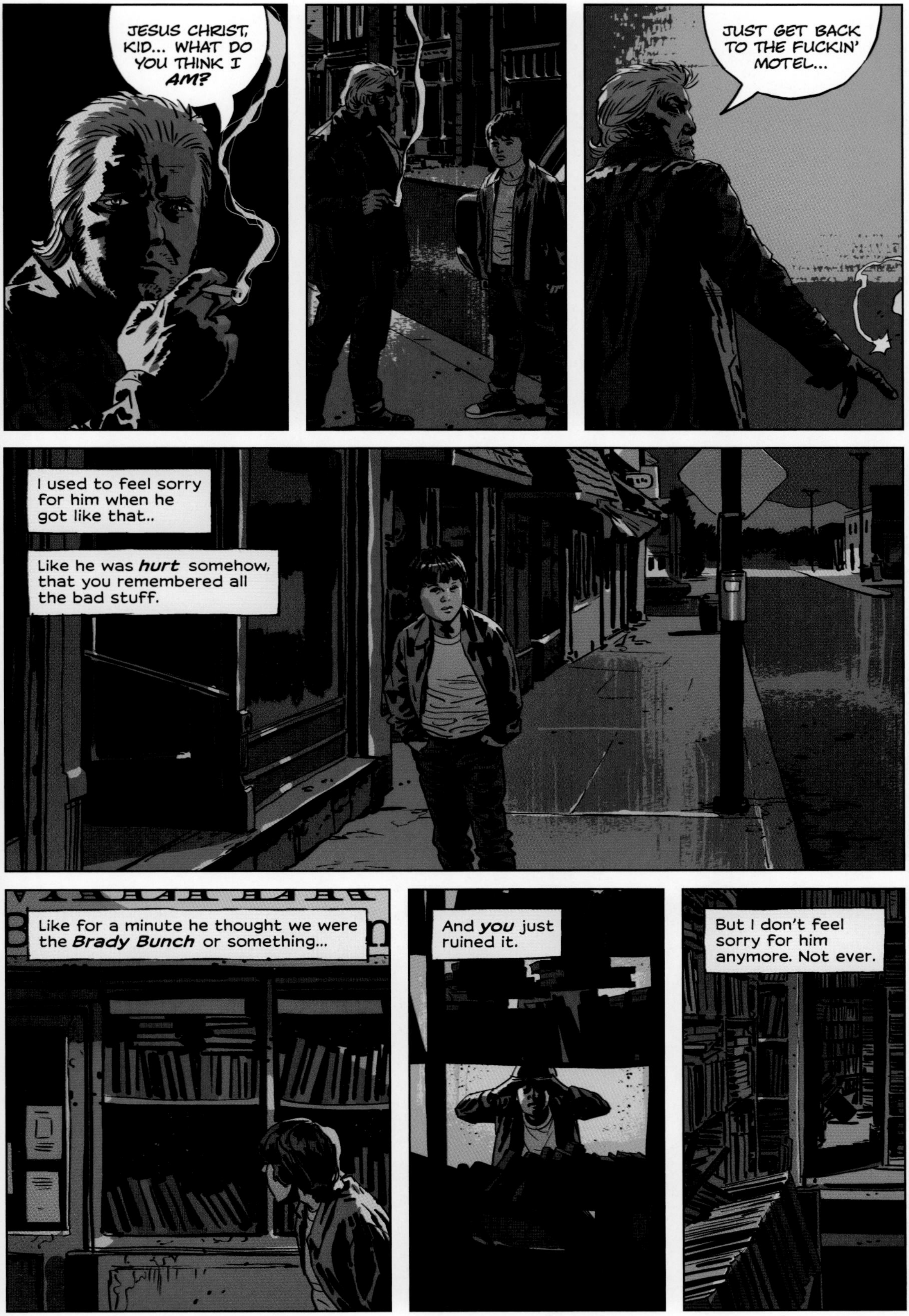
JESUS CHRIST, KID... WHAT DO YOU THINK I AM?
JUST GET BACK TO THE FUCKIN' MOTEL...
I used to feel sorry for him when he got like that..
Like he was hurt somehow, that you remembered all the bad stuff.
Like for a minute he thought we were the Brady Bunch or something...
And you just ruined it.
But I don't feel sorry for him anymore. Not ever.

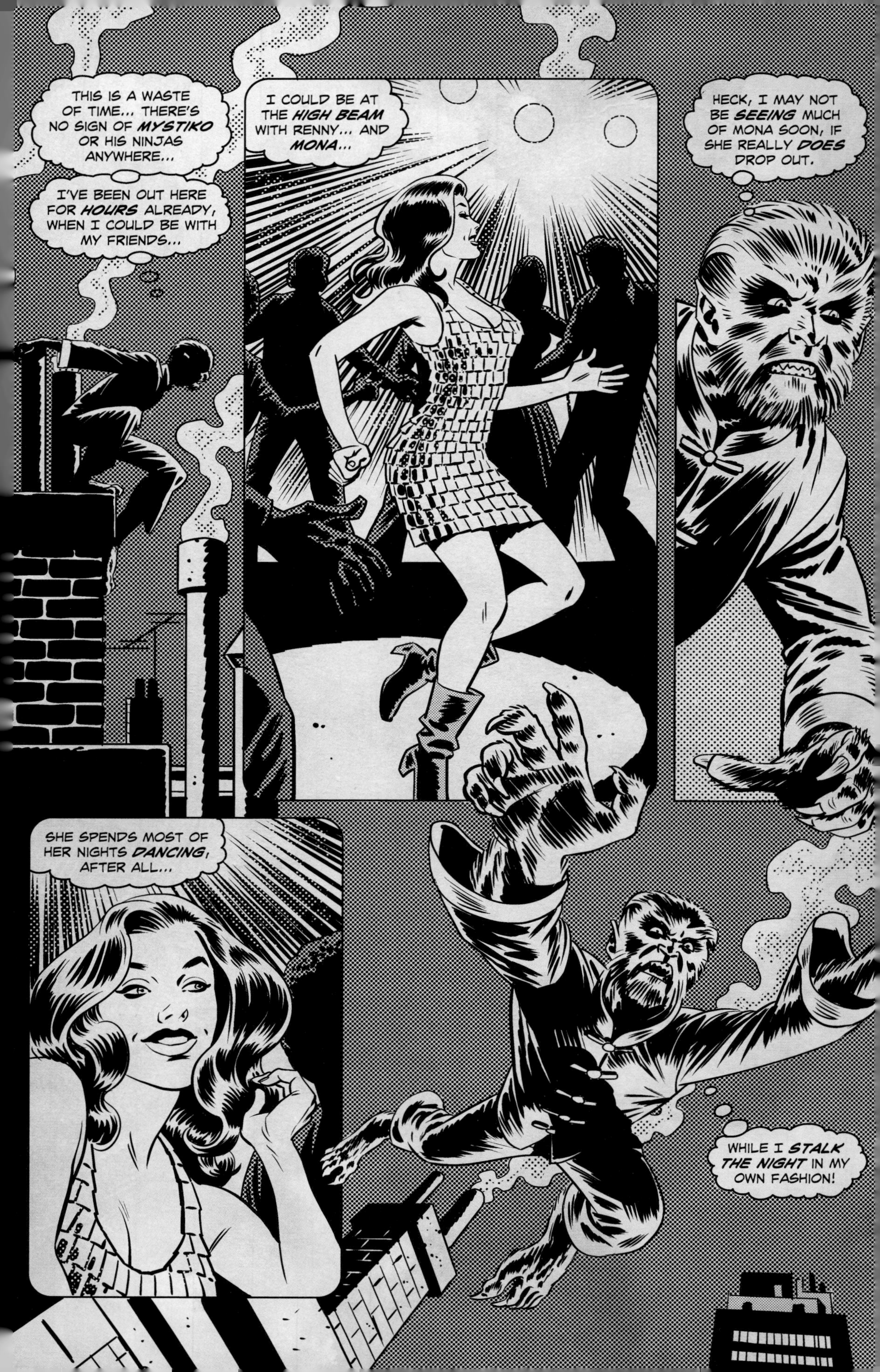
THIS IS A WASTE OF TIME... THERE'S NO SIGN OF MYSTIKO OR HIS NINJAS ANYWHERE...
I'VE BEEN OUT HERE FOR HOURS ALREADY, WHEN I COULD BE WITH MY FRIENDS...
I COULD BE AT THE HIGH BEAM WITH RENNY... AND MONA...
HECK, I MAY NOT BE SEEING MUCH OF MONA SOON, IF SHE REALLY DOES DROP OUT.
SHE SPENDS MOST OF HER NIGHTS DANCING, AFTER ALL...
WHILE I STALK THE NIGHT IN MY OWN FASHION!

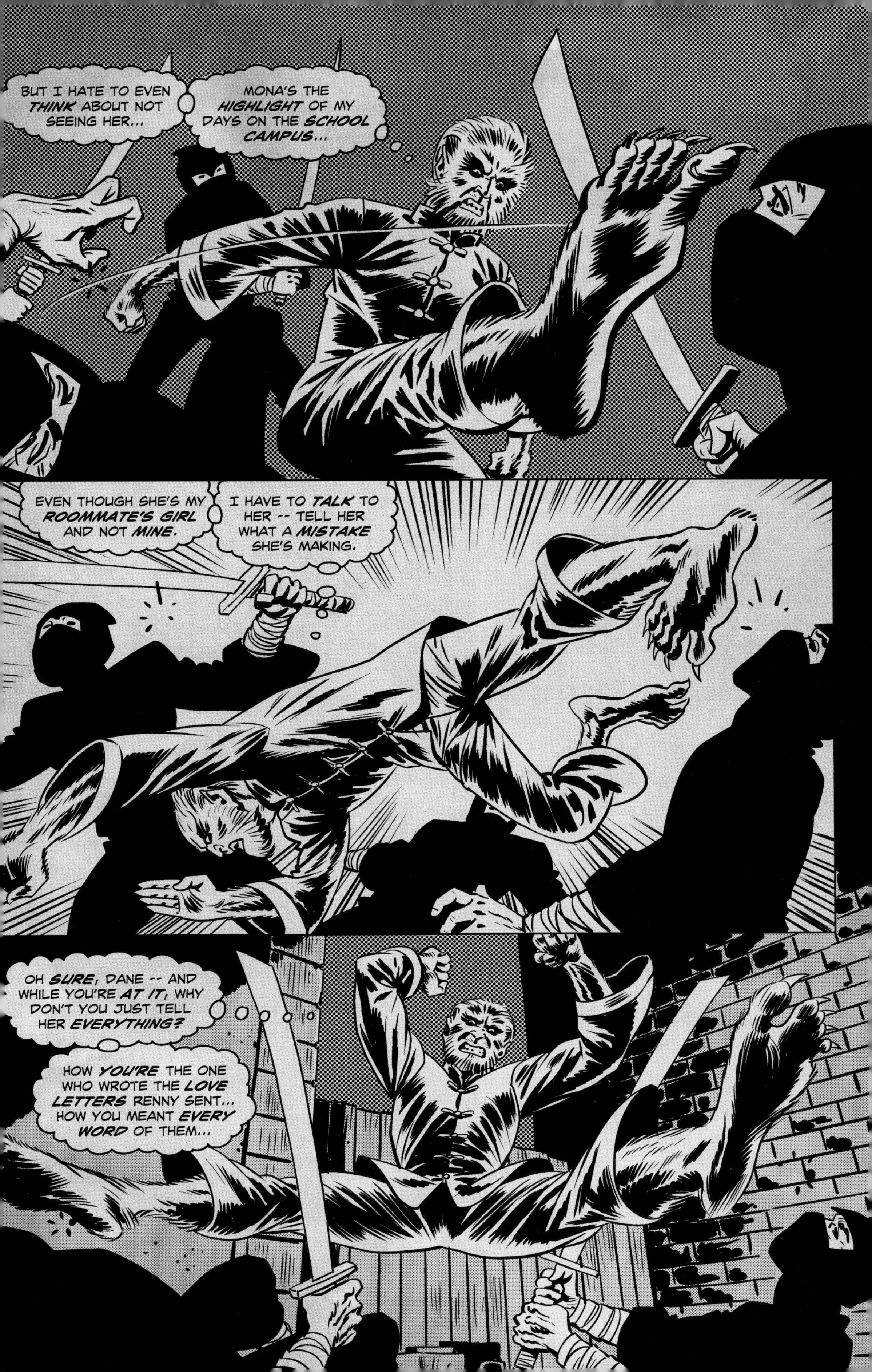
BUT I HATE TO EVEN THINK ABOUT NOT SEEING HER...
MONA'S THE HIGHLIGHT OF MY DAYS ON THE SCHOOL CAMPUS...
EVEN THOUGH SHE'S MY ROOMMATE'S GIRL AND NOT MINE.
I HAVE TO TALK TO HER -- TELL HER WHAT A MISTAKE SHE'S MAKING.
OH SURE, DANE -- AND WHILE YOU'RE AT IT, WHY DON'T YOU JUST TELL HER EVERYTHING?
HOW YOU'RE THE ONE WHO WROTE THE LOVE LETTERS RENNY SENT... HOW YOU MEANT EVERY WORD OF THEM...

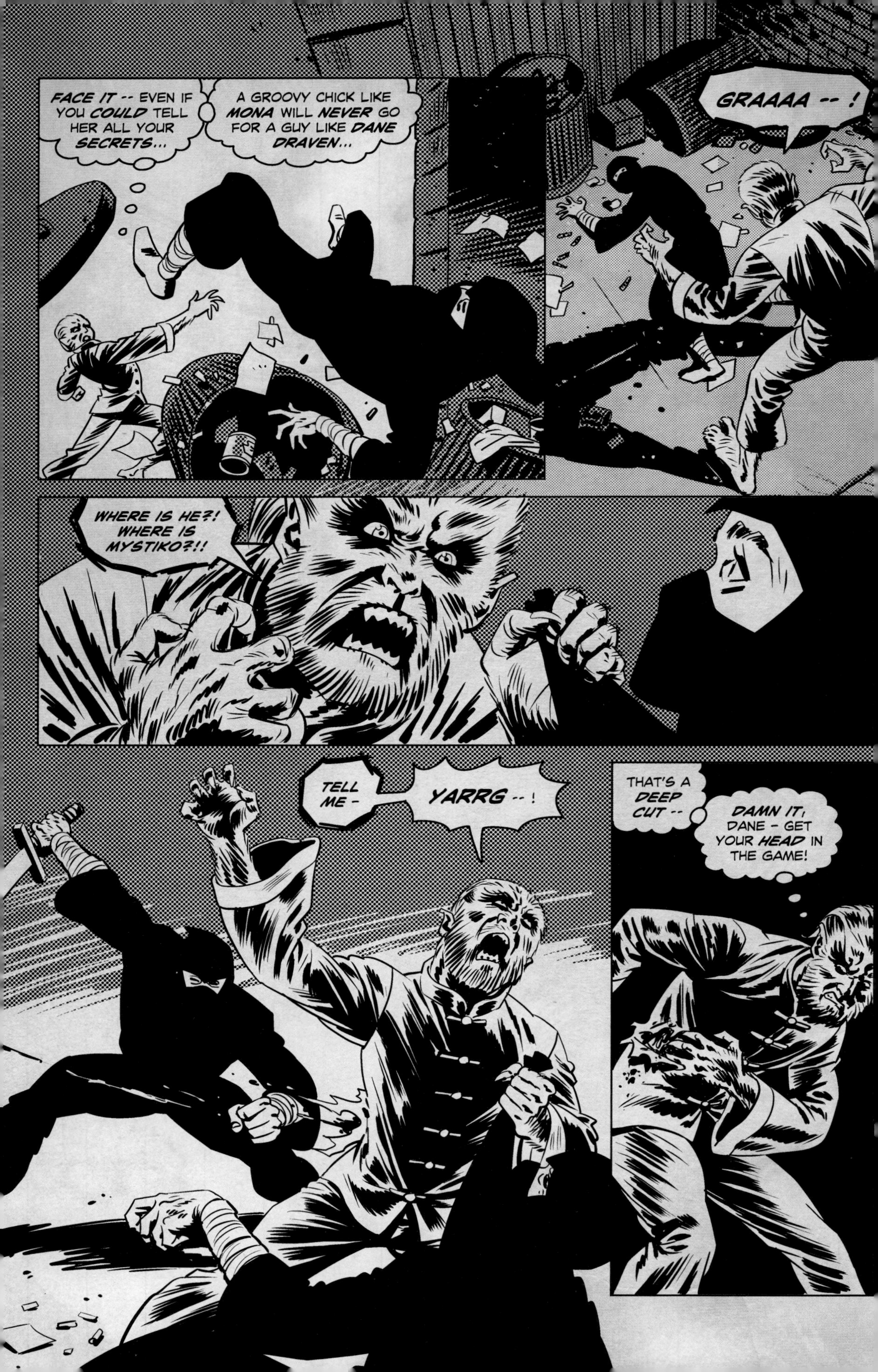
FACE IT -- EVEN IF YOU COULD TELL HER ALL YOUR SECRETS...
A GROOVY CHICK LIKE MONA WILL NEVER GO FOR A GUY LIKE DANE DRAVEN...
GRAAAA -- !
WHERE IS HE?! WHERE IS MYSTIKO?!!
TELL ME -
YARRG -- !
THAT'S A DEEP CUT --
DAMN IT, DANE - GET YOUR HEAD IN THE GAME!

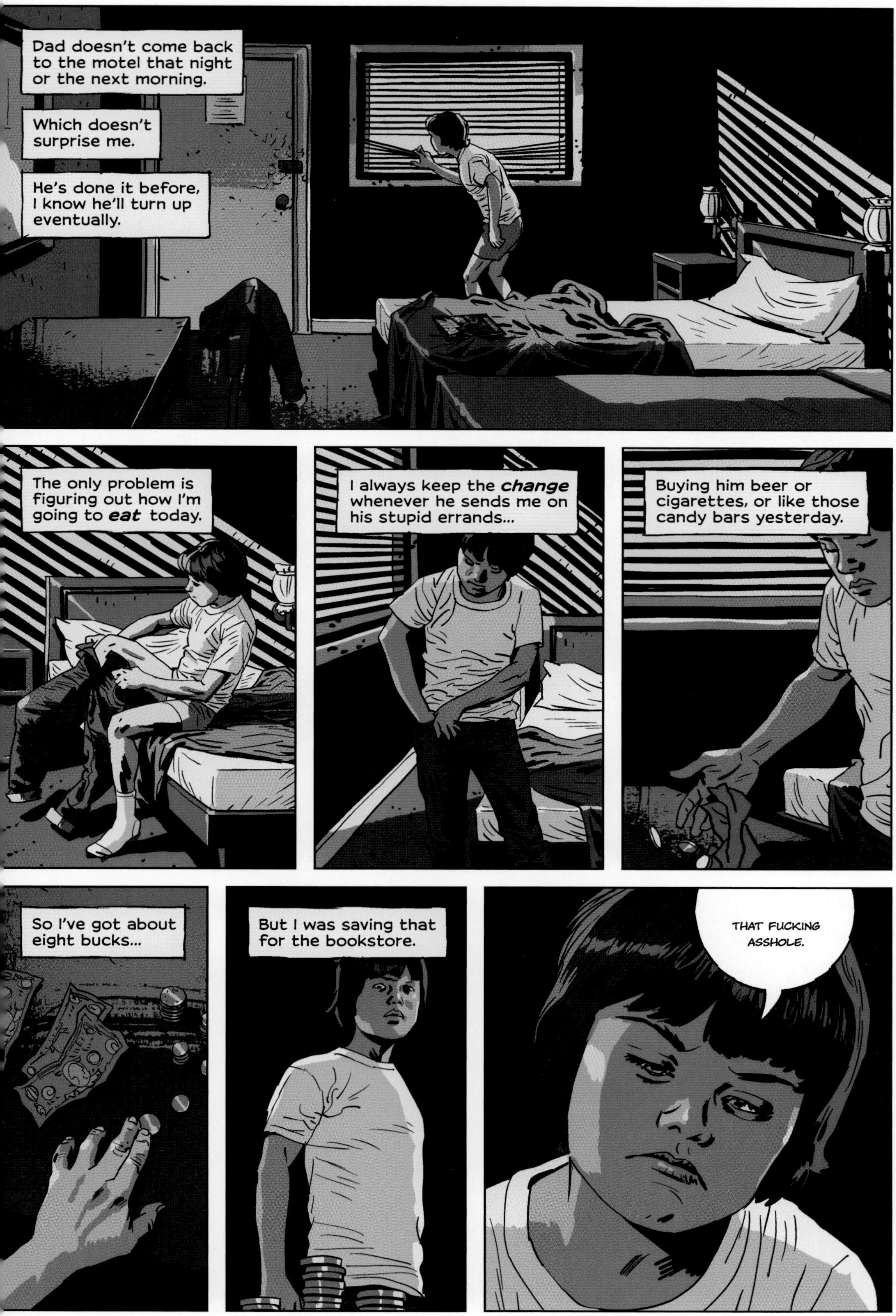
Dad doesn't come back to the motel that night or the next morning.
Which doesn't surprise me.
He's done it before, I know he'll turn up eventually.
The only problem is figuring out how I'm going to *eat* today.
I always keep the *change* whenever he sends me on his stupid errands...
Buying him beer or cigarettes, or like those candy bars yesterday.
So I've got about eight bucks...
But I was saving that for the bookstore.
THAT FUCKING ASSHOLE.

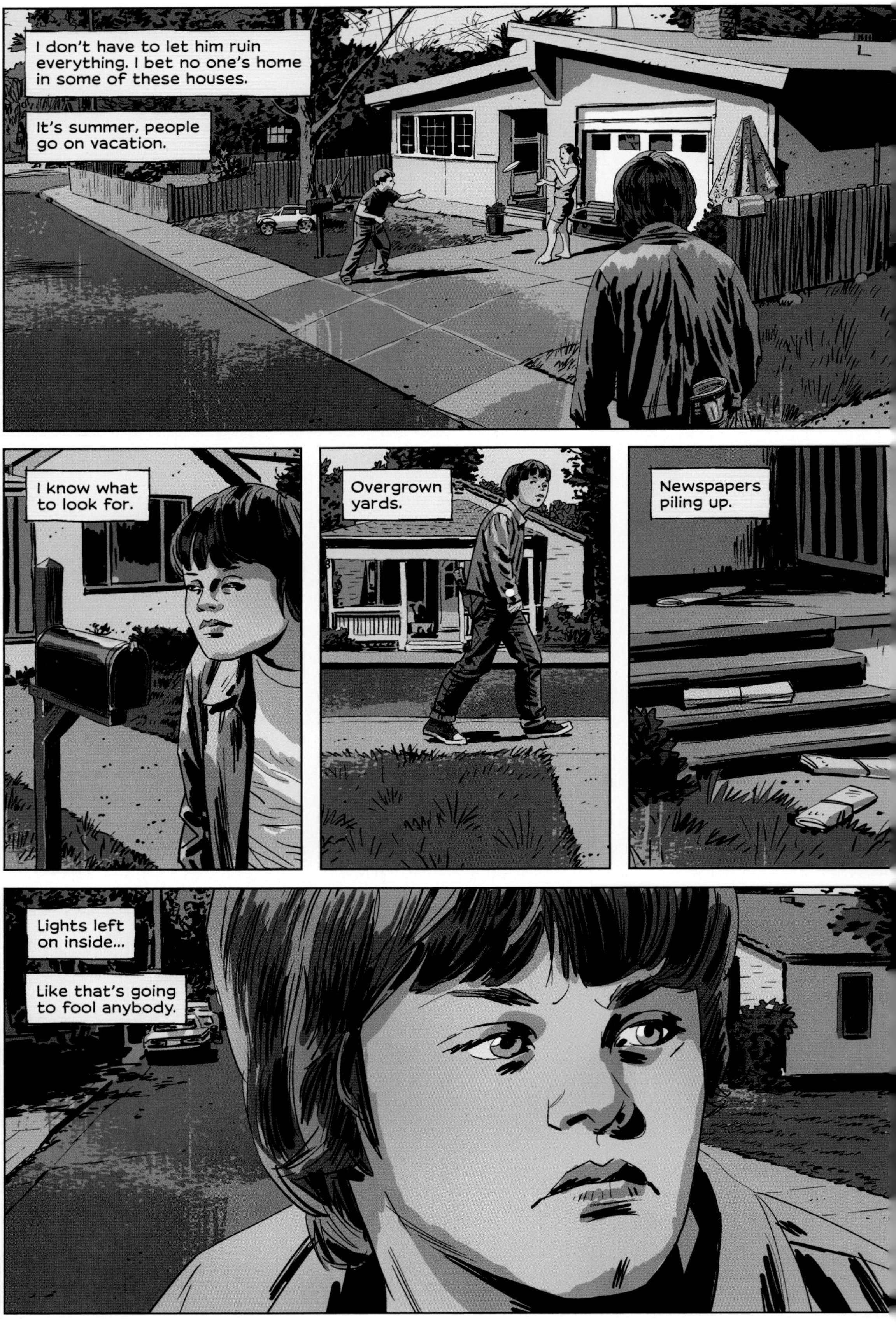

I don't have to let him ruin everything. I bet no one's home in some of these houses.
It's summer, people go on vacation.
I know what to look for.
Overgrown yards.
Newspapers piling up.
Lights left on inside...
Like that's going to fool anybody.

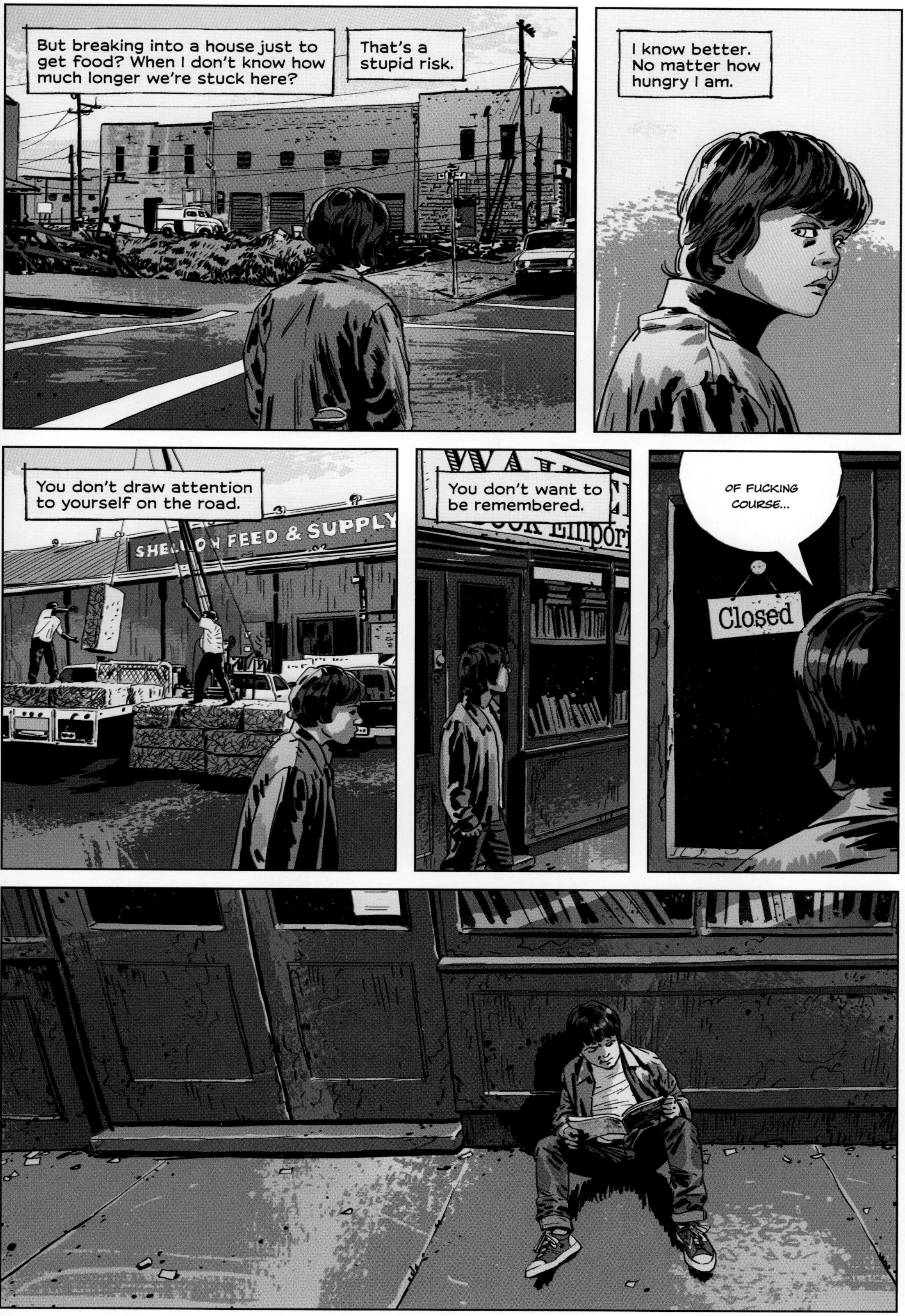
But breaking into a house just to get food? When I don't know how much longer we're stuck here?
That's a stupid risk.
I know better. No matter how hungry I am.
You don't draw attention to yourself on the road.
FEED & SUPPLY
You don't want to be remembered.
OF FUCKING COURSE...
Closed

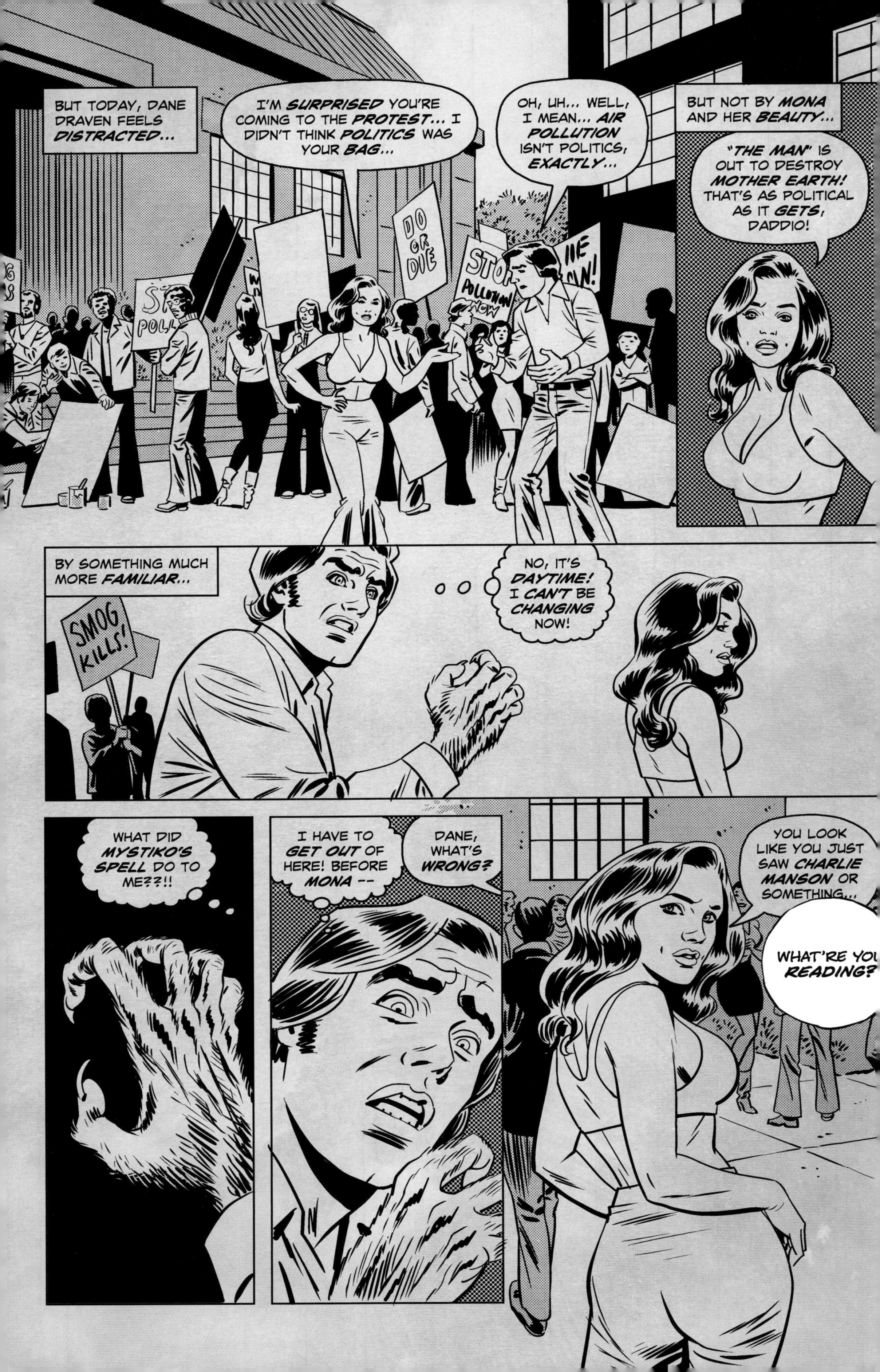

BUT TODAY, DANE DRAVEN FEELS DISTRACTED...
I'M SURPRISED YOU'RE COMING TO THE PROTEST... I DIDN'T THINK POLITICS WAS YOUR BAG...
OH, UH... WELL, I MEAN... AIR POLLUTION ISN'T POLITICS, EXACTLY...
DO OR DIE
STOP POLLUTION NOW
BUT NOT BY MONA AND HER BEAUTY...
"THE MAN" IS OUT TO DESTROY MOTHER EARTH! THAT'S AS POLITICAL AS IT GETS, DADDIO!
BY SOMETHING MUCH MORE FAMILIAR...
SMOG KILLS!
NO, IT'S DAYTIME! I CAN'T BE CHANGING NOW!
WHAT DID MYSTIKO'S SPELL DO TO ME??!!
I HAVE TO GET OUT OF HERE! BEFORE MONA --
DANE, WHAT'S WRONG?
YOU LOOK LIKE YOU JUST SAW CHARLIE MANSON OR SOMETHING...
WHAT'RE YOU READING?

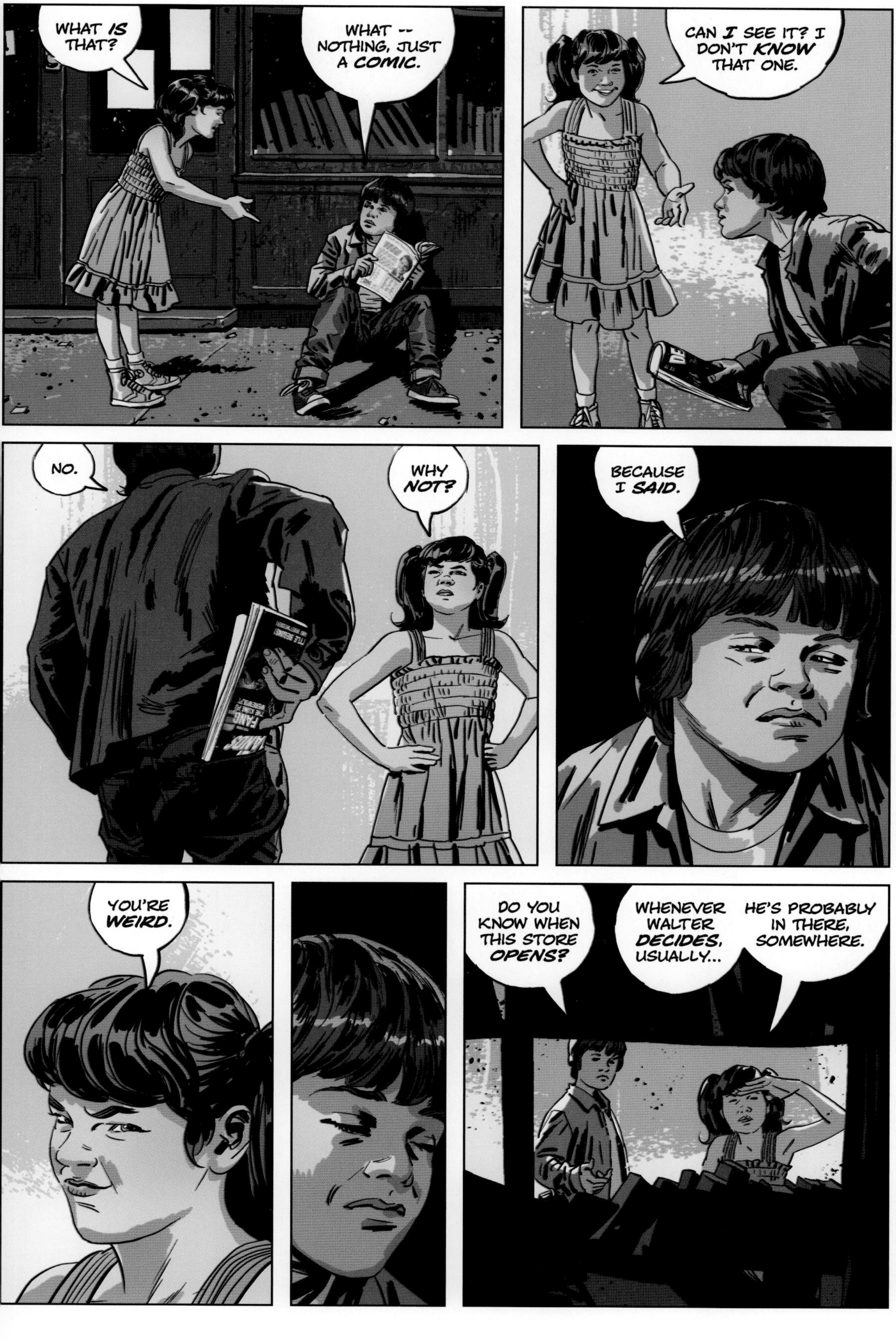
WHAT IS THAT?
WHAT -- NOTHING, JUST A COMIC.
CAN I SEE IT? I DON'T KNOW THAT ONE.
NO.
WHY NOT?
BECAUSE I SAID.
YOU'RE WEIRD.
DO YOU KNOW WHEN THIS STORE OPENS?
WHENEVER WALTER DECIDES, USUALLY...
HE'S PROBABLY IN THERE, SOMEWHERE.

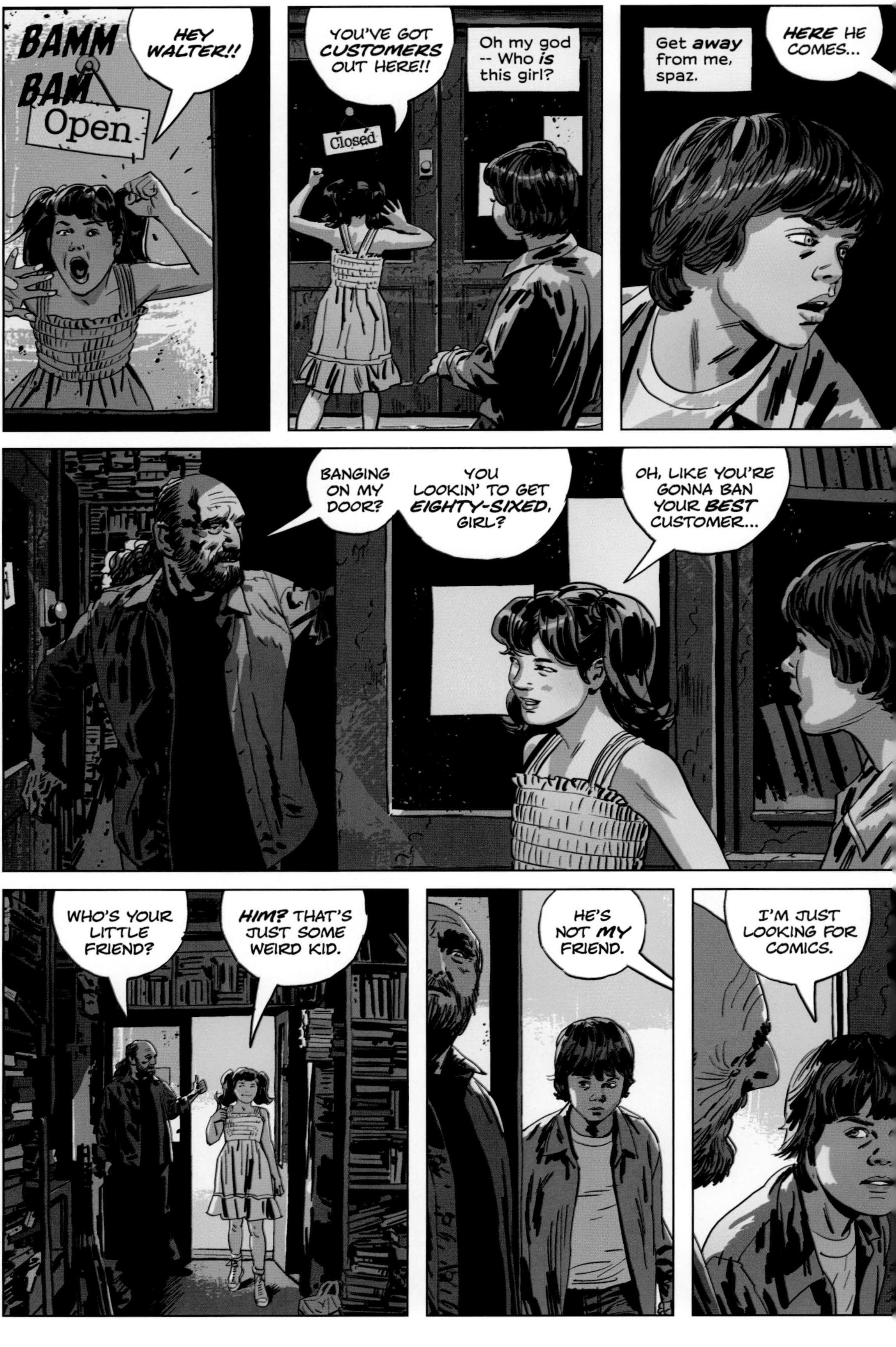
BAMM BAM
Open
HEY WALTER!!
YOU'VE GOT CUSTOMERS OUT HERE!!
Closed
Oh my god -- Who is this girl?
Get away from me, spaz.
HERE HE COMES...
BANGING ON MY DOOR?
YOU LOOKIN' TO GET EIGHTY-SIXED, GIRL?
OH, LIKE YOU'RE GONNA BAN YOUR BEST CUSTOMER...
WHO'S YOUR LITTLE FRIEND?
HIM? THAT'S JUST SOME WEIRD KID.
HE'S NOT MY FRIEND.
I'M JUST LOOKING FOR COMICS.

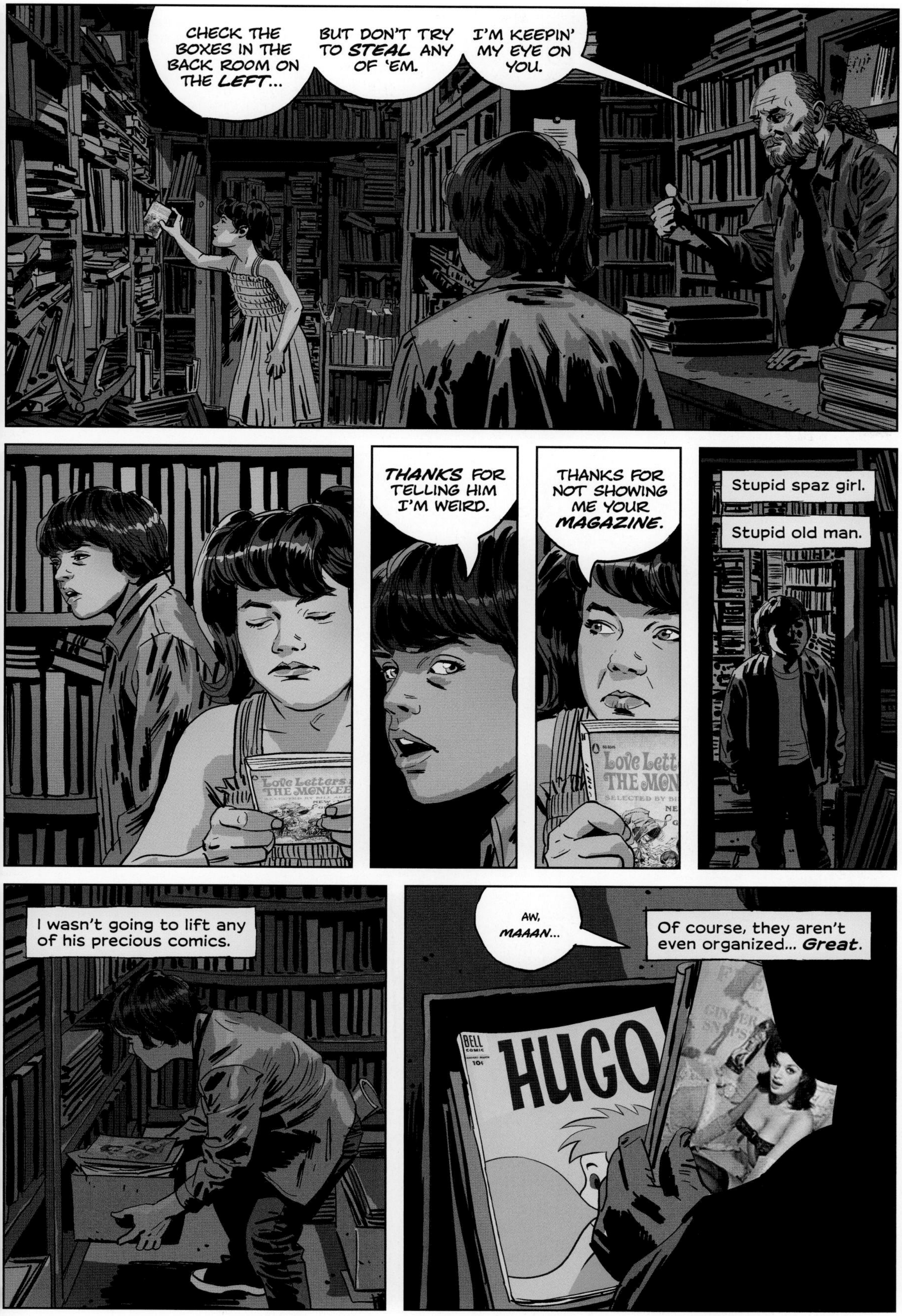
CHECK THE BOXES IN THE BACK ROOM ON THE *LEFT*...
BUT DON'T TRY TO *STEAL* ANY OF 'EM.
I'M KEEPIN' MY EYE ON YOU.
THANKS FOR TELLING HIM I'M WEIRD.
THANKS FOR NOT SHOWING ME YOUR *MAGAZINE*.
Stupid spaz girl.
Stupid old man.
I wasn't going to lift any of his precious comics.
AW, *MAAAN*...
Of course, they aren't even organized... *Great*.
BELL COMIC
10¢
HUGO

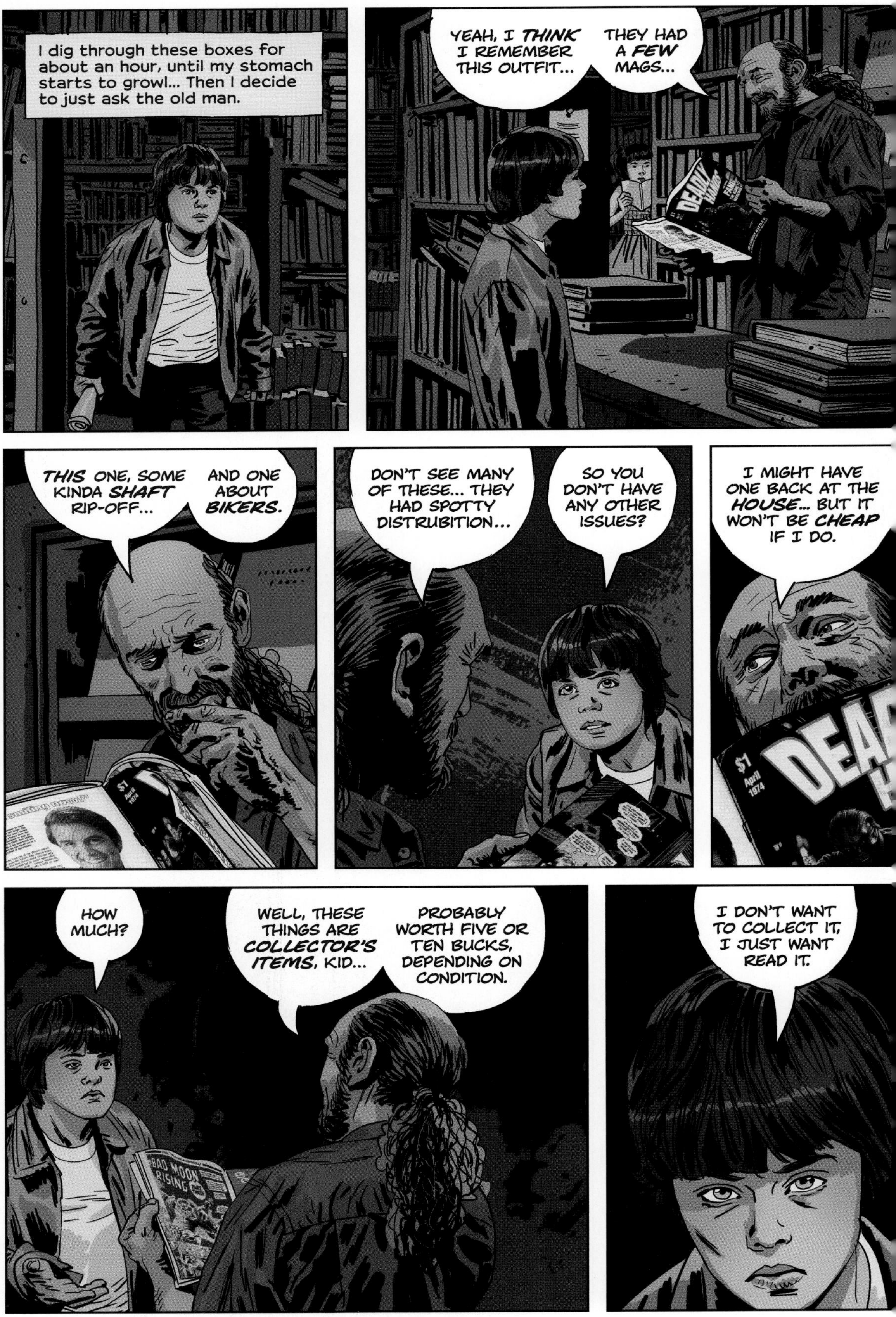

I dig through these boxes for about an hour, until my stomach starts to growl... Then I decide to just ask the old man.
YEAH, I *THINK* I REMEMBER THIS OUTFIT...
THEY HAD A *FEW* MAGS...
THIS ONE, SOME KINDA *SHAFT* RIP-OFF...
AND ONE ABOUT *BIKERS.*
$1 April 1974
DON'T SEE MANY OF THESE... THEY HAD SPOTTY DISTRUBITION...
SO YOU DON'T HAVE ANY OTHER ISSUES?
I MIGHT HAVE ONE BACK AT THE *HOUSE*... BUT IT WON'T BE *CHEAP* IF I DO.
$1 April 1974
HOW MUCH?
WELL, THESE THINGS ARE *COLLECTOR'S ITEMS,* KID...
PROBABLY WORTH FIVE OR TEN BUCKS, DEPENDING ON CONDITION.
BAD MOON RISING
I DON'T WANT TO COLLECT IT, I JUST WANT READ IT.

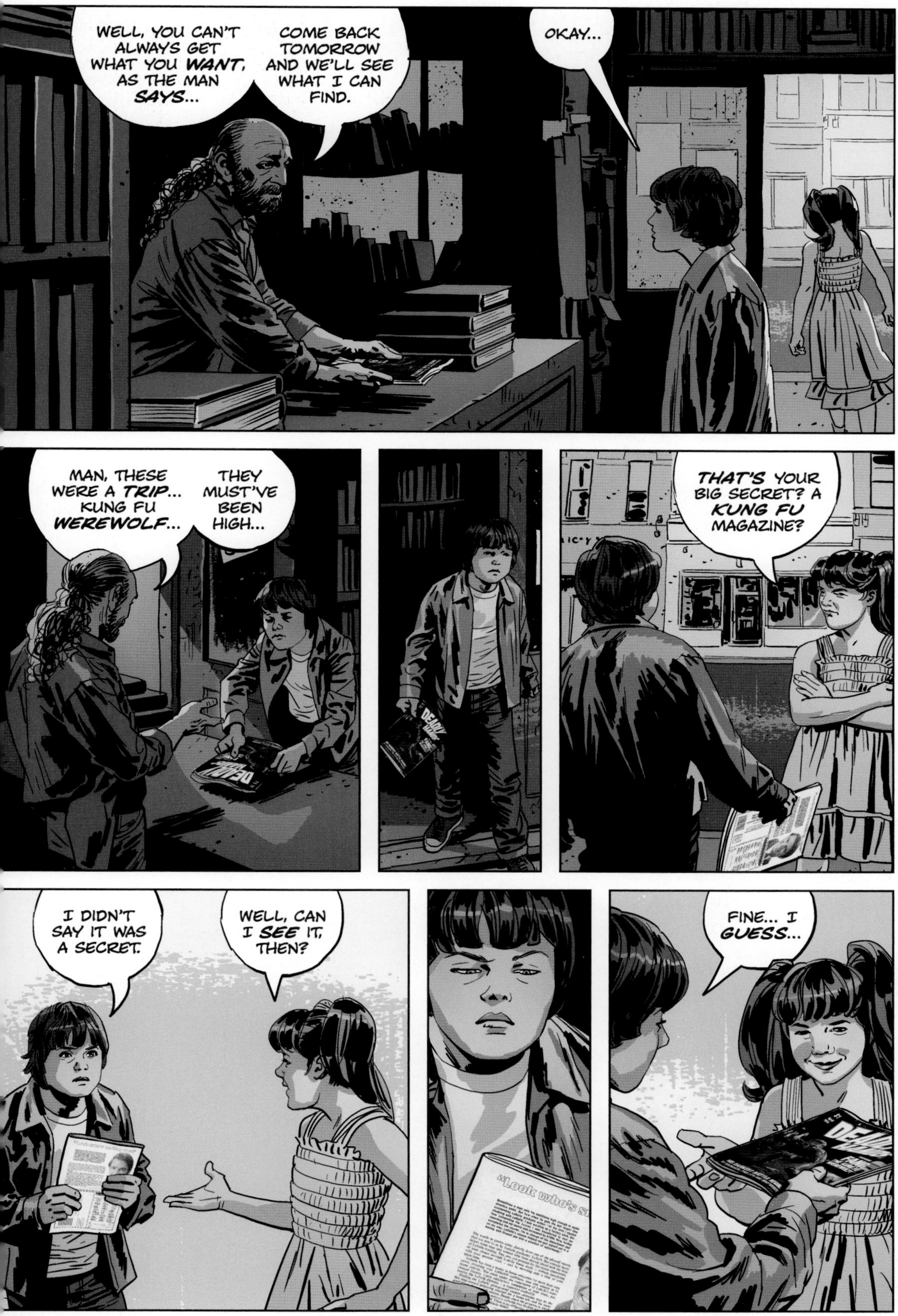
WELL, YOU CAN'T ALWAYS GET WHAT YOU *WANT*, AS THE MAN *SAYS*...
COME BACK TOMORROW AND WE'LL SEE WHAT I CAN FIND.
OKAY...
MAN, THESE WERE A *TRIP*... KUNG FU *WEREWOLF*...
THEY MUST'VE BEEN HIGH...
THAT'S YOUR BIG SECRET? A *KUNG FU* MAGAZINE?
I DIDN'T SAY IT WAS A SECRET.
WELL, CAN I *SEE* IT, THEN?
FINE... I *GUESS*...

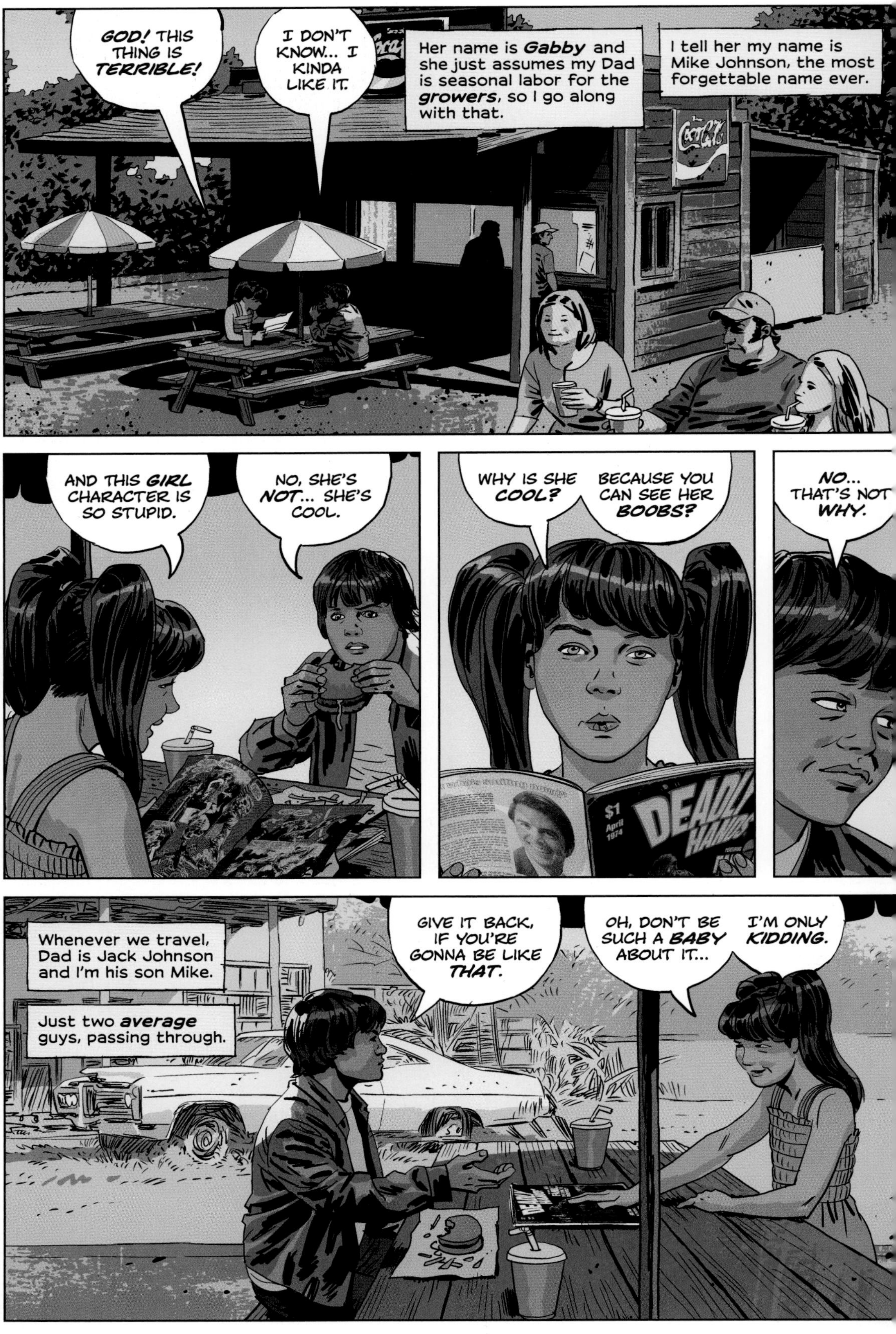
GOD! THIS THING IS TERRIBLE!
I DON'T KNOW... I KINDA LIKE IT.
Her name is Gabby and she just assumes my Dad is seasonal labor for the growers, so I go along with that.
I tell her my name is Mike Johnson, the most forgettable name ever.
AND THIS GIRL CHARACTER IS SO STUPID.
NO, SHE'S NOT... SHE'S COOL.
WHY IS SHE COOL?
BECAUSE YOU CAN SEE HER BOOBS?
$1
April 1974
NO... THAT'S NOT WHY.
Whenever we travel, Dad is Jack Johnson and I'm his son Mike.
Just two average guys, passing through.
GIVE IT BACK, IF YOU'RE GONNA BE LIKE THAT.
OH, DON'T BE SUCH A BABY ABOUT IT...
I'M ONLY KIDDING.

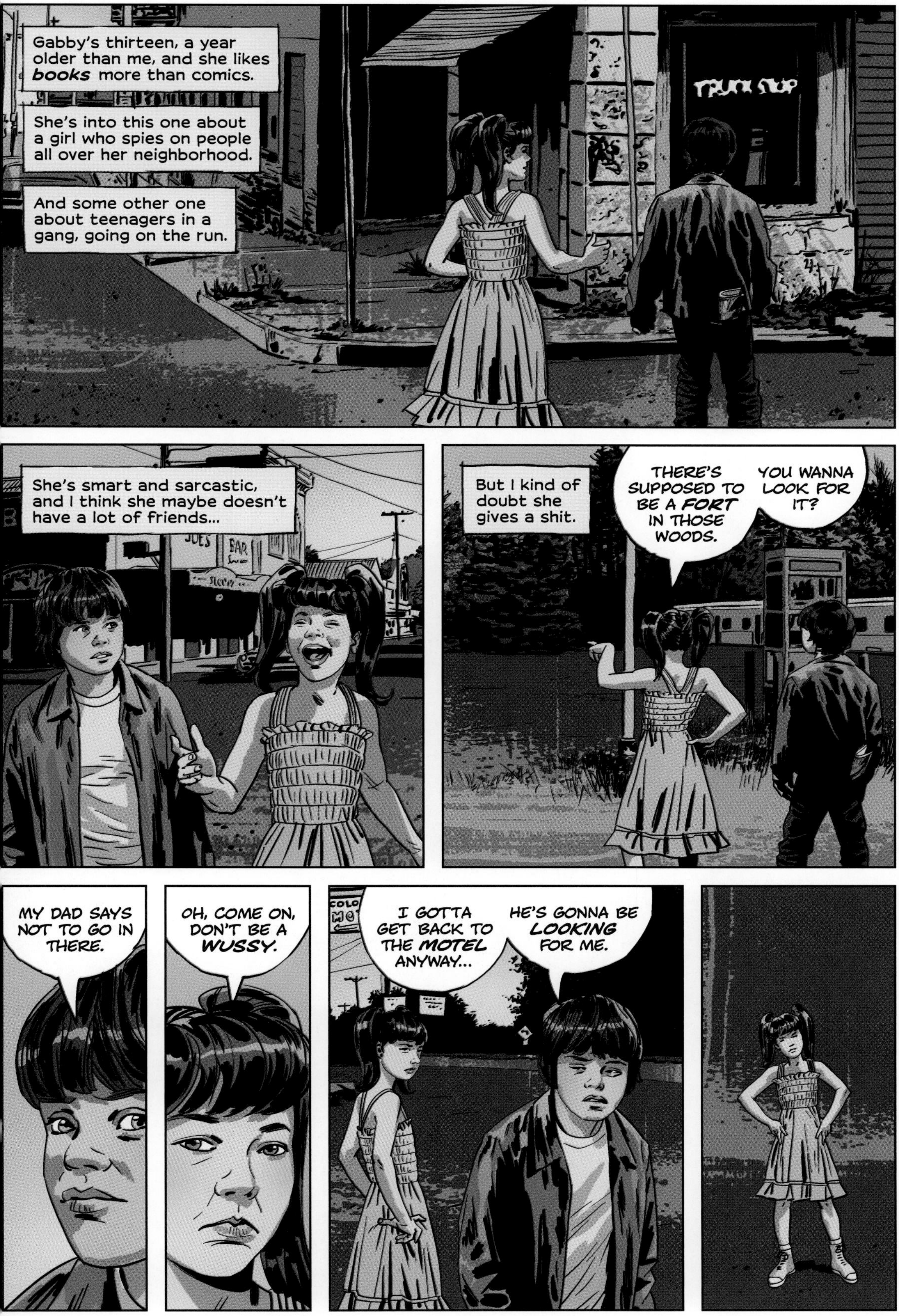
Gabby's thirteen, a year older than me, and she likes *books* more than comics.
She's into this one about a girl who spies on people all over her neighborhood.
And some other one about teenagers in a gang, going on the run.
She's smart and sarcastic, and I think she maybe doesn't have a lot of friends...
But I kind of doubt she gives a shit.
THERE'S SUPPOSED TO BE A *FORT* IN THOSE WOODS.
YOU WANNA LOOK FOR IT?
MY DAD SAYS NOT TO GO IN THERE.
OH, COME ON, DON'T BE A *WUSSY*.
I GOTTA GET BACK TO THE *MOTEL* ANYWAY...
HE'S GONNA BE *LOOKING* FOR ME.

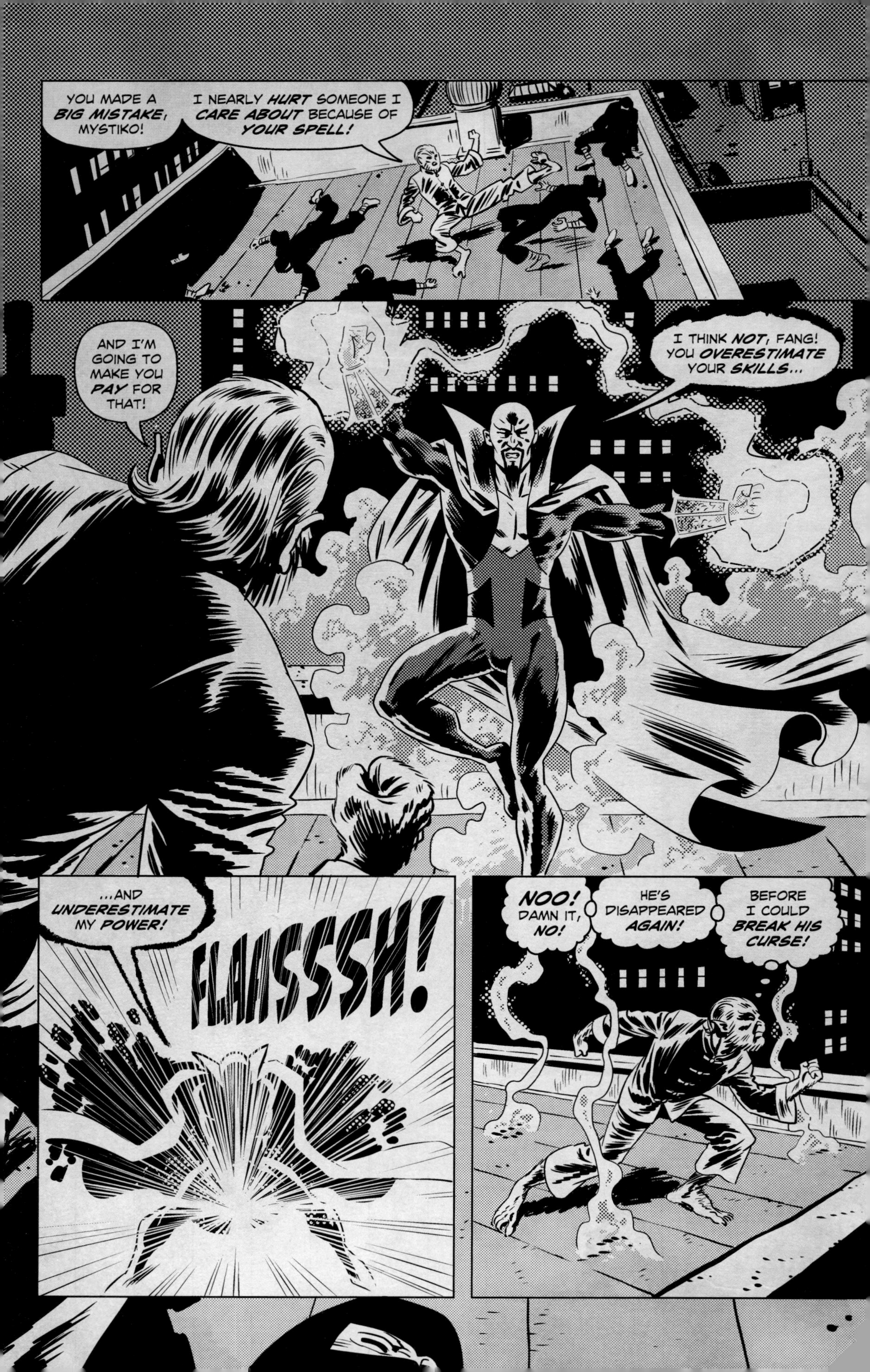
YOU MADE A BIG MISTAKE, MYSTIKO!
I NEARLY HURT SOMEONE I CARE ABOUT BECAUSE OF YOUR SPELL!
AND I'M GOING TO MAKE YOU PAY FOR THAT!
I THINK NOT, FANG! YOU OVERESTIMATE YOUR SKILLS...
...AND UNDERESTIMATE MY POWER!
FLAASSSH!
NOO! DAMN IT, NO!
HE'S DISAPPEARED AGAIN!
BEFORE I COULD BREAK HIS CURSE!

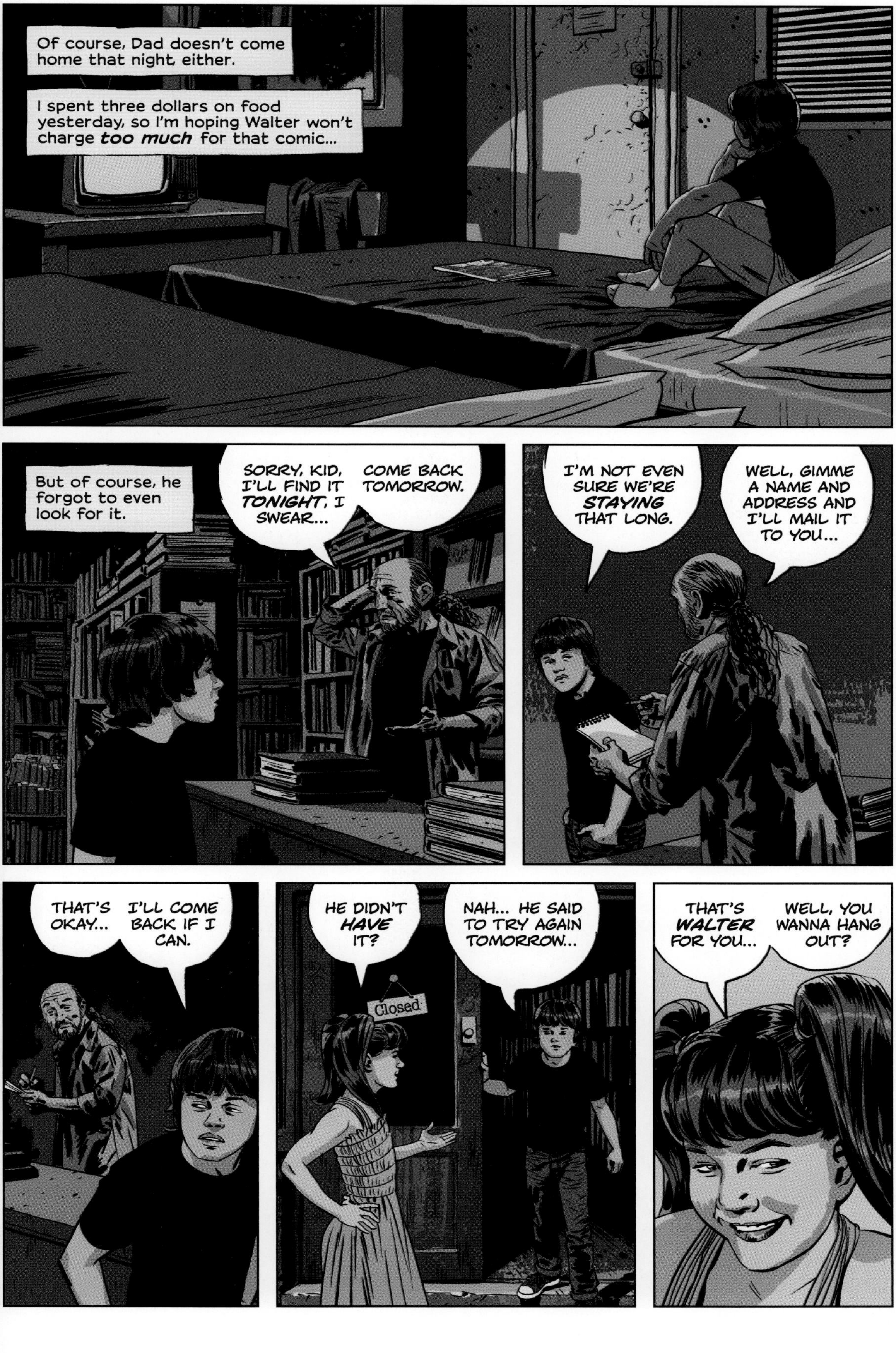

Of course, Dad doesn't come home that night either.
I spent three dollars on food yesterday, so I'm hoping Walter won't charge *too much* for that comic...
But of course, he forgot to even look for it.
SORRY, KID, I'LL FIND IT *TONIGHT*, I SWEAR...
COME BACK TOMORROW.
I'M NOT EVEN SURE WE'RE *STAYING* THAT LONG.
WELL, GIMME A NAME AND ADDRESS AND I'LL MAIL IT TO YOU...
THAT'S OKAY...
I'LL COME BACK IF I CAN.
HE DIDN'T *HAVE* IT?
Closed
NAH... HE SAID TO TRY AGAIN TOMORROW...
THAT'S *WALTER* FOR YOU...
WELL, YOU WANNA HANG OUT?

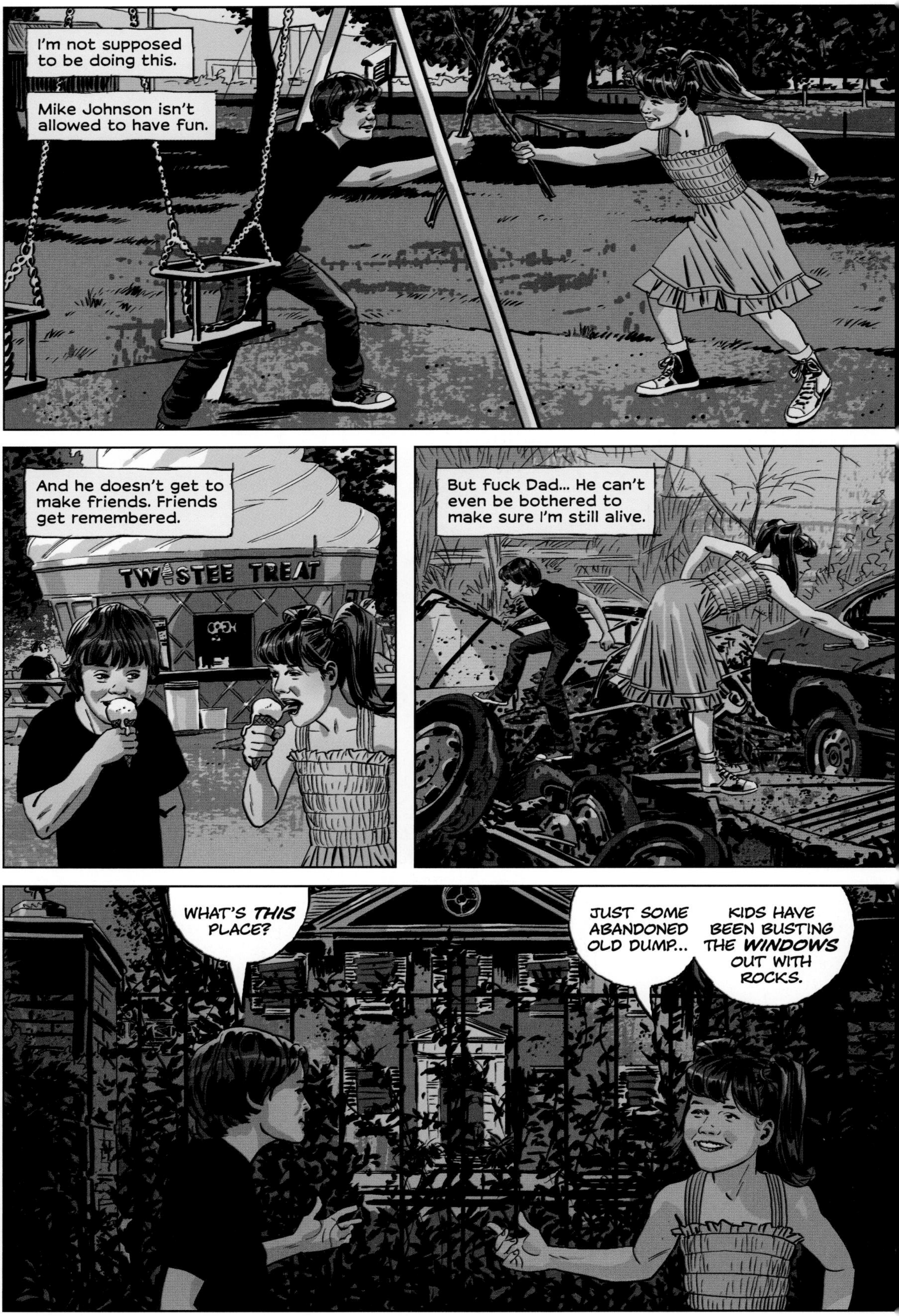
I'm not supposed to be doing this.
Mike Johnson isn't allowed to have fun.
And he doesn't get to make friends. Friends get remembered.
TWISTEE TREAT
OPEN
But fuck Dad... He can't even be bothered to make sure I'm still alive.
WHAT'S *THIS* PLACE?
JUST SOME ABANDONED OLD DUMP...
KIDS HAVE BEEN BUSTING THE *WINDOWS* OUT WITH ROCKS.

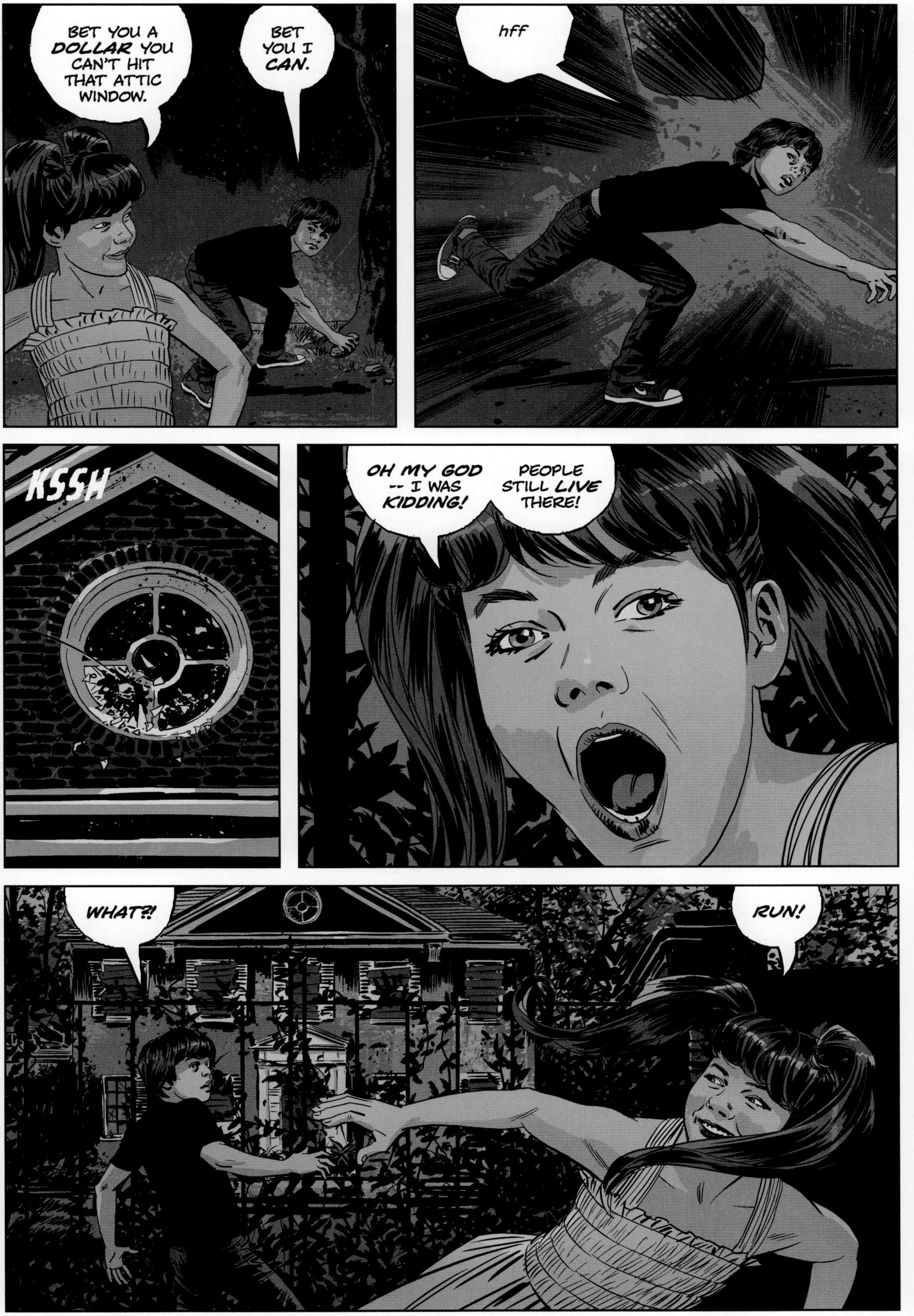
BET YOU A DOLLAR YOU CAN'T HIT THAT ATTIC WINDOW.
BET YOU I CAN.
hff
KSSH
OH MY GOD -- I WAS KIDDING!
PEOPLE STILL LIVE THERE!
WHAT?!
RUN!

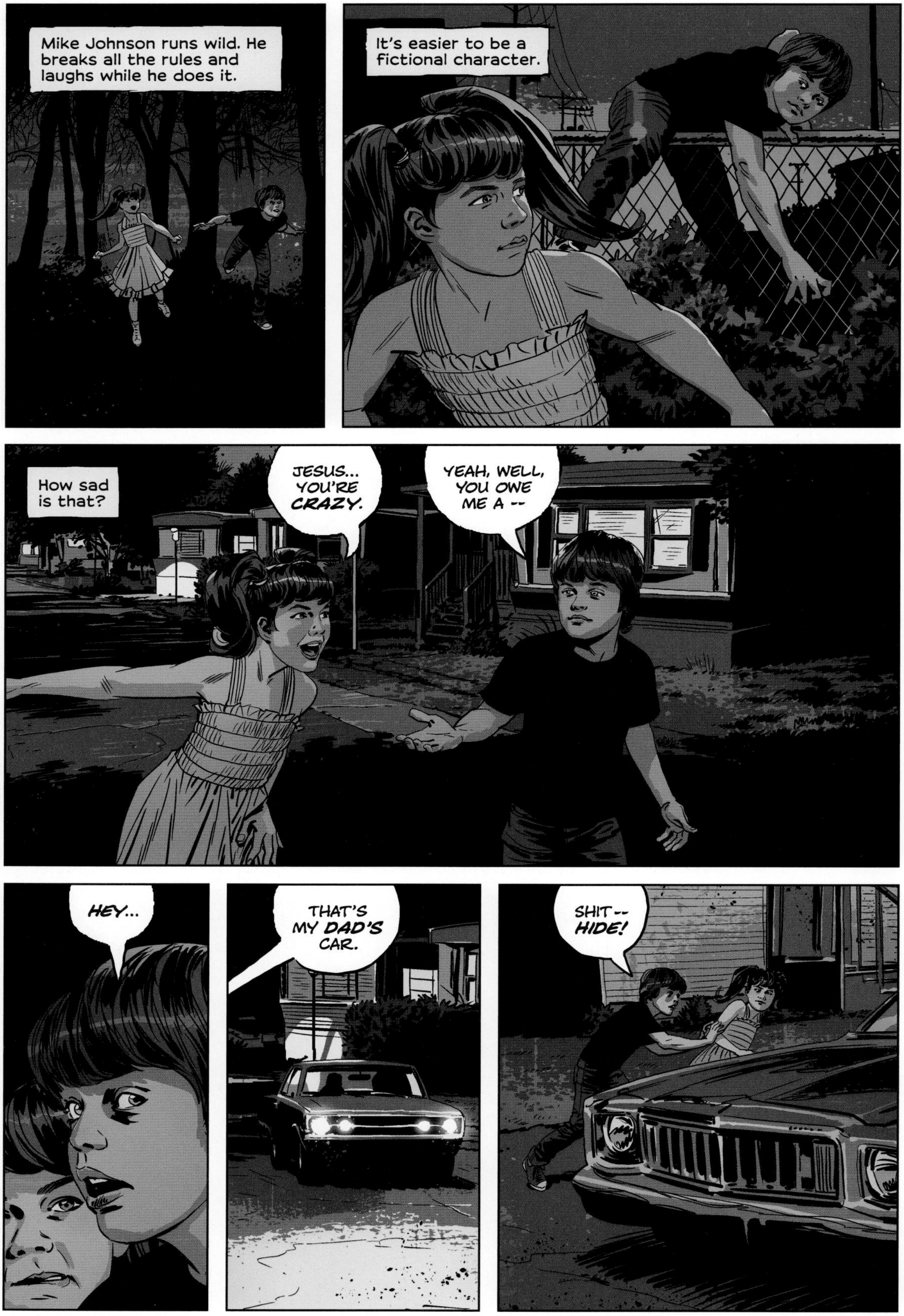
Mike Johnson runs wild. He breaks all the rules and laughs while he does it.
It's easier to be a fictional character.
How sad is that?
JESUS... YOU'RE CRAZY.
YEAH, WELL, YOU OWE ME A --
HEY...
THAT'S MY DAD'S CAR.
SHIT -- HIDE!

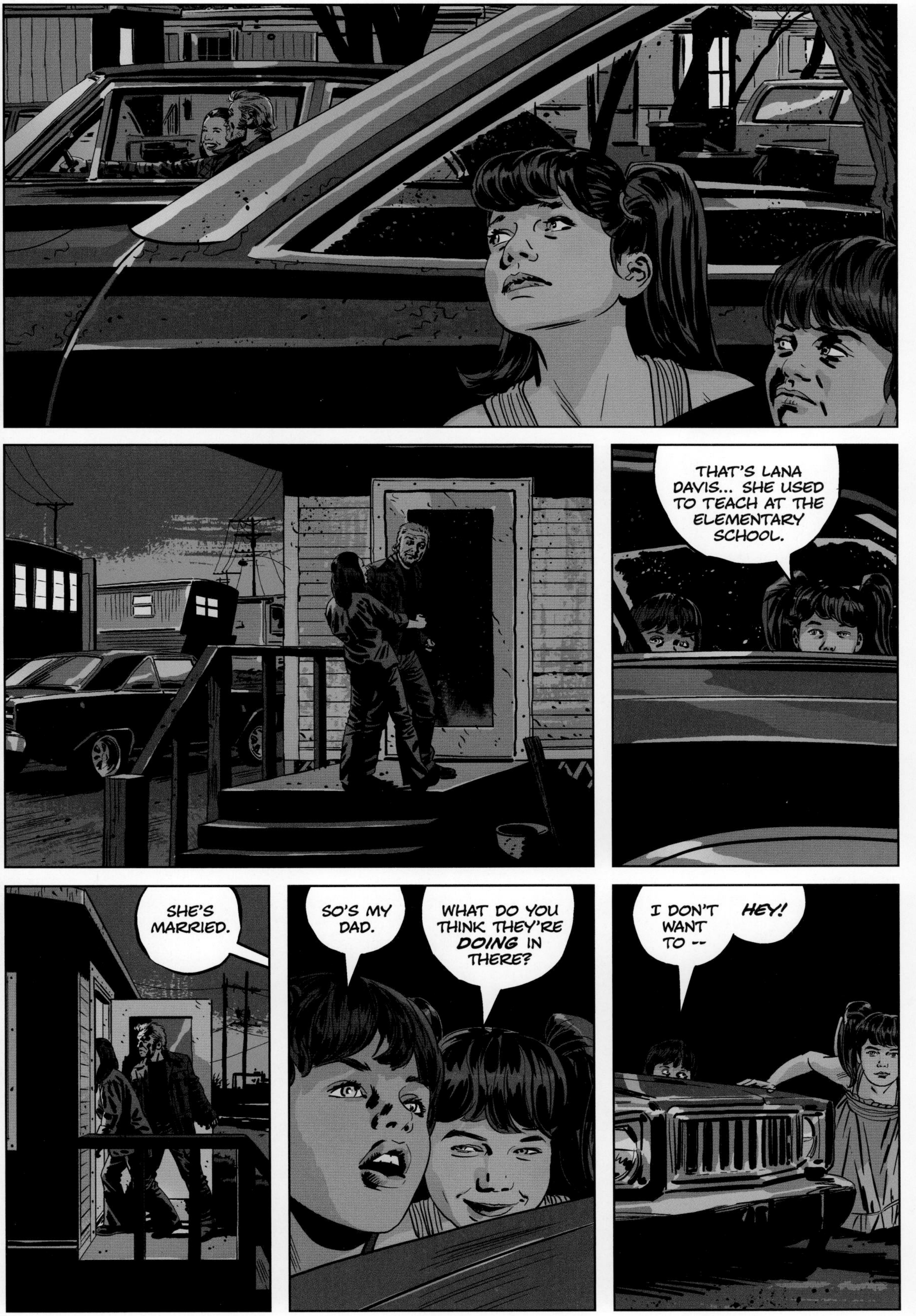
THAT'S LANA DAVIS... SHE USED TO TEACH AT THE ELEMENTARY SCHOOL.
SHE'S MARRIED.
SO'S MY DAD.
WHAT DO YOU THINK THEY'RE *DOING* IN THERE?
I DON'T WANT TO --
HEY!

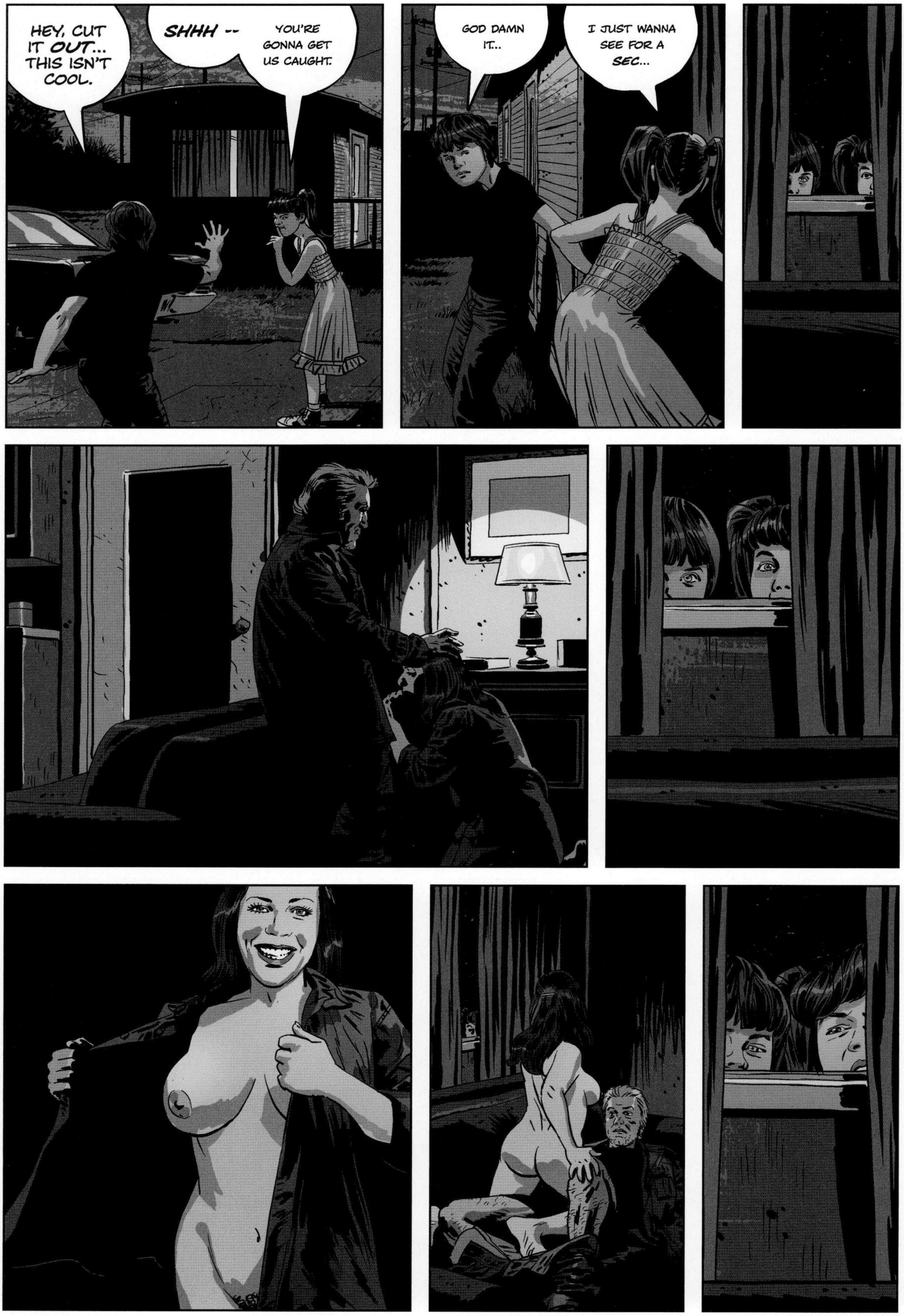
HEY, CUT IT OUT... THIS ISN'T COOL.
SHHH --
YOU'RE GONNA GET US CAUGHT.
GOD DAMN IT...
I JUST WANNA SEE FOR A SEC...

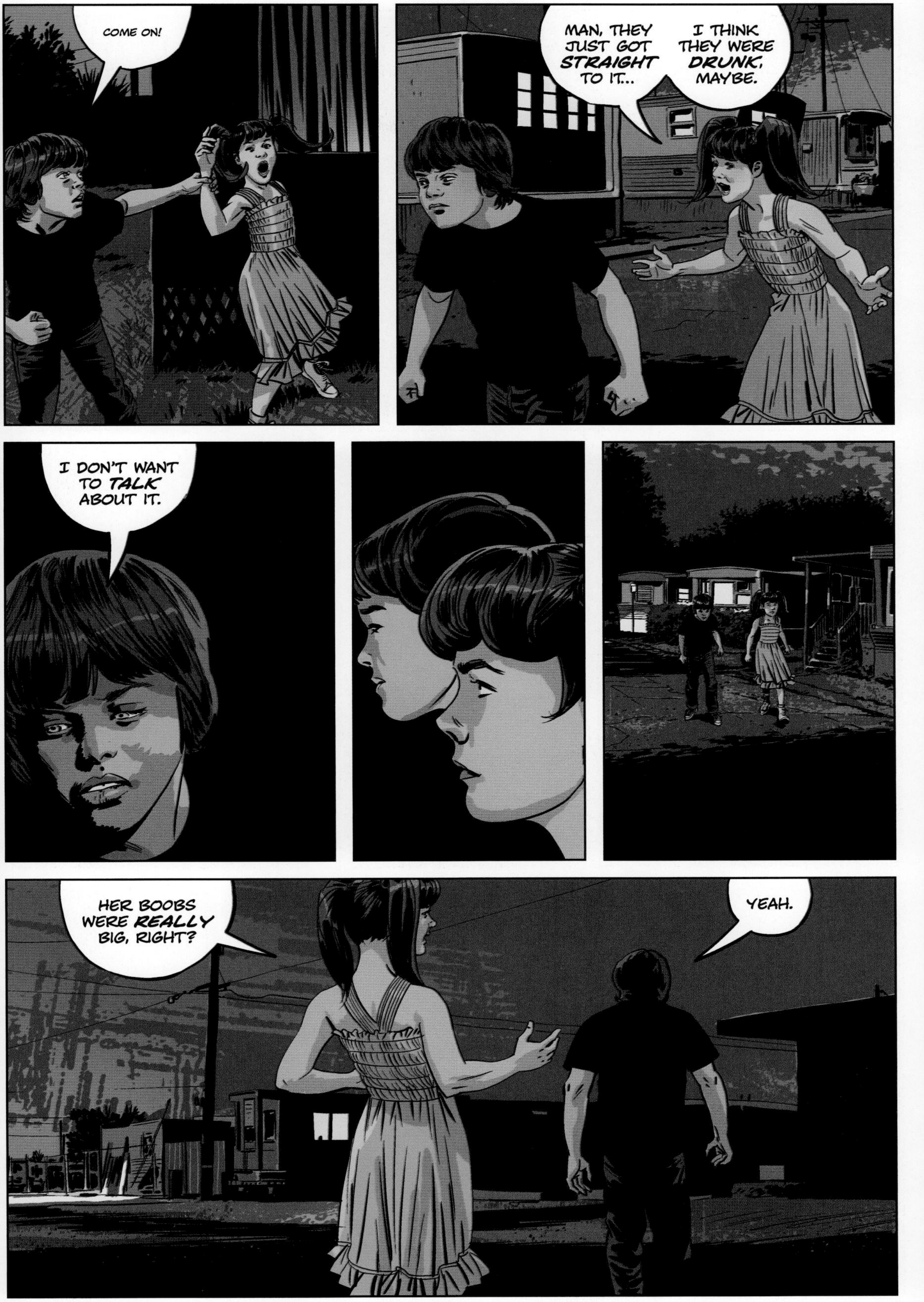
COME ON!
MAN, THEY JUST GOT STRAIGHT TO IT...
I THINK THEY WERE DRUNK, MAYBE.
I DON'T WANT TO TALK ABOUT IT.
HER BOOBS WERE REALLY BIG, RIGHT?
YEAH.

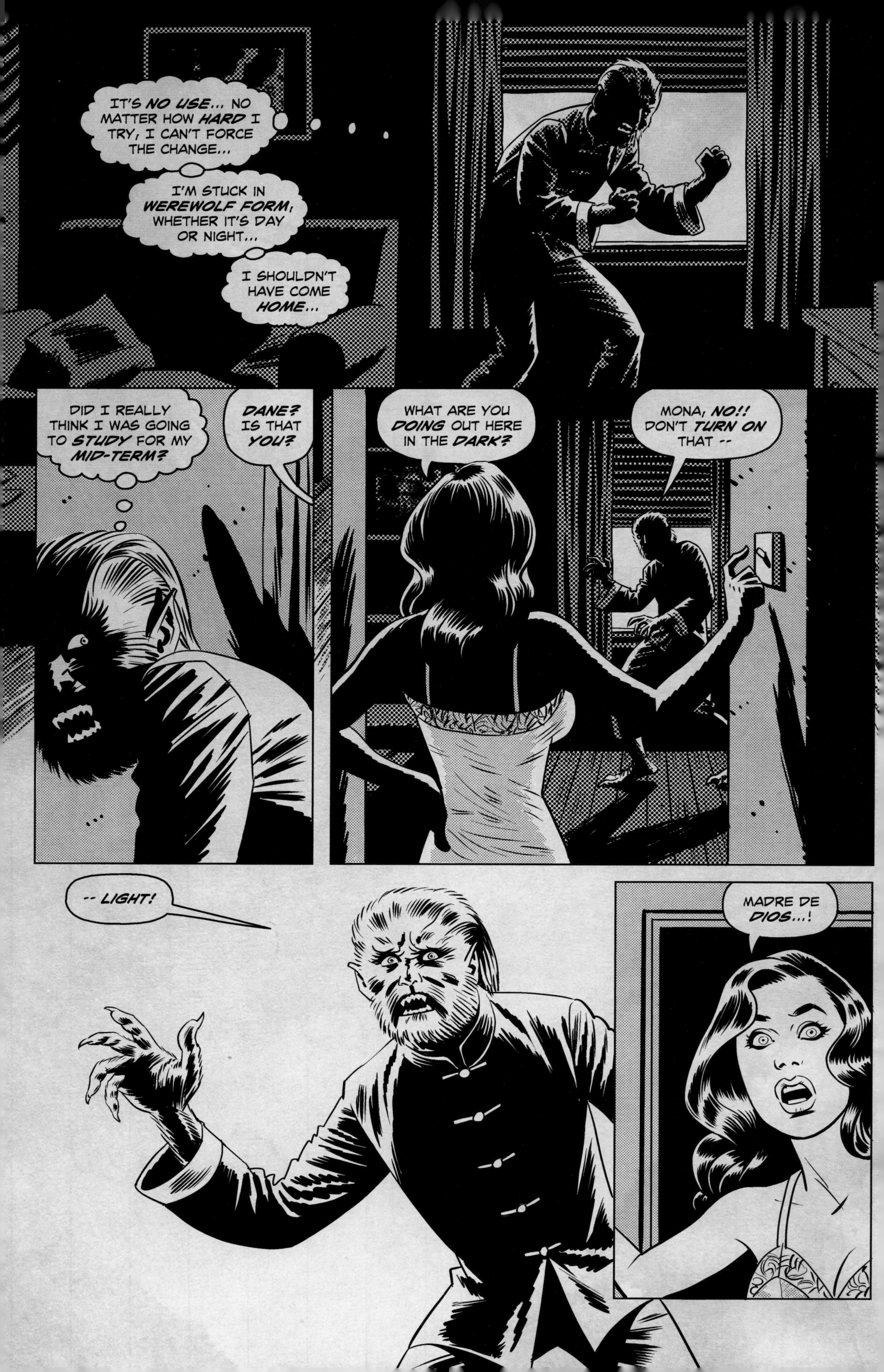

IT'S NO USE... NO MATTER HOW HARD I TRY, I CAN'T FORCE THE CHANGE...
I'M STUCK IN WEREWOLF FORM, WHETHER IT'S DAY OR NIGHT...
I SHOULDN'T HAVE COME HOME...
DID I REALLY THINK I WAS GOING TO STUDY FOR MY MID-TERM?
DANE? IS THAT YOU?
WHAT ARE YOU DOING OUT HERE IN THE DARK?
MONA, NO!! DON'T TURN ON THAT --
-- LIGHT!
MADRE DE DIOS...!

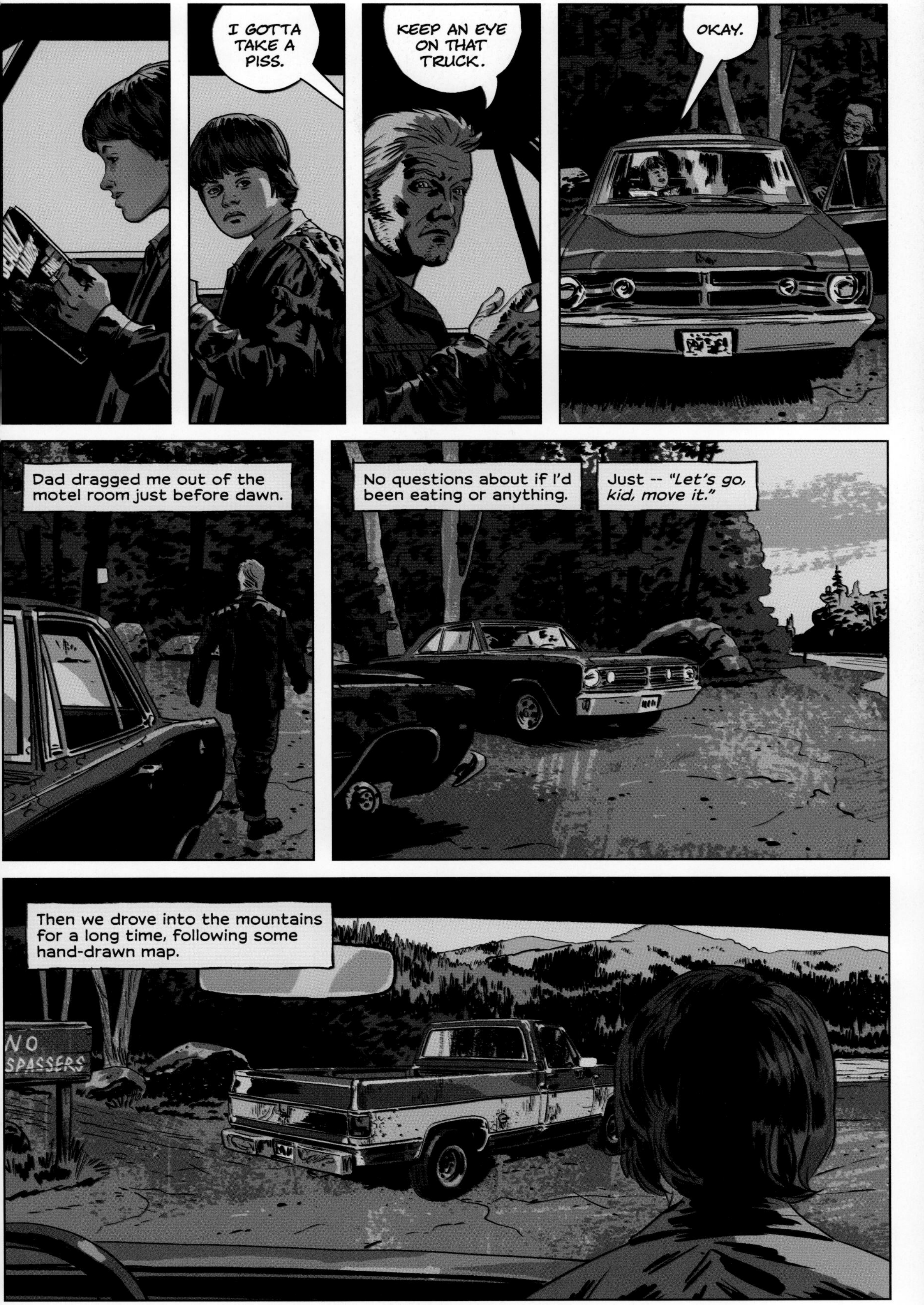
I GOTTA TAKE A PISS.
KEEP AN EYE ON THAT TRUCK.
OKAY.
Dad dragged me out of the motel room just before dawn.
No questions about if I'd been eating or anything.
Just -- *"Let's go, kid, move it."*
Then we drove into the mountains for a long time, following some hand-drawn map.
NO
SPASSERS

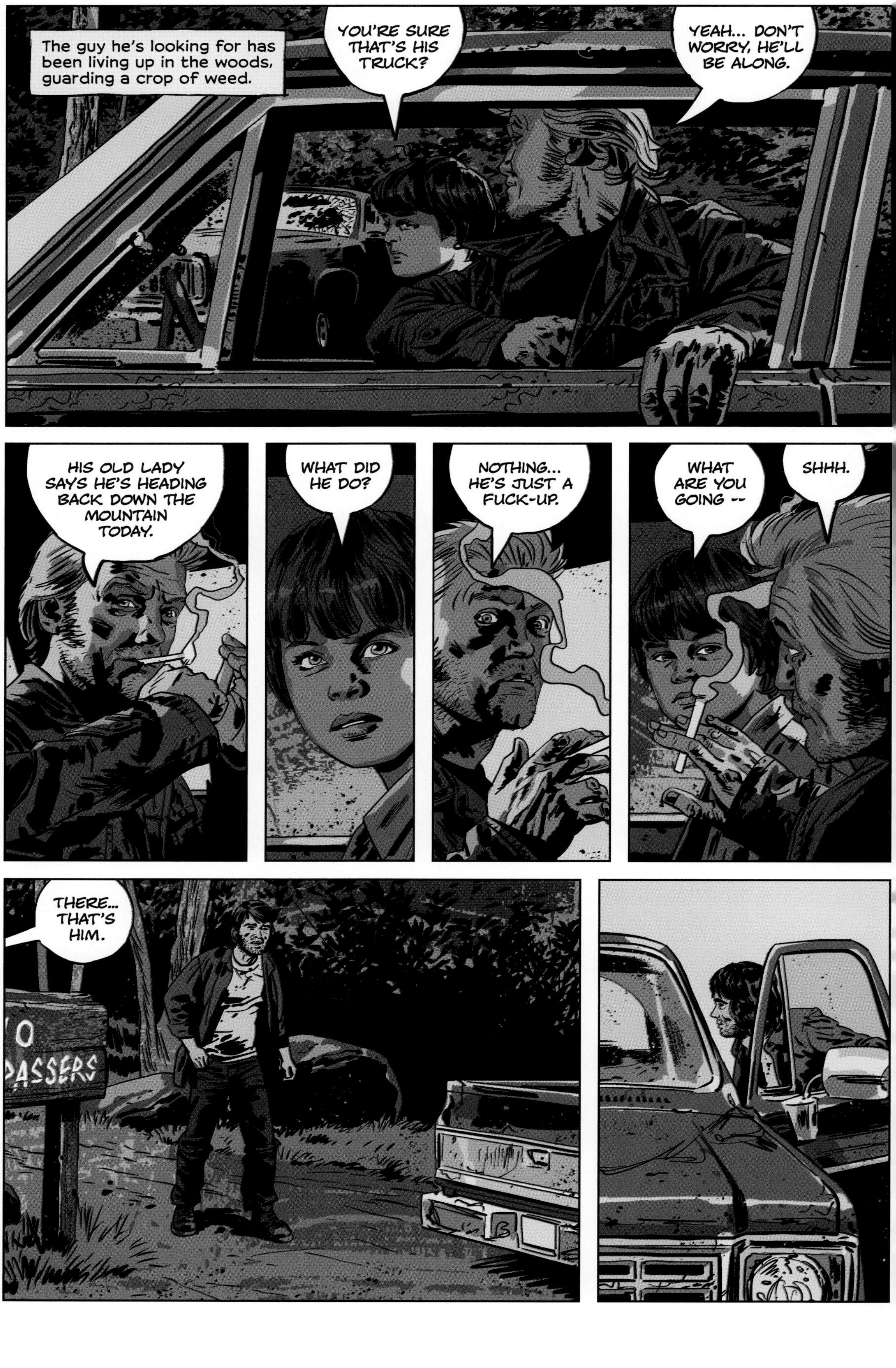
The guy he's looking for has been living up in the woods, guarding a crop of weed.
YOU'RE SURE THAT'S HIS TRUCK?
YEAH... DON'T WORRY, HE'LL BE ALONG.
HIS OLD LADY SAYS HE'S HEADING BACK DOWN THE MOUNTAIN TODAY.
WHAT DID HE DO?
NOTHING... HE'S JUST A FUCK-UP.
WHAT ARE YOU GOING --
SHHH.
THERE... THAT'S HIM.

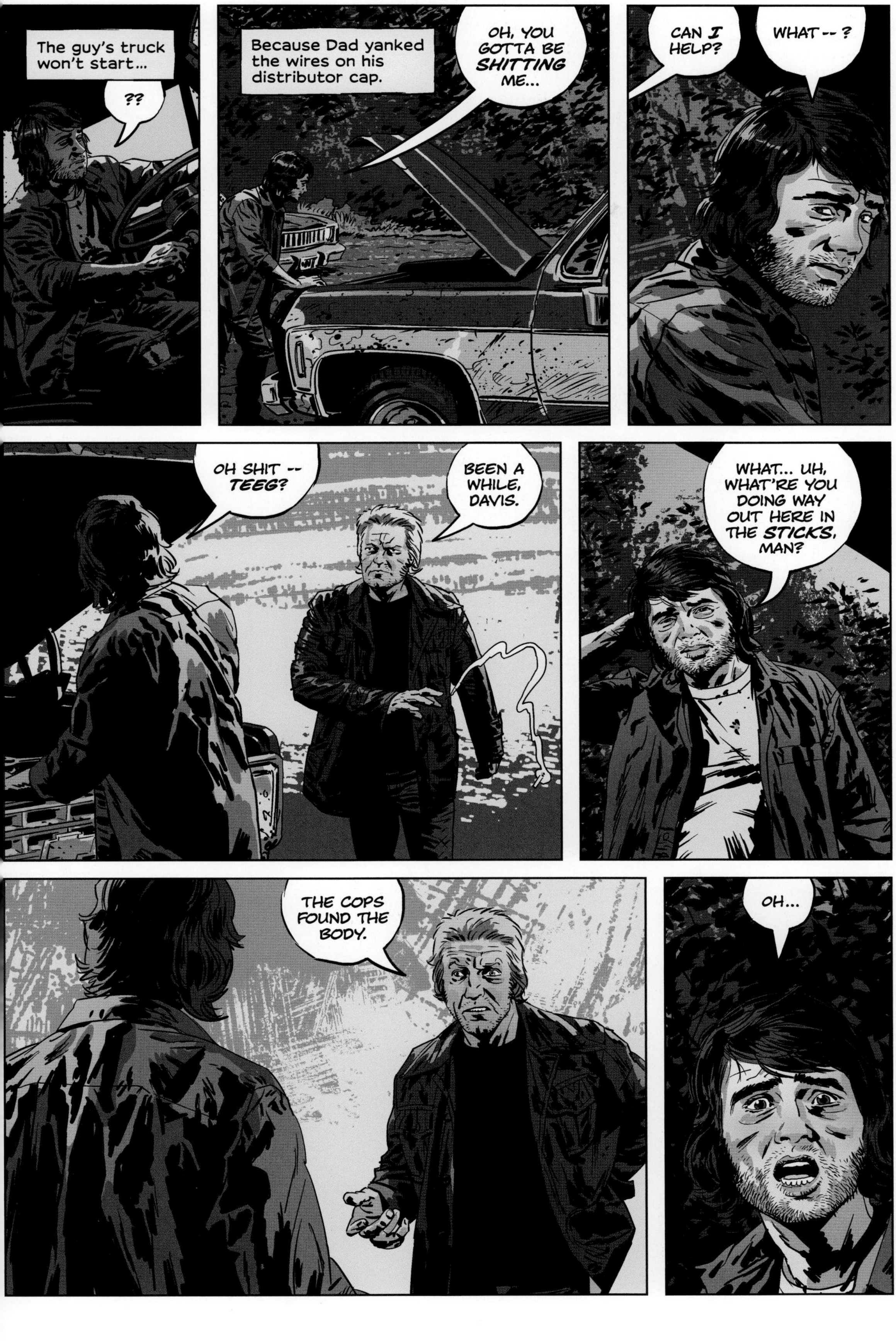
The guy's truck won't start...
??
Because Dad yanked the wires on his distributor cap.
OH, YOU GOTTA BE SHITTING ME...
CAN I HELP?
WHAT -- ?
OH SHIT -- TEEG?
BEEN A WHILE, DAVIS.
WHAT... UH, WHAT'RE YOU DOING WAY OUT HERE IN THE STICKS, MAN?
THE COPS FOUND THE BODY.
OH...

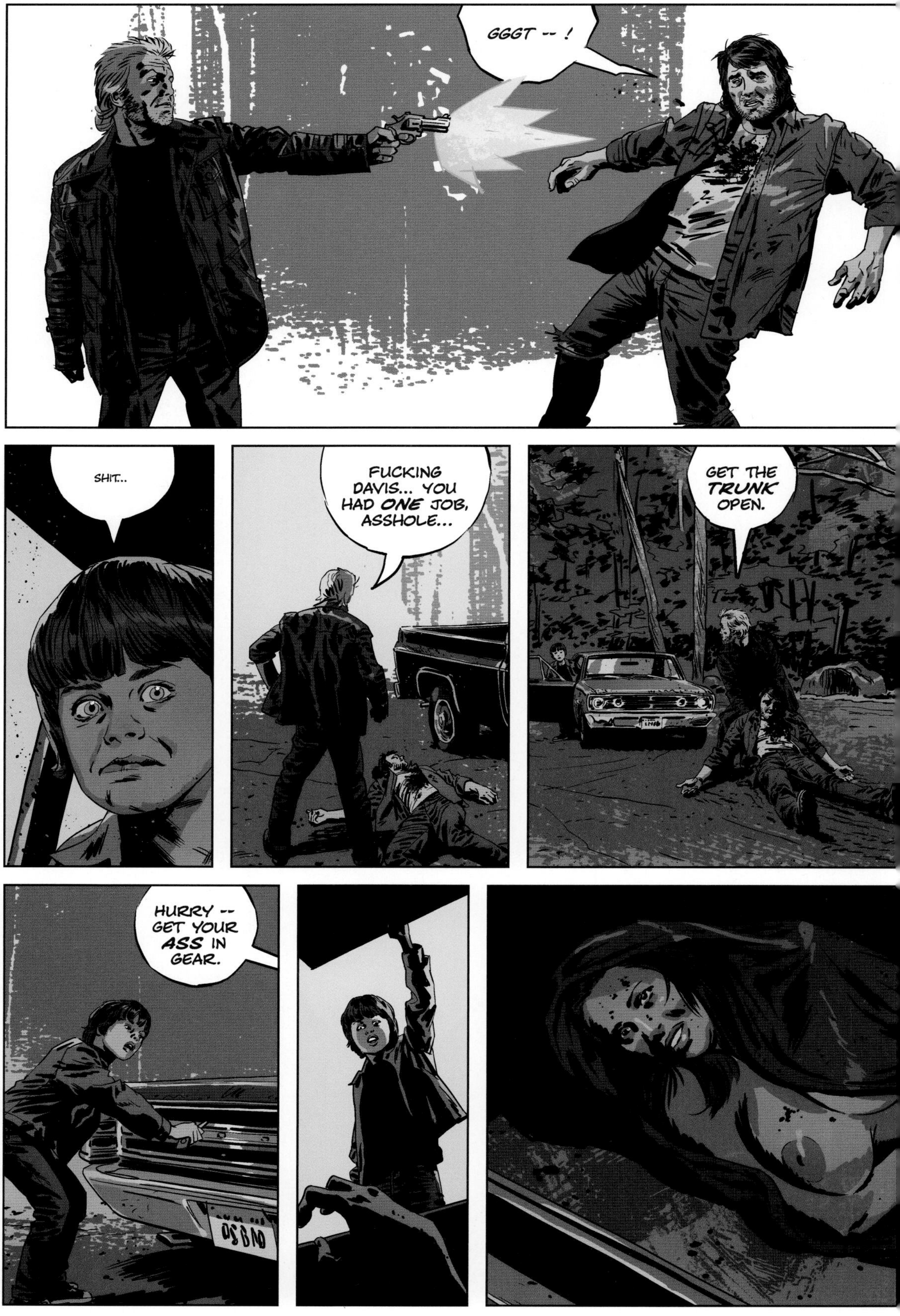
GGGT -- !
SHIT...
FUCKING DAVIS... YOU HAD ONE JOB, ASSHOLE...
GET THE TRUNK OPEN.
HURRY -- GET YOUR ASS IN GEAR.

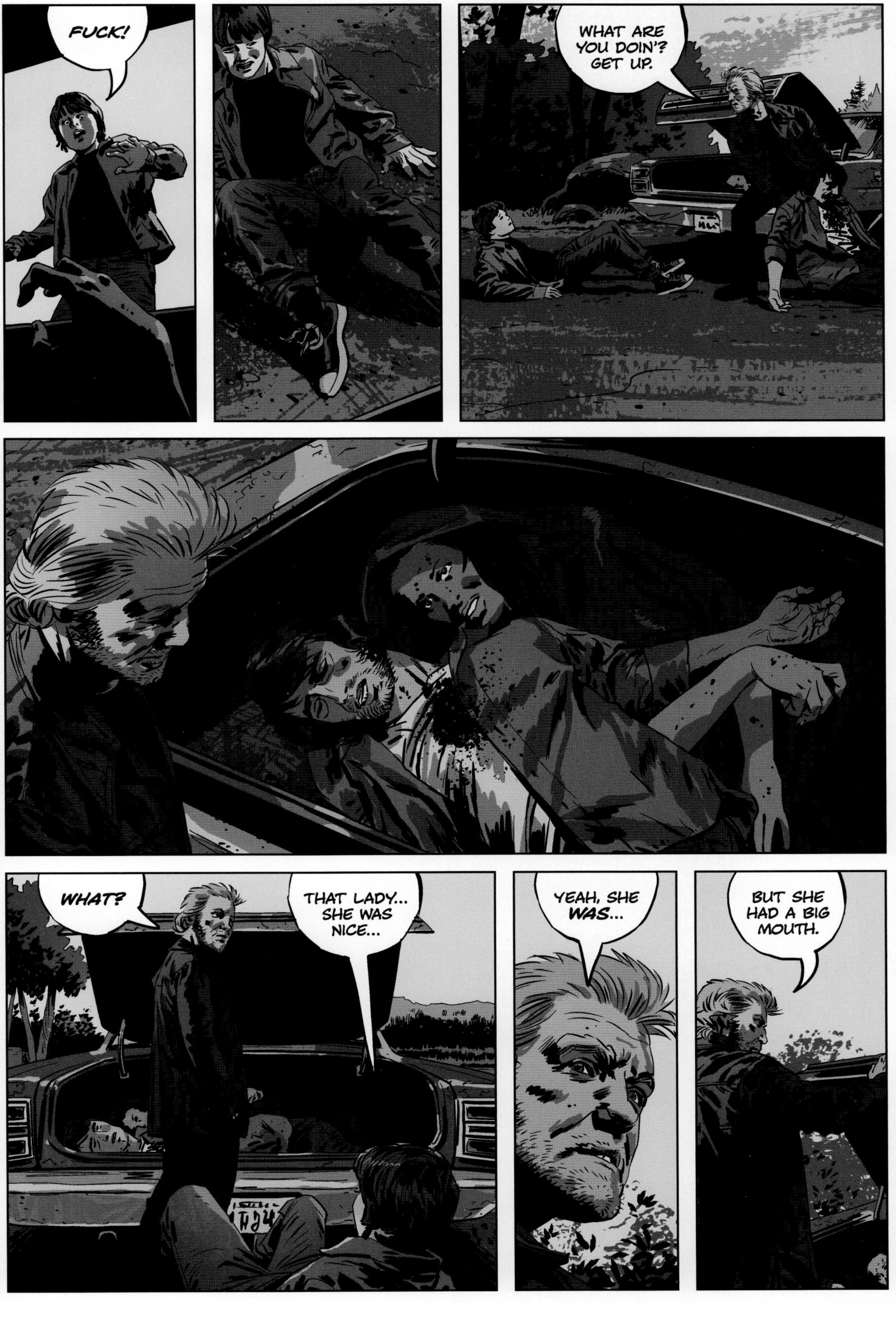
FUCK!
WHAT ARE YOU DOIN'? GET UP.
WHAT?
THAT LADY... SHE WAS NICE...
YEAH, SHE *WAS*...
BUT SHE HAD A BIG MOUTH.

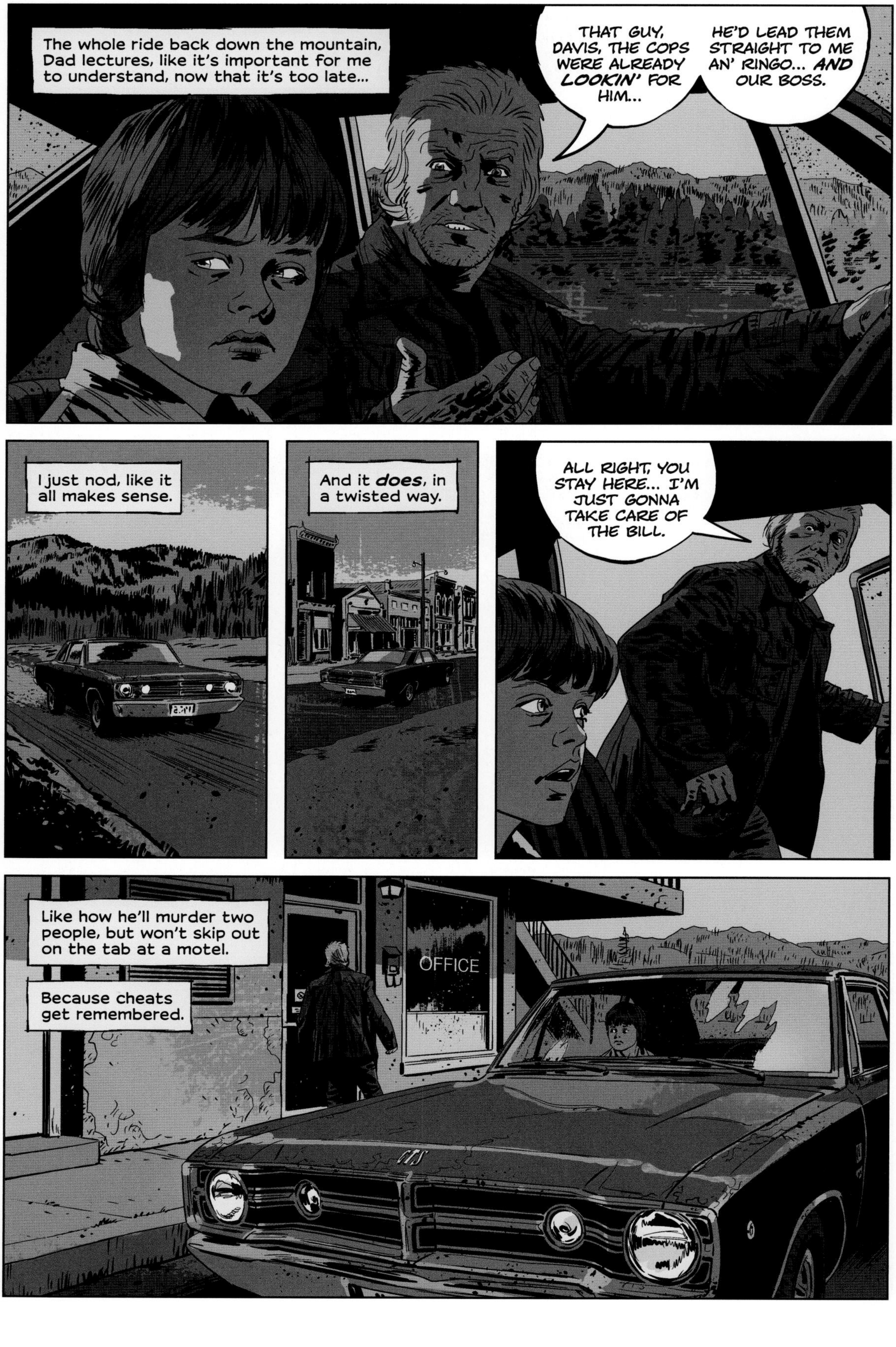
The whole ride back down the mountain, Dad lectures, like it's important for me to understand, now that it's too late...
THAT GUY, DAVIS, THE COPS WERE ALREADY *LOOKIN'* FOR HIM...
HE'D LEAD THEM STRAIGHT TO ME AN' RINGO... ***AND*** OUR BOSS.
I just nod, like it all makes sense.
And it ***does***, in a twisted way.
ALL RIGHT, YOU STAY HERE... I'M JUST GONNA TAKE CARE OF THE BILL.
Like how he'll murder two people, but won't skip out on the tab at a motel.
Because cheats get remembered.
OFFICE

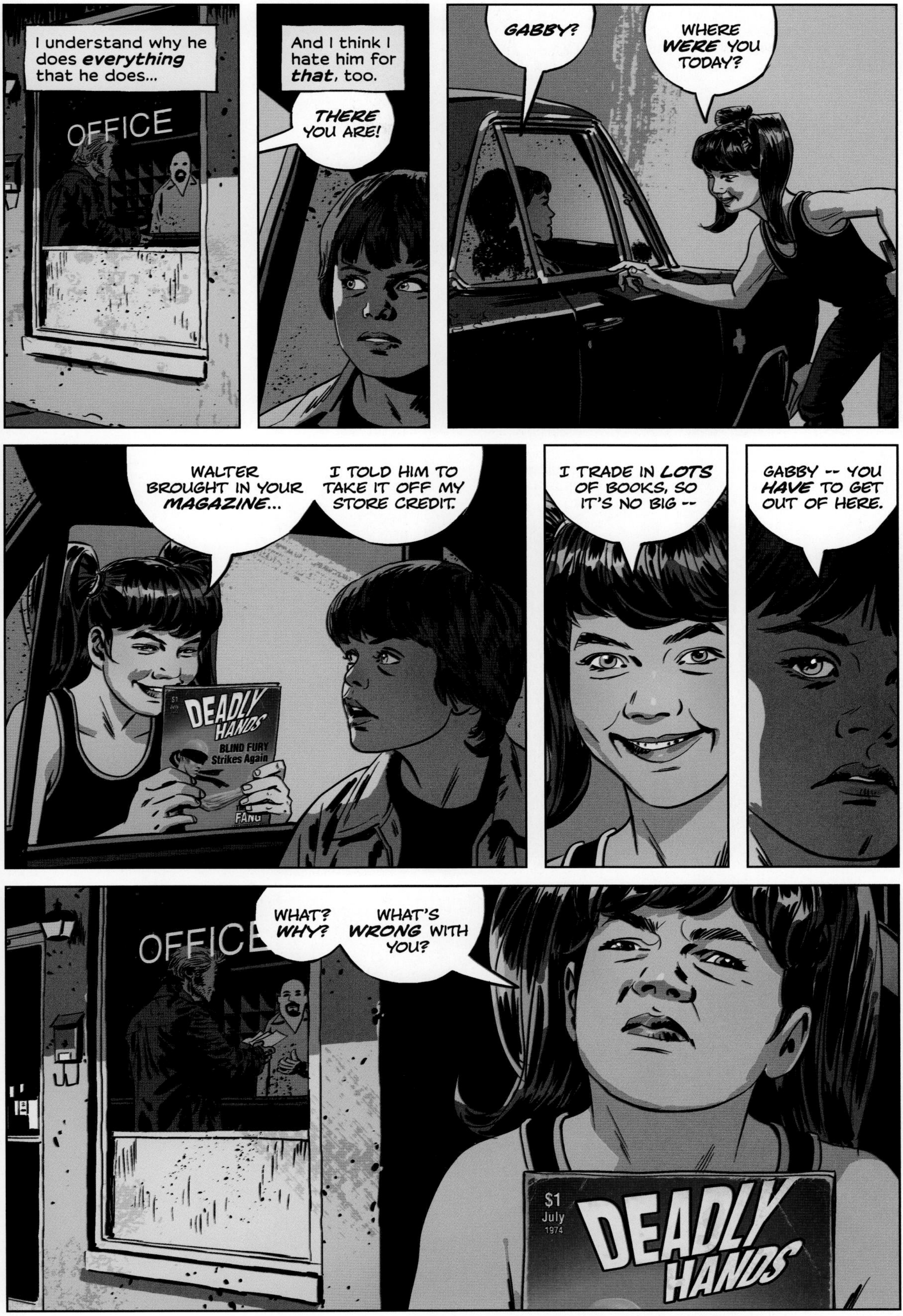
I understand why he does *everything* that he does...
OFFICE
And I think I hate him for *that*, too.
THERE YOU ARE!
GABBY?
WHERE *WERE* YOU TODAY?
WALTER BROUGHT IN YOUR *MAGAZINE*...
I TOLD HIM TO TAKE IT OFF MY STORE CREDIT.
DEADLY HANDS
BLIND FURY Strikes Again
I TRADE IN *LOTS* OF BOOKS, SO IT'S NO BIG --
GABBY -- YOU *HAVE* TO GET OUT OF HERE.
OFFICE
WHAT? *WHY?*
WHAT'S *WRONG* WITH YOU?
$1 July 1974
DEADLY HANDS

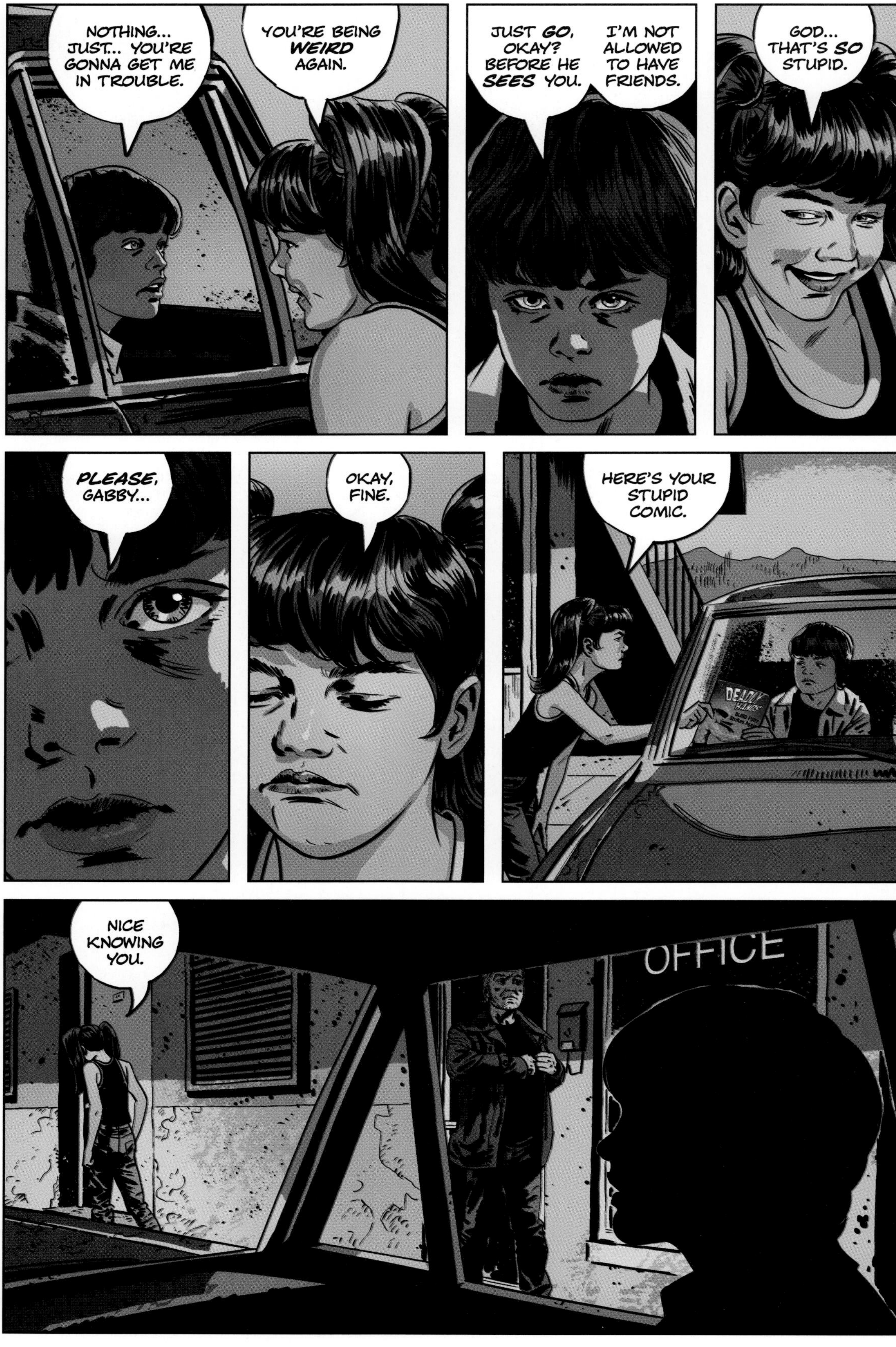
NOTHING... JUST... YOU'RE GONNA GET ME IN TROUBLE.
YOU'RE BEING WEIRD AGAIN.
JUST GO, OKAY? BEFORE HE SEES YOU.
I'M NOT ALLOWED TO HAVE FRIENDS.
GOD... THAT'S SO STUPID.
PLEASE, GABBY...
OKAY, FINE.
HERE'S YOUR STUPID COMIC.
NICE KNOWING YOU.
OFFICE

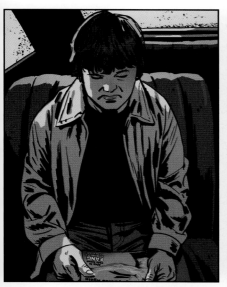

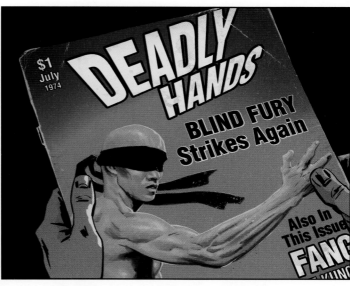

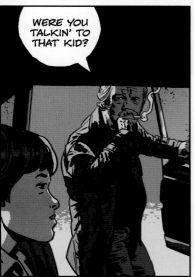

$1
July
1974
DEADLY HANDS
BLIND FURY Strikes Again
Also In This Issue
FANG
WERE YOU TALKIN' TO THAT KID?
YEAH. SHE WANTED CHANGE FOR THE CANDY MACHINE.
WHY DIDN'T SHE ASK IN THE OFFICE?
I DON'T KNOW. SHE'S JUST SOME DUMB *GIRL*...
WHO CARES?
SO ARE WE HEADING *HOME* NOW OR WHAT?

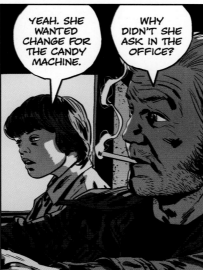

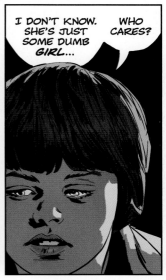

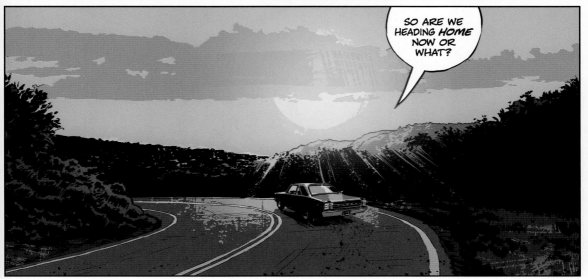

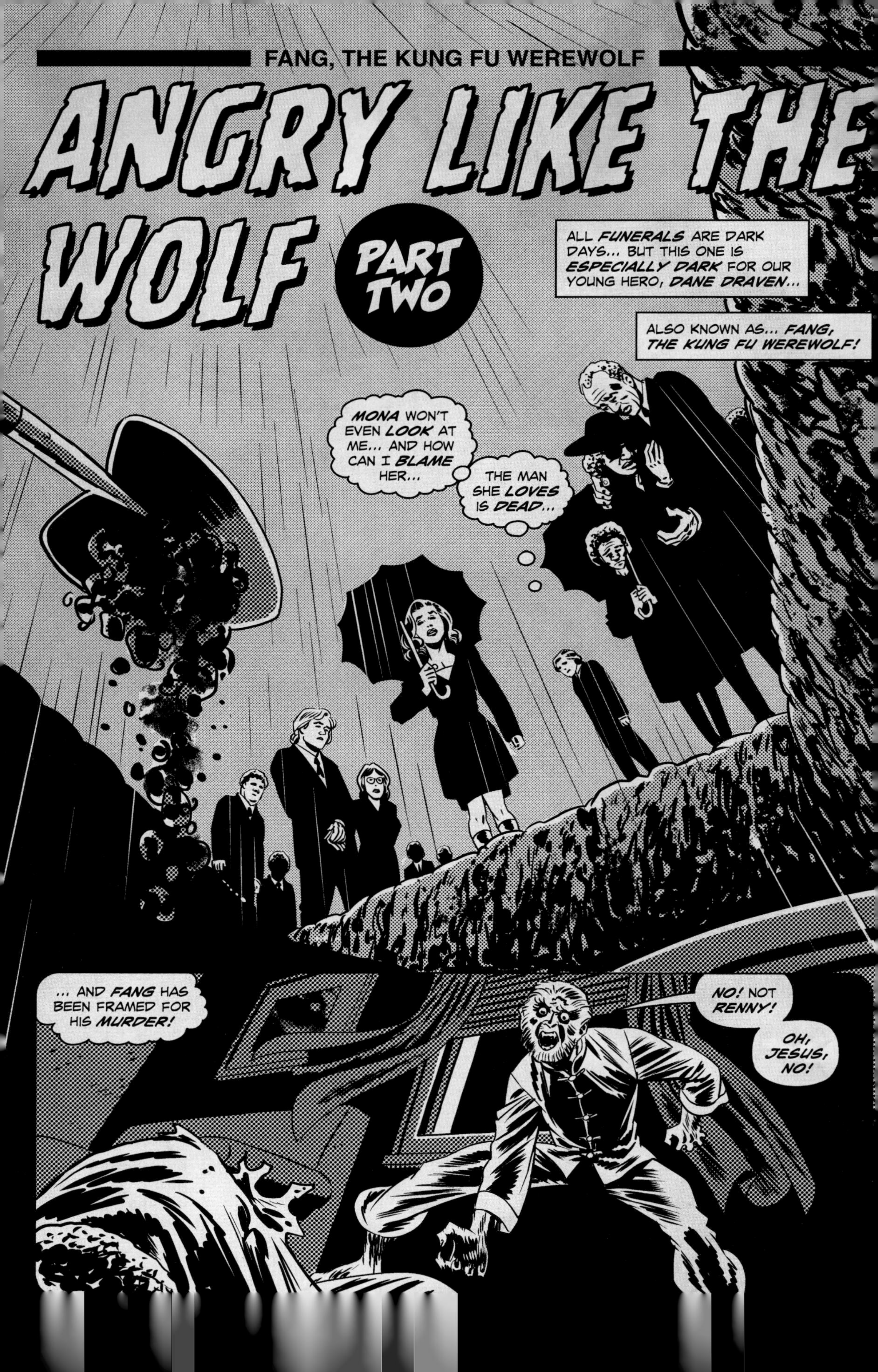
FANG, THE KUNG FU WEREWOLF
ANGRY LIKE THE WOLF
PART TWO
ALL FUNERALS ARE DARK DAYS... BUT THIS ONE IS ESPECIALLY DARK FOR OUR YOUNG HERO, DANE DRAVEN...
ALSO KNOWN AS... FANG, THE KUNG FU WEREWOLF!
MONA WON'T EVEN LOOK AT ME... AND HOW CAN I BLAME HER...
THE MAN SHE LOVES IS DEAD...
... AND FANG HAS BEEN FRAMED FOR HIS MURDER!
NO! NOT RENNY!
OH, JESUS, NO!

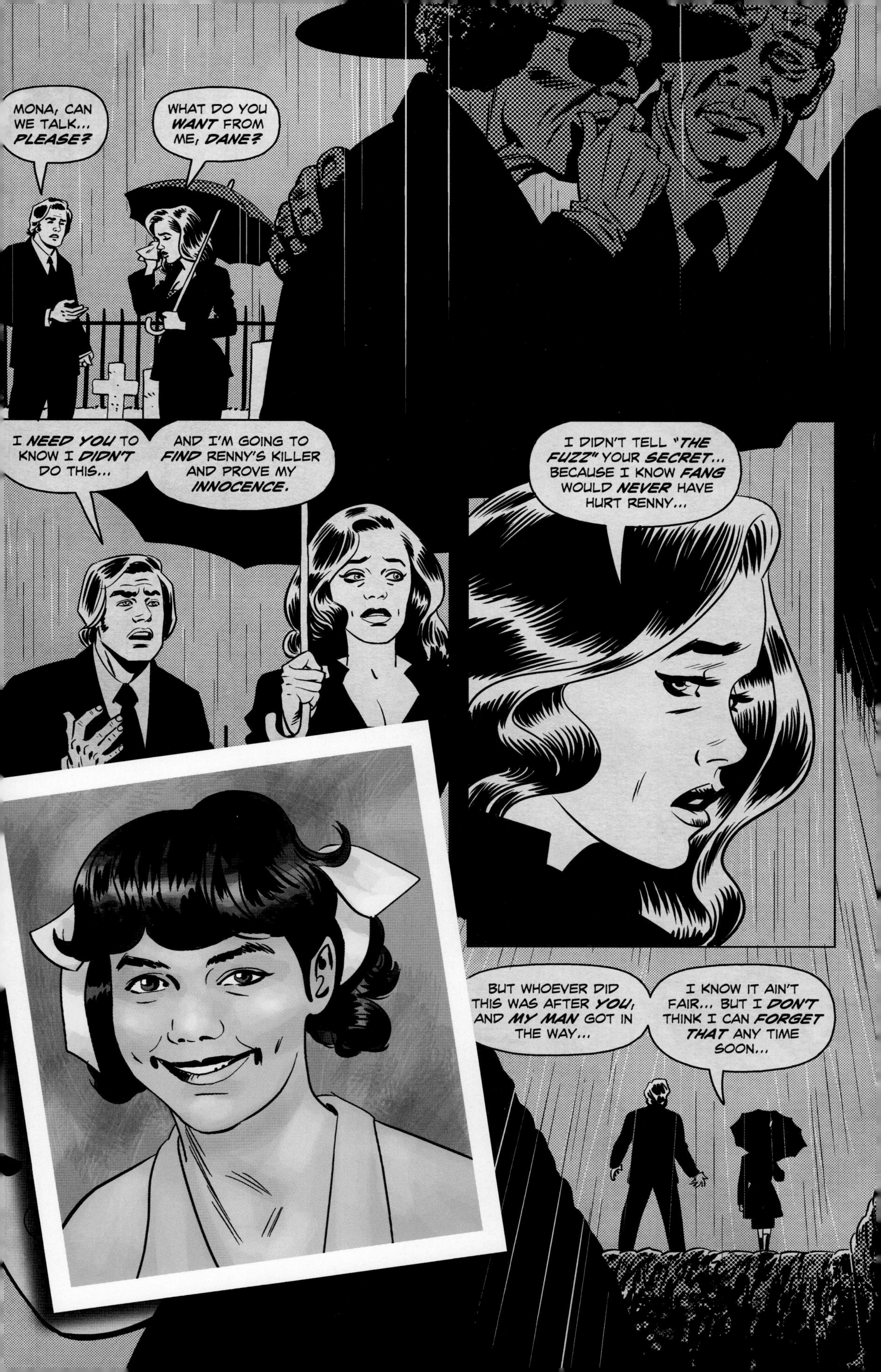
MONA, CAN WE TALK... PLEASE?
WHAT DO YOU WANT FROM ME, DANE?
I NEED YOU TO KNOW I DIDN'T DO THIS...
AND I'M GOING TO FIND RENNY'S KILLER AND PROVE MY INNOCENCE.
I DIDN'T TELL "THE FUZZ" YOUR SECRET... BECAUSE I KNOW FANG WOULD NEVER HAVE HURT RENNY...
BUT WHOEVER DID THIS WAS AFTER YOU, AND MY MAN GOT IN THE WAY...
I KNOW IT AIN'T FAIR... BUT I DON'T THINK I CAN FORGET THAT ANY TIME SOON...

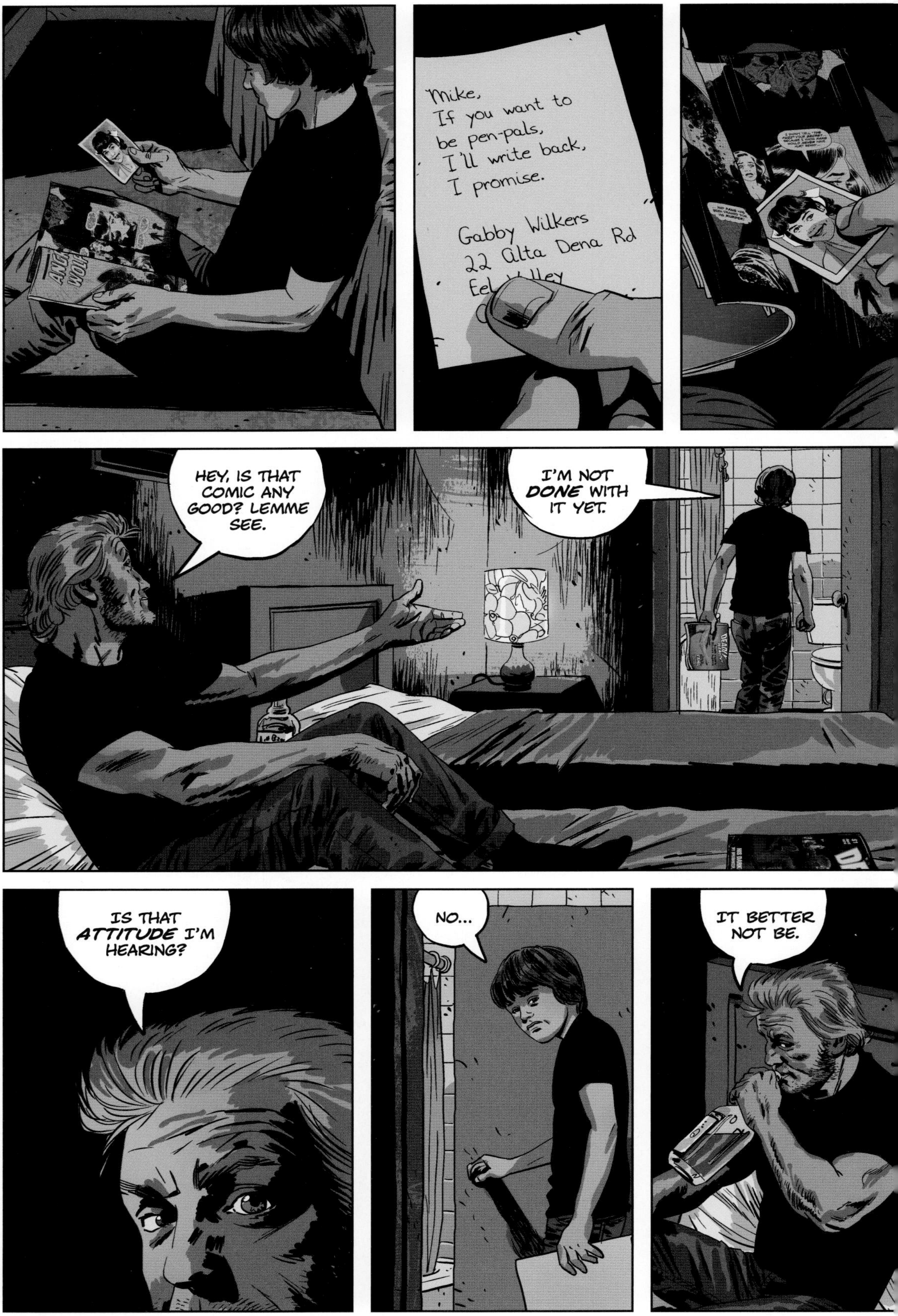
Mike,
If you want to
be pen-pals,
I'll write back,
I promise.
Gabby Wilkers
22 Alta Dena Rd
Eel
HEY, IS THAT COMIC ANY GOOD? LEMME SEE.
I'M NOT *DONE* WITH IT YET.
IS THAT *ATTITUDE* I'M HEARING?
NO...
IT BETTER NOT BE.

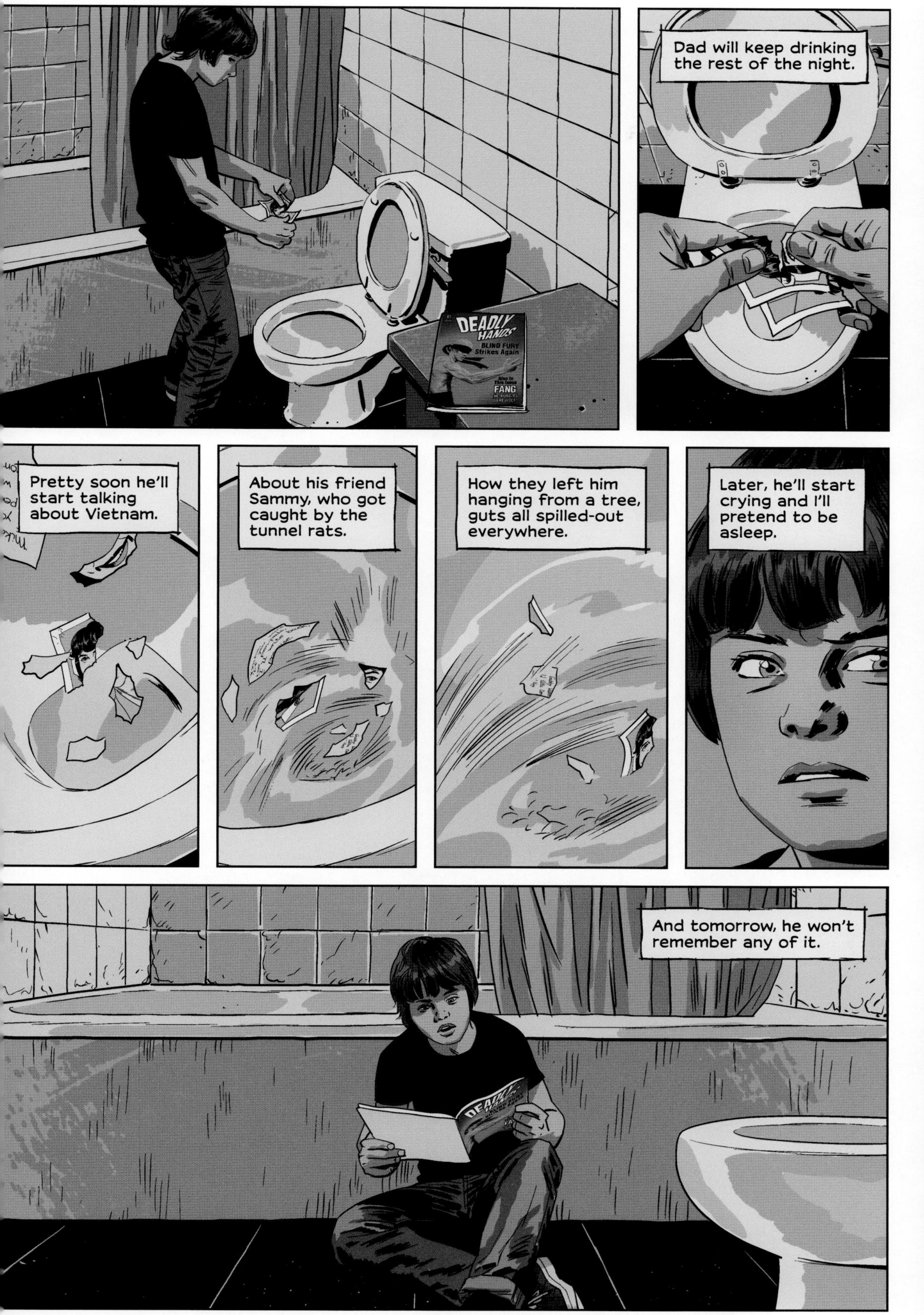
DEADLY HANDS
BLIND FURY Strikes Again
FANG
Dad will keep drinking the rest of the night.
Pretty soon he'll start talking about Vietnam.
About his friend Sammy, who got caught by the tunnel rats.
How they left him hanging from a tree, guts all spilled-out everywhere.
Later, he'll start crying and I'll pretend to be asleep.
And tomorrow, he won't remember any of it.

Enter the World of World of Brubaker and Phillips...

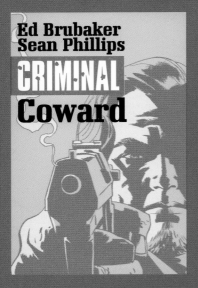

Ed Brubaker
Sean Phillips

CRIMINAL
Coward

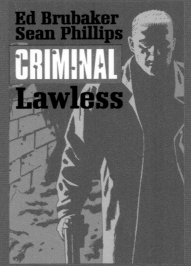

Ed Brubaker
Sean Phillips

CRIMINAL
Lawless

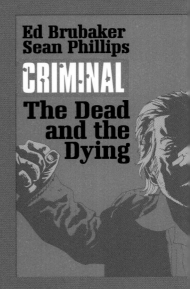

Ed Brubaker
Sean Phillips

CRIMINAL
**The Dead
and the
Dying**

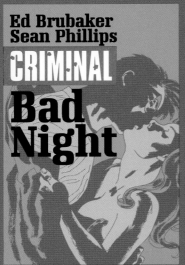

Ed Brubaker
Sean Phillips

CRIMINAL
**Bad
Night**

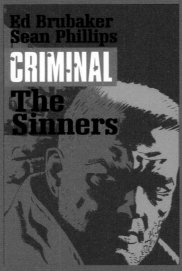

Ed Brubaker
Sean Phillips

CRIMINAL
**The
Sinners**

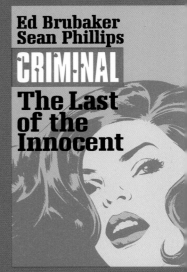

Ed Brubaker
Sean Phillips

CRIMINAL
**The Last
of the
Innocent**

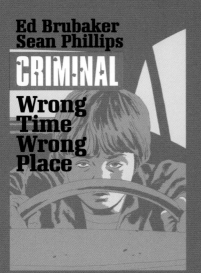

Ed Brubaker
Sean Phillips

CRIMINAL
**Wrong
Time
Wrong
Place**

"**CRIMINAL** is equal parts John Woo's **THE KILLER** Stanley Kubrick's **THE KILLING**, and Francis Ford Coppola's **THE GODFATHER**."
- **Playboy Magazine**

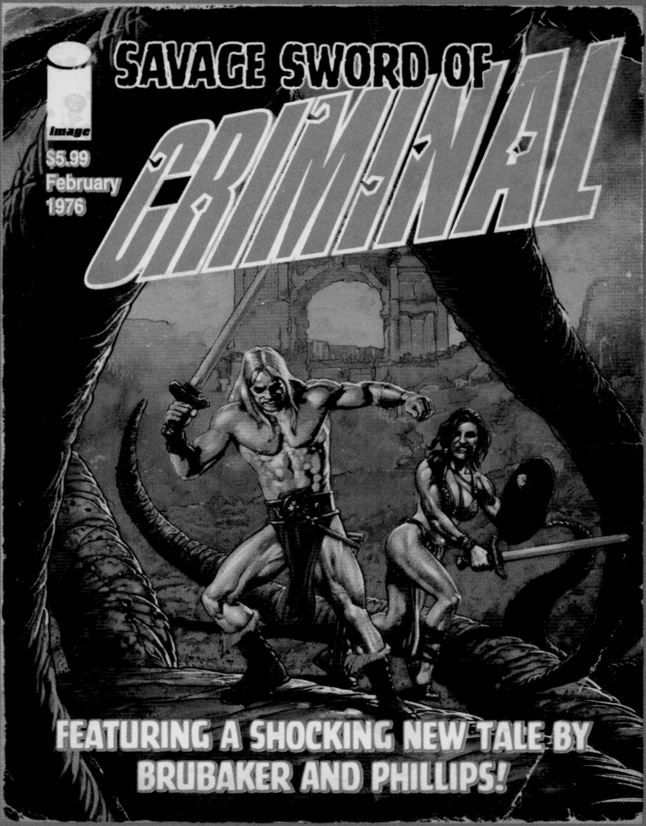
SAVAGE SWORD OF
CRIMINAL
$5.99
February
1976
FEATURING A SHOCKING NEW TALE BY
BRUBAKER AND PHILLIPS!

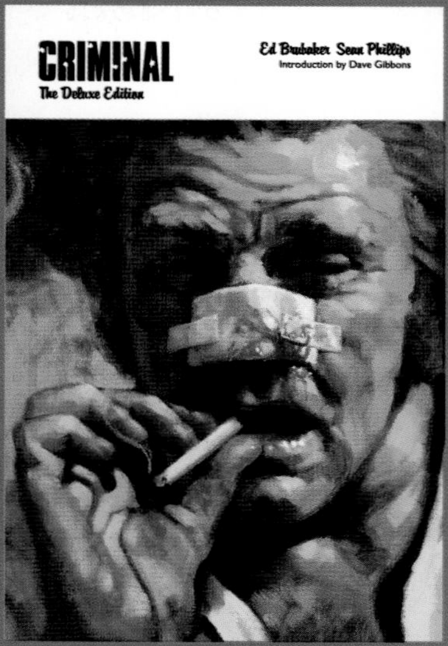
CRIMINAL
The Deluxe Edition
Ed Brubaker Sean Phillips
Introduction by Dave Gibbons

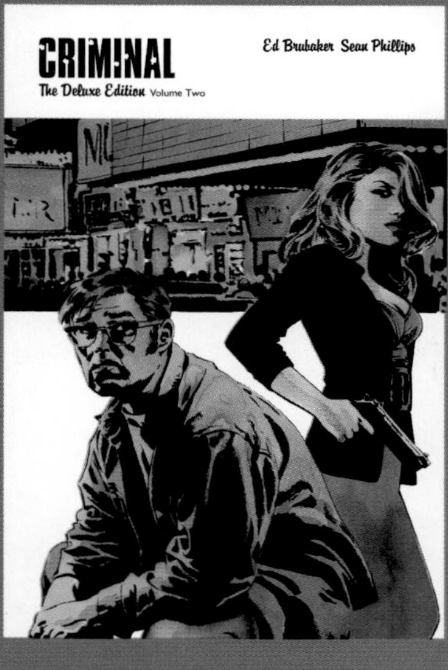
CRIMINAL
The Deluxe Edition Volume Two
Ed Brubaker Sean Phillips

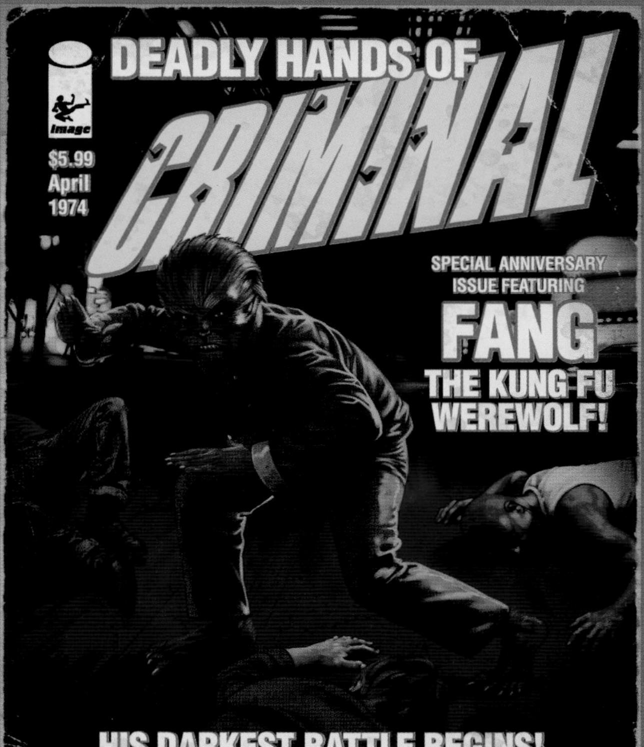
DEADLY HANDS OF
CRIMINAL
$5.99
April
1974
SPECIAL ANNIVERSARY
ISSUE FEATURING
FANG
THE KUNG FU
WEREWOLF!
HIS DARKEST BATTLE BEGINS!
BY BRUBAKER, PHILLIPS AND BREITWEISER!

Multiple Eisner Award-Winning Series

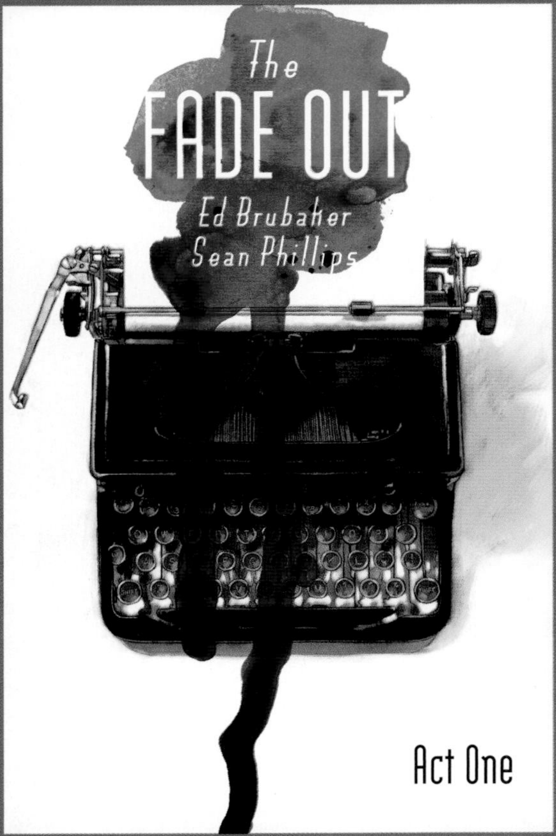
The
FADE OUT
Ed Brubaker
Sean Phillips
Act One

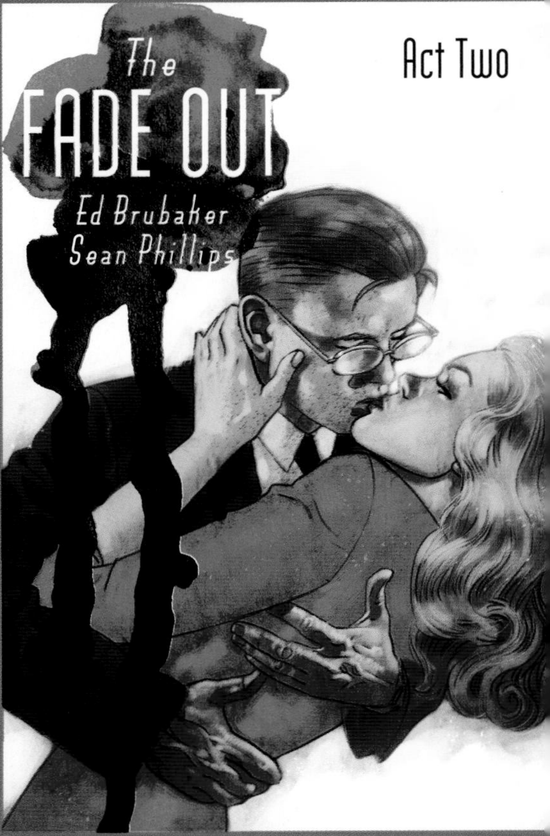
The
FADE OUT
Ed Brubaker
Sean Phillips
Act Two

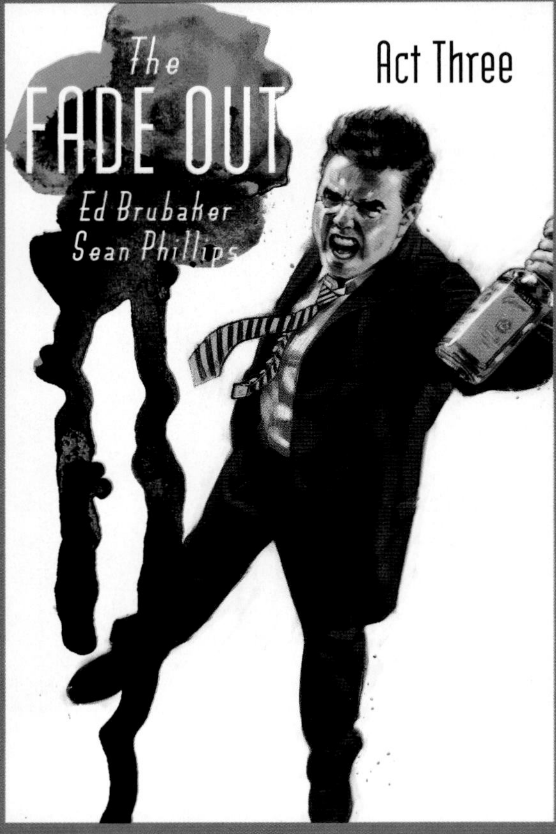
The
FADE OUT
Ed Brubaker
Sean Phillips
Act Three

"One of comics dream teams delivers their best story yet in **THE FADE OUT**, an old Hollywood murder mystery draped against HUAC and the Red Scare."

- **New York Magazine**

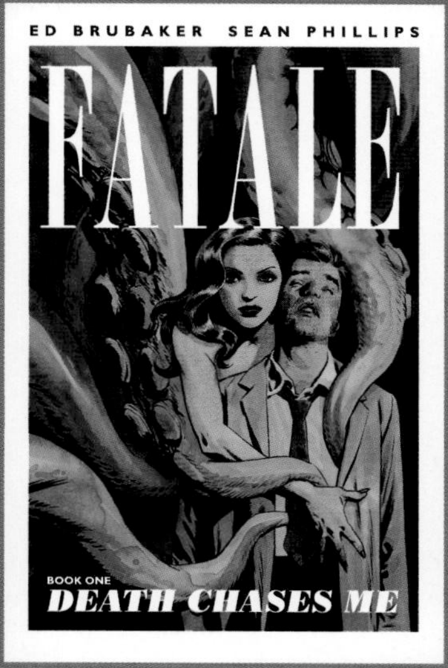
ED BRUBAKER SEAN PHILLIPS
FATALE
BOOK ONE
DEATH CHASES ME

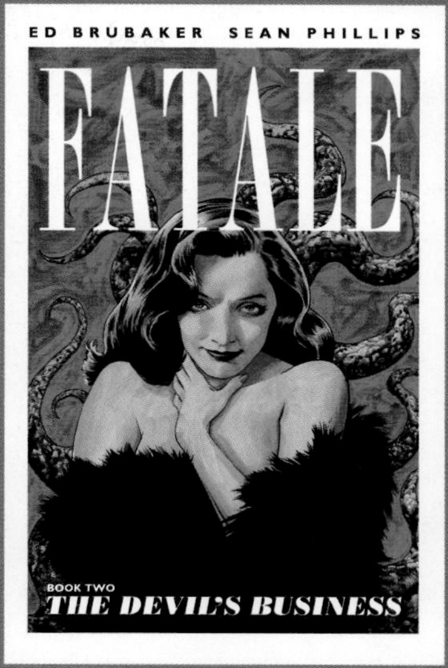
ED BRUBAKER SEAN PHILLIPS
FATALE
BOOK TWO
THE DEVIL'S BUSINESS

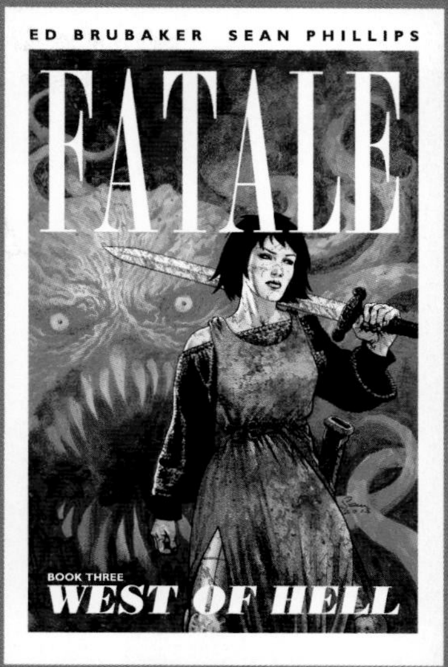
ED BRUBAKER SEAN PHILLIPS
FATALE
BOOK THREE
WEST OF HELL

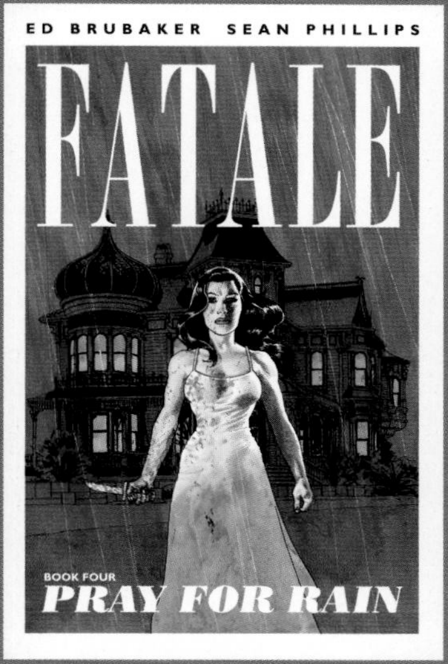
ED BRUBAKER SEAN PHILLIPS
FATALE
BOOK FOUR
PRAY FOR RAIN

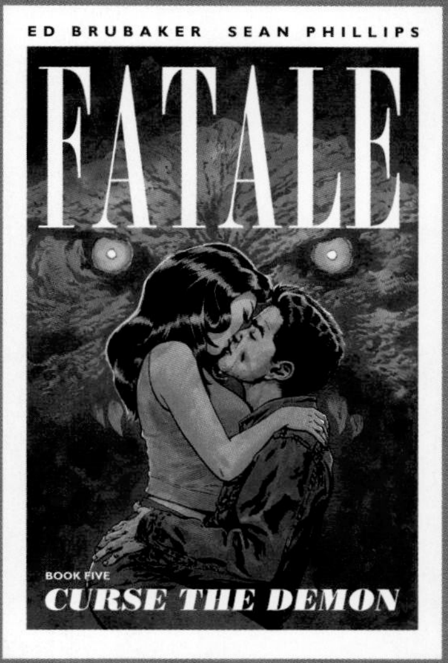
ED BRUBAKER SEAN PHILLIPS
FATALE
BOOK FIVE
CURSE THE DEMON

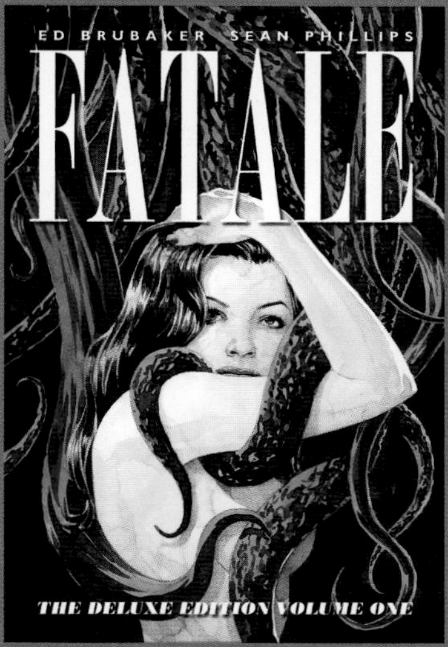
ED BRUBAKER SEAN PHILLIPS
FATALE
THE DELUXE EDITION VOLUME ONE

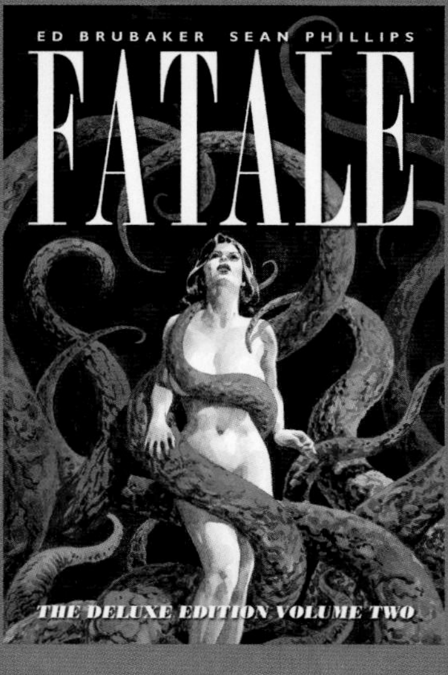
ED BRUBAKER SEAN PHILLIPS
FATALE
THE DELUXE EDITION VOLUME TWO

"Immortality may be a double-edged sword, but it's one the intoxicating Jo wields with a boundless grace in this addictive page-turner."
- **Publishers Weekly**

sleeper

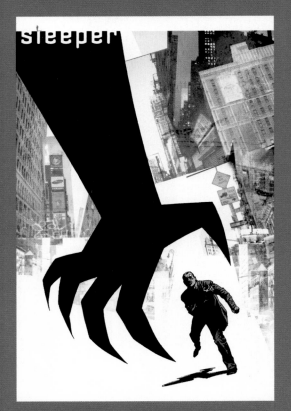

"**SLEEPER** is a perfect noir story that just happens to star people who can do fantastic things."
- **io9**

"**SCENE OF THE CRIME** is one of the very few books in the entire world to make me growl 'Ugh, I should have thought of this!'"
- **Brian Michael Bendis**

Ed Brubaker
Michael Lark
Sean Phillips
SCENE OF THE CRIME

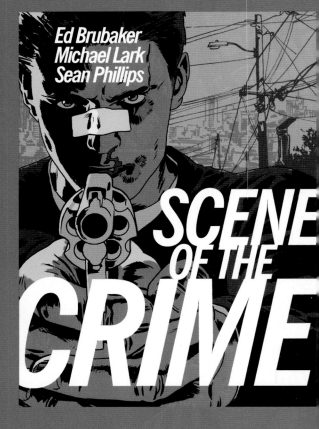